D0047295

JOSEPH TELLER

GUILTY AS SIN

MIRA®

MIRA®

Recycling programs
for this product may
not exist in your area.

ISBN-13: 978-0-7783-1233-8

GUILTY AS SIN

For questions and comments about the quality of this book please contact us at
Customer_eCare@Harlequin.ca.

www.MIRABooks.com

Printed in U.S.A.

For Herb ("Whitey") Rein.
Classmate, teammate, neighbor, friend.
Left the party before the end.

1

The guiltiest man there ever was

Alonzo Barnett died last week.

There wasn't any obituary announcement that ran in the *Times,* or even the *Daily News* or the *Post.* It seems the Alonzo Barnetts of the world don't rate obituary announcements.

In fact, Jaywalker might never have found out, had he not gotten a phone call from a mutual acquaintance named Kenny Smith. Smith had originally met Barnett through Jaywalker, and had somehow gotten word on the street of Barnett's death.

Not that the death was a particularly tragic one, as deaths go. Barnett was seventy-six, after all, and even though he'd spent a good portion of those years in state prison, seventy-six is still a pretty fair number, by any yardstick.

There was no funeral or memorial service held for Alonzo Barnett. Still, Jaywalker and Smith did get together to pay a brief condolence call. Though for Jaywalker, it felt like something much more than that. Because over the twenty-five years since their first meeting, he'd come to regard Barnett not just as a former client and a good friend but as a defendant sent his way by something very close to Providence. Not that Jaywalker would ever admit believing in that kind of stuff, not even if his life depended on it.

Still, a year before the Barnett case, he'd represented another defendant, also a likable African-American with a long record, who, like Barnett, had been charged with selling drugs. The guy had been considering taking a plea, but Jaywalker had talked him out of it, telling him the offer wasn't good enough and there was an excellent chance they could beat the case at trial. So when the jury inexplicably came back with a conviction, Jaywalker had gone into a deep depression. He'd failed his client, he realized, not only by losing but by pushing him to go to trial in the first place. He'd been a "cowboy," a "gunslinger," an unpardonable sin in Jaywalker's book. The resulting funk left him nearly suicidal. He stopped taking on new cases and could barely show up for his existing ones. He might have walked away from his practice altogether, had he not had a wife and daughter to support and tuition payments to meet.

So when Barnett's case came along, it meant more than just another client, more than just another payday. It represented something of a second chance for Jaywalker, an opportunity to atone for having failed so terribly the last time out. A chance, if you will, for redemption.

That had been then. But there was more to it. Over the twenty-five years that had passed since Alonzo Barnett first came into Jaywalker's life, his name has become the answer to a trivia question of sorts. A question Jaywalker's been asked hundreds of times by now, perhaps even thousands. Though to Jaywalker, there's nothing the least bit trivial about it. It goes like this:

"How can you possibly represent somebody you know is guilty?"

He's heard it so many times, in fact, that he long ago developed a stock response to it, a little civics lecture he trots out and delivers on cue, punctuated with timeworn phrases like *passionate belief in the process, foundation of the adversarial system of justice,* and *love of the underdog.*

And his words seem to satisfy most folks, at least up to a point. Others, he's come to learn, are never going to get it. Like the earnest young man who appeared to listen intently before smiling and saying, "That's very nice. I hope you lose all your trials."

Every once in a while, though, the questioner presses Jaywalker further, and sounds as though he or she is really interested in getting beyond the catchphrases and truly understanding why it is that the guiltiest of defendants, particularly those who readily admit their guilt, nevertheless deserve a champion every bit as much as the wrongly accused. And at that point Jaywalker will look around the room, searching for a couple of empty chairs off in a quiet corner. Then he'll suggest that the two of them sit down. And once they've done so, he'll look the person hard in the eye. "Do you really, *really* want to know the answer to that question?" he'll ask. And if he happens to get a "Yes," he'll lean back and close his eyes for a long moment, the better to take himself back over the twenty-five years that have passed since the event. And then, once he's completed the journey in his mind, he'll open his eyes again. And if the other chair isn't empty by that time—as it actually was once—Jaywalker will draw in a deep breath.

"Let me tell you a story," he'll say to his listener. "A story about the guiltiest man there ever was. A guy who was, as the old saying goes, guilty as sin."

2

The Tombs

Although his client's name may have been Alonzo Barnett, for as long as anyone could remember he'd been known simply as AB. Which made the two of them a pretty good match, considering that years earlier, long before he'd become Jaywalker the criminal defense lawyer, he himself had been born into the world as Harrison J. Walker.

Barnett came his way in the mid-1980s, which for many New Yorkers was a time of crime, cocaine and crack in epidemic proportions. For Jaywalker, it was also a time to hustle to pay the mortgage and his daughter's tuition. And one of the ways he hustled was to accept court-appointed cases. The Legal Aid Society, where he himself had been broken in not too long ago, could handle only so many indigent defendants. The rest were doled out to private lawyers. Not the big-firm partners or the hotshots who were even then billing out their services for hundreds of dollars an hour. No, the ones who lined up to take the overflow were the young, the old and the journeymen who hung on but never got rich in the business. The Jaywalkers. Who else, after all, would be willing to work for forty dollars an hour for in-court time and twenty-five for out-of-court?

When a person gets arrested and is lucky enough to have money to hire a lawyer—or when his family is—he gets to choose the lawyer. When he doesn't, the constitutions of both the United States and the State of New York guarantee him free representation. But the catch is, he no longer gets to choose the lawyer; the system chooses for him. Not that money necessarily insures quality representation. To this day, it's Jaywalker's firm belief that overall, there's as much talent at Legal Aid and on the assigned counsel rolls as there is in the private bar. But when somebody else is doing the choosing, the defendant finds himself totally at the mercy of the luck of the draw.

According to Alonzo Barnett, the luck of the draw hadn't been particularly good to him, and he'd been through two free lawyers already by the time Jaywalker was asked if he was interested in picking up a defendant charged with sale and possession of drugs.

"What is he, a troublemaker?" was his first question.

"No," said Lorraine Wilson, the clerk who'd phoned him after he'd finally let it be known that he was ready to start accepting court-appointed cases again. "At least it doesn't seem that way. I mean, I don't see any 'DD' notation next to his name." DD's were Difficult Defendants, who earned the designation by punching or spitting at their lawyers, bringing frivolous pro se lawsuits, or lodging spurious complaints to some bar association they picked out of the phone book. Alonzo Barnett had apparently done none of those things, at least so far. The only things that stood out about him, as best as Lorraine could tell, were the multiple previous lawyers and the fact that by now his case was beginning to grow whiskers.

More than a year and a half had passed since his arrest, something of an anomaly in a system that owed its very survival to its unfailing ability to rapidly dispose of huge numbers of cases. "Maybe he just tires lawyers out," she suggested. "Want to give it a try?"

Jaywalker thought about it for a good second or two. Lawyers didn't tend to tire out all that easily, especially when they were working on the clock. If anything, they were far more likely to be the ones that tired other people out. So chances were there had to be *something* wrong with the guy. But a major tuition payment was coming due the end of the month, with close to nothing in the bank to cover it.

"Sure," he said. "Why not?"

As Lorraine read off the particulars of the case to him, he jotted down the indictment number, the courtroom and the adjourned date. "Let me know how it turns out," she said.

He promised he would.

Most lawyers who take assignments wait until the day the case appears in court to start working on it. Whether consciously or not, they're immediately relegating the court-appointed client to a status inferior to that of the retained one. Jaywalker was different, even back then. Although he was trying hard to develop a private practice and would eventually succeed, he never would differentiate between the defendants who could afford to pay him and the ones who couldn't. Those who noticed—and they included not only colleagues but prosecutors and judges, as well—were by turns impressed with his dedication and astounded by his stupidity. The object of being a lawyer, they all understood, was to make money.

But Jaywalker and money have always had something

of an uneasy relationship, and he knew even then, even back in the '80s, that he'd never be a big earner. So already he'd begun to measure success not in terms of dollars and cents, but by other, vaguer yardsticks, such as the appreciation of those he worked for and the respect of those he worked in front of, against or alongside. To his way of thinking, this difference in how he looked at things didn't deserve medals or accolades. The truth was, he'd simply dropped out of the money chase because he was genetically ill-suited to compete in it. Sort of like how a dog might concentrate on fetching a stick instead of trying to drive a car. Focusing on getting the best possible results for his clients, regardless of their means, and along the way treating them more like family than freeloaders, didn't necessarily make Jaywalker a better person than his colleagues.

But it did tend to make him a better lawyer.

Not the lawyer he'd eventually become, winning ninety percent of his cases in a business where he wasn't supposed to win half that many. But already, even back then, he was doing things no other lawyers were doing, and the results had begun to show.

So even though Alonzo Barnett wasn't scheduled to be back in court for another week and a half, on the day following his conversation with Lorraine Wilson, Jaywalker made a trip to Part 91, the courtroom on the fifteenth floor of 100 Centre Street where Barnett's case was pending, right up to and including a trial, if there was to be one. There he found a friendly clerk and traded a notice of appearance for a look at the file.

To Jaywalker's way of thinking, reading through a file before meeting the defendant had to be something like a doctor's studying a patient's workup before the actual exam. You weren't going to learn everything, but you were going to get a pretty good idea of just how good or bad things were going to be. You'd learn the person's name, as well as any other names he might be known by, his sex and his age. There'd be a printout of his past history, always important to factor in. Next there'd be a bunch of numbers, totally indecipherable to a layman but immediately telling to the trained eye. Finally, there'd be a little narrative of sorts, a paragraph or two describing just what it was that had brought the person in—whether the "in" happened to be to the office, the emergency room or, as was the case in Alonzo Barnett's situation, the criminal justice system. But it didn't much matter, the point being that from studying the reading materials, you were generally going to get a pretty good idea of what you were looking at and how bad it was.

For Alonzo Barnett, the news wasn't good.

To begin with, his past history was absolutely terrible. It took Jaywalker a good five minutes just to read and decipher the NYSIS sheet, the computer printout of Barnett's prior arrest record. By the time he'd finished jotting down the relevant highlights, he was able to count no less than five felony convictions amassed over the past thirty years. Almost all of them were for drugs, either sale or possession. In addition to the felonies, there was a scattering of misdemeanor convictions, somewhere between eight and twelve of them. And while incomplete sentencing data made it impossible to determine exactly how much time Barnett had actually served, it was apparent that he'd been behind bars for well over half of his fifty years. Make that fifty-one, since the printout was by this time more than a year old.

There was no dearth of names, either. In addition to Alonzo Barnett, the name the defendant had given at this latest arrest, he'd also been know at various times of his adult life as Alonzo Brown, Alvin Brown, Alonzo Black, Alonzo Bell and AB. Simply from the repeated recurrence of the first name, Jaywalker guessed that at least the Alonzo part was correct. The true last name was anyone's guess. Not that it mattered. With only one name himself, Jaywalker had always made it a habit to address his clients using their first names, and he always would.

Next there were the numbers. The ones that stood out were 2, 4, 220.43 and 220.21. Again, not much to a layperson, except perhaps one interested in playing them in some combination, whether on the street or in some Lotto game. But to Jaywalker, they immediately told a story, and once again, it wasn't a good one. The 2 was for the number of ounces of a narcotic drug that Barnett—or whatever his name was—was charged with selling; the 4 was for the ounces he was accused of possessing. And the fancier numbers, the 220.43 and the 220.21, were the particular sections of the New York State Penal Law that he'd allegedly violated in the process of doing so, the first representing Criminal Sale of a Controlled Substance in the First Degree, the second Criminal Possession of a Controlled Substance in the First Degree. Both charges were A-1 felonies, indistinguishable from murder in terms of the sentences they carried. Thanks to a long-ago governor named Rockefeller and a never-ending succession of lawmakers panicked at the notion of being branded soft on crime, each charge carried a maximum sentence of twenty-five years to life, the absolute *minimum* being fifteen to life.

Finally, there was the narrative. Jaywalker knew better than to look for it in the indictment. That was merely the instrument drawn up by some computer in the D.A.'s office and rubber-stamped by a grand jury. It would be couched in legalese and contain the formal accusations, but little in the way of helpful detail. So he looked instead at the Criminal Court complaint, a single sheet of yellow paper typed out the old-fashioned way the day or night Barnett had been brought to 100 Centre Street to make the first of a long series of appearances before one judge or another.

It was in affidavit form, the named deponent being the detective who'd sworn to its truth and accuracy a year and a half ago.

> The defendant, Alonzo Barnett, on or about the 5th day of October, 1984, at 1830 hours, in the vicinity of 127th Street and Broadway, in the County of New York, State of New York, did unlawfully sell to a law enforcement officer known to deponent a quantity of heroin in excess of 2 ounces, and did unlawfully possess a quantity of heroin in excess of 4 ounces.

In other words, Alonzo Barnett was looking at a direct sale to an undercover cop. That said, the phrase "law enforcement officer" caused Jaywalker to pause for just a moment. The usually language was "a police officer." But then he looked back at the deponent's command and noticed for the first time the initials "JCSFTF." Although he'd never before heard of such a unit, Jaywalker felt he was on pretty safe ground translating it as "Joint City, State and Federal Task Force." Which would explain the "law enforcement officer" bit. The undercover cop hadn't necessarily been a cop at all; he might just as easily have been a state trooper or a federal agent on loan from the New York State Police, the DEA or the FBI, called in to work on a major investigation.

Your tax dollars at work.

There was still one more item in the file that caught Jaywalker's attention. It was a small color photo of the defendant, no larger than the ones they stick on passports. Not your traditional mug shot with a pair of images—one full face and one in profile—above a series of numbers. No, this one was a single exposure, a shot of the defendant looking directly into the camera, taken hours after his arrest. He was dark-skinned, but not so dark that Jaywalker didn't have to check his race under the pedigree section, where he found it listed as "black," "African-American" not really being in vogue yet in law enforcement circles. Barnett was described as five-foot-seven inches and one hundred and sixty pounds. His graying hair made him look every bit of his fifty-one years and then some. Staring out at Jaywalker, as he'd stared at the camera a year and a half earlier, he looked neither belligerent nor defiant, the way a younger man might have. If anything, he looked sad. If he was angry, he was angry only at himself.

Before returning the file, Jaywalker jotted down the A.D.A.'s name and number. He took a look at the earlier notices of appearance that had been filed in the case. There turned out to be three of them, not two, as Lorraine Wilson had thought. The two court-appointed lawyers— Jaywalker now being number three—had been preceded by a private attorney, some guy who'd walked away from the case after making a single appearance. Maybe he hadn't been paid enough, or maybe he had suspected early on that Mr. Barnett was going to be hard to deal with. Whichever had been the case, later on he'd somehow managed to sneak the words *For Arraignment Only* onto his notice. It was the different color ink that gave the notation away as an afterthought. So one thing was certain, at least. Whether it was Alonzo Barnett's long record, his lack of money or his disinclination to take a plea, it seemed nobody wanted any part of him.

Nobody, at least, until Jaywalker.

Having done the unusual by looking through the file a full week before the case was scheduled to appear in court, Jaywalker next did the unthinkable. He went to visit Barnett.

He would have done it the hard way, killing a full day by making the round-trip out to Rikers Island and back. That's where the vast majority of the city's detainees were housed while awaiting trial or some other disposition of their cases. But it turned out Jaywalker didn't have to go that far. Barnett was a guest of what was at that time known as the Manhattan Detention Center. In its later incarnations it would become the Bernard B. Kerik Complex, and then—following Mr. Kerik's indictment, conviction and fall from grace—the Manhattan Detention Complex. But to everyone familiar with it, whether as an insider or an outsider, it had always been, and would always be, the Tombs.

The good thing about the Tombs was that, rather than being plunked down in the middle of a river, it was conveniently located at 125 White Street, at the northern end of 100 Centre Street. So in order to get to it from the Criminal Court Building, all you had to do was walk around the corner. In fact, if you were unlucky enough to be a guest of the city, you didn't even have to do that. Both an underground passageway and a twelfth-floor covered bridge—imaginatively referred to as "the bridge"—saved you the trouble. Jaywalker, who'd been a guest of the city on more than one occasion—whether for mouthing off to a judge or committing some other minor breach of courtroom etiquette—took the trouble on this occasion of walking around the corner.

The other thing about the Tombs was that it was then, and continues to be to this day, reserved for the more desirable detainees in the system. Not that there's any written policy decreeing it as such. But it can't be purely by accident that at any given moment the population of the Tombs is considerably older, whiter, more fluent in English and less prone to committing crimes of violence than the inhabitants of Rikers Island.

An hour after arrival, Jaywalker found himself sitting across a table from Alonzo Barnett. It was an old wooden table, covered with peeling paint and cigarette burn marks, and it was securely bolted to the floor. But sitting across it sure beat trying to carry on a conversation through iron bars or bulletproof glass, or using telephone handsets manufactured sometime during the last Ice Age.

Barnett looked about like he had in his photograph, only older. And not just a year and a half older. Even in the Tombs, time has a tendency to take its toll. But other than that, he was the same man the photo had promised. Relaxed, mature, self-aware, sad and somehow dignified despite the predicament in which he found himself. And if you think it's easy to look dignified while wearing an orange jumpsuit and paper slippers, sitting at a bolted-down table in a room walled by steel and cinder blocks, try it sometime.

"I suspect my previous attorneys have warned you that I'm a bit of a pain," were the first words out of Barnett's mouth. "And the prosecutor, as well."

Which wasn't quite the opening line Jaywalker had expected. Defendants didn't generally make a habit of using terms like *suspect, previous* and *as well.* Or even *attorney,* for that matter. Not to mention *prosecutor.* Evidently, what Mr. Barnett was trying to say was, "I bet all my otha lawyers and that muthafuckin' no-good D.A. been bad-mouthin' me, huh?"

But he hadn't said it that way, and the almost quaint manner he'd used to express himself instead brought a smile to Jaywalker's face. "Actually," he said, "I haven't spoken with any of them."

"Oh? Why not?"

"Well," said Jaywalker, "if I understand the way things are supposed to work, I'm assigned to represent you, not them. So I figured I'd come in here and see what you have to say first, before I talk to any of them. If that's okay with you."

Which evened the score at one smile apiece.

They talked for an hour that first day, maybe a little more. Alonzo Barnett came across as a gentle, thoughtful and intelligent man. Born on a farm in central Alabama, he'd had almost nothing in the way of formal education, finally earning his GED at the age of forty-eight in a place called Green Haven. A GED is a high school equivalency degree, a not-quite-diploma that the state corrections system used to hand out, back when there was enough money to hold classes behind bars. And despite its bucolic name, Green Haven was and continues to be a maximum security prison surrounded by a huge wall topped with miles of razor wire. It was no doubt given its name by someone who never set eyes on it.

Barnett had made his way north at the age of fourteen, alone. He slept on the floor of a Harlem shooting gallery, a large room shared by upward of twenty men and women who otherwise would have been out on the street. In summer, it was cooled by a single window cracked

open at the top. In winter, it was heated by the open lit
burners of a gas range. And lest there be any confusion,
there are no targets to shoot at in a shooting gallery, and
no trophies awarded for marksmanship. What is shot is
heroin, what are aimed at are veins, and the only prize
for hitting one is an hour or so of oblivion.

Days, Barnett worked for street corner dealers as a
gofer. A gofer is someone who's willing to go for this
and go for that. This and that might include coffee, soda,
lunch, cigarettes, change or more product. The product
could be heroin, cocaine, marijuana or pills. At the end
of the day the gofer would get paid in the form of a few
dollars or, more typically, a few glassine bags filled with
white powder.

Barnett's first arrest came shortly after his fifteenth
birthday and was for possession. Too young to be brought
to criminal court, he was treated as a juvenile delinquent
and placed on probation. He succeeded for a full twenty-
seven days, before being rearrested for sale. This time
he was sent to Spofford. Until 1998, the Spofford Juvenile Justice Center, located in the Bronx, was the facility
where they sent boys so they could learn how to grow up
to be adult criminals. Although the curriculum did indeed
include mandatory education classes, that fact had little
or nothing to do with how its residents referred to it.

They called it *Crime School*.

The juvenile justice system has jurisdiction over its
subjects until they reach their twenty-first birthdays. Most
are released much sooner, so they can be supervised while
on the equivalent of parole. At the time of Alonzo Barnett's stay at Spofford, probation officers typically carried caseloads upward of two hundred juveniles apiece.
Which allowed an officer to spend four minutes with each
of his charges, oh, every six weeks or so. When it came

to Alonzo Barnett, they didn't even bother. Seeing that he'd already flunked probation once, they weren't about to give him another chance. Instead, he was released outright two years later, having been outfitted with a shirt, a pair of pants, a pair of ill-fitting shoes and a subway token, all courtesy of the Fortune Society, and a ten-dollar bill, thanks to the largesse of the taxpayers of New York State.

He was seventeen at the time.

As interested as he was in Barnett's account of the years that followed, Jaywalker figured that could wait for another day. With eight dollars in commissary funds and no bail set, Barnett certainly wasn't going anywhere. Besides which, Jaywalker knew the odds. No doubt there were some uneducated, unemployed, unskilled, seventeen-year-old African-Americans with no families who came out of lockup, defied the odds and went on to succeed. But a look at Barnett's rap sheet had already told Jaywalker more than he needed to know. In addition to Green Haven, he'd seen the sights at Sing Sing, Great Meadow, Fishkill, Dannemora, Auburn and Attica. As for the little time he'd spent out on the street between visits, it didn't require all that much imagination to fill in the blanks.

What Jaywalker was more interested in right now was the case at hand, the one that looked like it might turn out to be Alonzo Barnett's final encounter with the court system. Not that it didn't promise to at last provide Barnett with something he hadn't had since his fourteenth birthday.

A permanent address.

As seamlessly as he could, Jaywalker gently steered the conversation toward the current charges. Unsure if, GED or no GED, Barnett could read—Jaywalker had made that mistake once with a client, and like most mistakes he made, he would never repeat it—he read the complaint aloud and then summarized the ten counts of the indictment.

"Funny," said Barnett. "You're my fourth lawyer on this case. But you're the first one who's bothered to read me the charges. Thank you."

Jaywalker nodded but resisted commenting. He didn't make criticizing other lawyers a habit, not unless he recognized their names and knew they were $750-an-hour blowhards. None of the ones listed on the previous notices of appearance came close to fitting into that category. So he simply said, "What can you tell me about them?"

"The lawyers?"

"No, the charges."

He half expected Barnett to deny them, to say he was being framed, that he was the wrong guy, that he had an alibi, that he hadn't known it was heroin. Once a client of Jaywalker's had explained that he had diplomatic immunity. The guy was an American citizen, born and raised in Bayonne, New Jersey, who worked as a pipe fitter and had never once been out of the country. But he'd taken a few correspondence courses from an outfit he'd seen advertised on a matchbook, after which they'd mailed him a piece of paper with the word *Diploma* printed across the top of it. So having received the diploma, he'd figured immunity came along with it.

Kind of like fries, he'd explained.

Alonzo Barnett wasn't asserting diplomatic immunity. Nor was he claiming frame, ignorance, alibi or mistaken identity. Without missing a beat, he looked Jaywalker squarely in the eye and said, "The charges are true. Every word of them."

3

I did a favor

"So there you have it in a nutshell," Jaywalker would tell his listener. "Here was a five-time loser, a man who'd spent the better part of his life in state prison, charged this time with selling a pretty hefty amount of heroin, freely and unequivocally admitting that he'd done exactly that."

To make matters worse, what Barnett had been accused of went far beyond the single sale and possession spelled out in the Criminal Court complaint. If you were to read the indictment—as Jaywalker had read it first to himself and then aloud to Alonzo Barnett—you soon realized that the case involved more than the October 5 sale and possession. In addition to those crimes, the grand jury had signed off on two earlier heroin sales made to the same "law enforcement official," although both of those had been for amounts smaller than the two ounces required to turn them into A-1 felonies.

Jaywalker hated drug cases back then and does to this day. Which isn't the same as saying he hates the defendants themselves. Not by any means. In fact, he's always found it far easier to empathize with a drug defendant than he has with the vast majority of the muggers, burglars,

drunk drivers and con men who come his way. Those
sorts deliberately prey on their victims, or by their conduct place others in grave danger. The drug defendant's
biggest victim turns out to be himself. Sure, the politicians
will tell you otherwise. They'll tell you that drug dealers
disseminate poison and destroy not only their own lives
but those of their customers and their customers' families,
and that they end up costing society billions of dollars
annually in health care and social services. To Jaywalker,
those words pretty much describe what the tobacco and
liquor companies do, year in and year out. The only difference, so far as he can tell, is that they happen to have
lobbyists. And whatever you do, don't get him started
talking about the gun manufacturers.

Jaywalker's years as a DEA agent, especially on those
occasions when he was working undercover, had brought
him face-to-face with enough small-time, midlevel and
even major dealers to know that they were pretty much
like other people, just trying to get by. If one dealer got
caught—whether by Jaywalker, or some other agent or
cop—there was always another one waiting in line right
behind him to take his place. No, it wasn't the dealers
who were the problem, either individually or as a group.
It was the system itself that perpetuated the charade. By
pouring so much money into interdiction, enforcement
and imprisonment, and so little into education, treatment
and rehabilitation, all the lawmakers ever succeeded in
doing was driving up the price of the product until it was
literally worth more than gold itself. That in turn insured
that people would risk everything—their health, their
freedom and their very lives—to grow it, import it, dis-
tribute it and even look the other way when it was worth
their while to. So no, he didn't hate the dealers. Most of
them were beaten-down users themselves, and almost all

of the ones he encountered were getting worse than they deserved. If not this time, then surely the next.

What he hated were the cases.

He hated them because they made him sad. Sad in their testimony to human frailty and human suffering. Sad in their needless futility and ultimate folly. Sad in their dreary same-old, same-old familiarity. There were the direct sale, the observation sale, the buy-and-bust, and the cash-and-stash uncovered in some roach-infested tenement apartment during the execution of a search warrant. It was almost like ordering from one of those old Chinese take-out menus. Choose one from Column A, one from Column B, one from Column C. But it made no difference. You could forget about the names of the different generals and whether you wanted white rice or brown rice. Whatever you ordered was going to taste pretty much like everything else, and would come with the same stale fortune cookie. And whether they got you for possession or sale, direct or observation, you were going to end up with a one-way ticket to state prison.

They talked some more that day, Jaywalker and Barnett, but not all that much more. It was already apparent to Jaywalker that, like most cases, this one wasn't going to trial. It couldn't. Sooner or later Alonzo Barnett was going to have to plead guilty, even if it meant copping to an A-2 felony and accepting a minimum sentence of eight years to life. And since there was little likelihood that a parole board was going to give him yet another chance, Barnett might not die in prison, but he was going to be one very old man by the time he came out the other end of the meat grinder.

But that realization by no means ended Jaywalker's job. Just as he'd been the first of four lawyers to bother

to read the charges to Barnett, so would he be the first to
listen to the rest of the man's story, and to come to know
him as an individual and not just a defendant. He would
make it his business to draw Barnett out and make him
talk, make him explain just why an intelligent-sounding
man who had to have known better had succumbed yet
again to the lure of easy money. Jaywalker would describe
in detail the trial process itself, since despite all Barnett's
arrests and convictions he'd never been through a trial,
having pleaded guilty each time. Jaywalker would point
out the futility of changing that pattern now, and the dire
consequences of being convicted after trial, when all bets
were off.

In a word, he would become a friend.

Only not now.

Having resisted taking a plea for a year and a half,
Barnett evidently had his reasons, whatever they were
and however foolish they might be, for wanting to go to
trial this time. For Jaywalker to begin that conversation
now, at the very first meeting between lawyer and client,
would have been totally counterproductive. It would have
marked Lawyer Number 4 as no different from Numbers
1, 2 and 3. It would have undermined the very foundation
of something Jaywalker needed to build between himself
and his client.

Something called trust.

So they talked some more, but about other things.
Jaywalker learned that Barnett had two young daughters who were somewhere in foster care. That he'd been
a heroin addict beginning at age fifteen, but had been
clean for almost eight years now. That, like Jaywalker, he
was a Yankees fan. That not only had he taught himself
how to read and write, but that he'd begun composing

poems, a sample of which he agreed to show Jaywalker sometime.

They didn't teach you in law school to ask about that kind of stuff. You didn't need it in order to pass the bar exam or to hang up a shingle on the outside of your office door. Nor did the supervisors at Legal Aid talk about it. But it mattered; it mattered hugely. And even back then, back in 1986, without ever having been taught about it, Jaywalker knew and understood that. And the best thing about doing it was that it cost absolutely nothing, just like saying "please" or "thank you," or pausing for a second to hold a door open for someone a few steps behind you. So the only thing about doing all that stuff that mystified Jaywalker was that nobody else seemed to realize how terribly, terribly important it was.

He didn't go home after meeting with Barnett, or to court or his office. Instead he went back around the corner and walked south, downtown. He passed both entrances to 100 Centre Street on his left. Even though the district attorney's office was located there—albeit listed under the side street address of One Hogan Place—Jaywalker knew he wouldn't find the assistant D.A. in charge of Alonzo Barnett's case there. No, he'd noticed from a telephone number on the file that the case was assigned to someone in Special Narcotics.

Despite the promising name, Special Narcotics are not high-quality drugs. Created with an infusion of municipal, state and federal funds in 1971 to help deal with the city's mushrooming drug problem, the Office of the Special Narcotics Prosecutor for the City of New York was, and continues to be, located one block farther south, at 80 Centre Street. Its chief function is to handle a portion of the thousands of drug cases that would otherwise overwhelm the regular district attorney's office. It's headed by a Special Narcotics Prosecutor and staffed by a fluctuating number of lawyers who act as assistant district attorneys. Except that they handle nothing but drug cases.

Twenty minutes later, Jaywalker was sitting in a medium-sized office across the desk from the A.D.A. in charge of the prosecution of Alonzo Barnett. It was a medium-sized office rather than a small one, because the assistant also happened to be a supervisor, one of a half dozen who oversaw ten or fifteen other assistants and reported directly to the Special Narcotics Prosecutor himself. Though these days that would be *her*self.

Times change.

The name of the assistant was Daniel Pulaski. He was a good-looking man in his forties, careful with his three-piece suits and his slicked-back dark hair. He was also, at least according to the general consensus of the local defense bar, a Class A prick.

Jaywalker has never had qualms about going up against a prosecutor with sharp elbows. In fact, when it comes time to go to trial, he generally prefers that his adversaries are able to take care of themselves. He's found over the years that weak prosecutors tend to arouse the sympathies of both judges and juries, sympathies that Jaywalker would far sooner have directed at the defendant.

But there's sharp, and then there's nasty. And at least by reputation, Daniel Pulaski fell squarely into the latter category. That said, Jaywalker had never tried a case against him. He'd stood up opposite him on a few matters in court, but none of them had ended up going to trial, or even to an evidentiary hearing, for that matter. So he was willing to suspend judgment on Pulaski for the moment, and even determined to give the man the benefit of doubt, at least until he demonstrated he didn't deserve it.

It wouldn't take long.

"So," said Pulaski, "I see you're the latest flavor-of-the-month for Alonzo the Malingerer."

"I'm his new lawyer," Jaywalker deadpanned. "If that's what you mean."

"Right," said Pulaski, checking his wristwatch in what struck Jaywalker as a crude parody of impatience. And, he wondered, who wore cuff links these days? Especially *gold* cuff links?

"If this is a bad time—"

"No, no," said Pulaski. "It's as good a time as any. What can I do for you?"

"Well," said Jaywalker, "I was hoping you might have copies of papers for me, discovery material. That sort of stuff."

"Listen, Mr. Jaywalker—"

"Jay."

"Mr. Jay—"

"Just Jay."

"Whatever. The point is, you're this scumbag's fourth lawyer. I'm out of copies and have better things to do than run off more of them. You want copies, why don't you go see your predecessors?"

"I guess I can do that," Jaywalker conceded. "I just thought that since it seems like you and I might have to try this case, we might start off on the right—"

"We're not going to try this case," said Pulaski. "Your guy is going to jerk you around for six months, just like he did with all the others. Then he's going to say he can't communicate with you and ask the judge to give him a new lawyer. We both know that."

"Actually," said Jaywalker, "he seems to be communicating with me pretty well."

"You've met him?"

Jaywalker nodded matter-of-factly. Pulaski countered with a look of surprise. Evidently he didn't know any lawyers who went to the trouble of going to the jail and visiting their assigned clients even before their cases came on in court.

"So if you've met him," said Pulaski, "maybe you can tell me what he's waiting for before he takes his plea."

"As I said earlier, I'm not at all sure he's going to take a plea." It wasn't exactly the truth. Jaywalker was actually pretty sure Barnett would come around, sooner or later. But Pulaski's certainty about that had been enough to prompt Jaywalker to suggest he was mistaken.

"You understand," said Pulaski, "that eight to life is the best he can possibly get under the law, don't you? And that's on a *plea,* to an A-2. He goes to trial, the minimum starts at fifteen."

"We both know that," said Jaywalker. "But he doesn't seem particularly interested."

"Then fuck him. He can go to trial and get twenty-five to life, for all I care. It'll be my pleasure." Followed by another look at the wristwatch, this one even more deliberate and more dismissive than the first.

The meeting, for all intents and purposes, was over. Nine minutes after it had begun.

Well, thought Jaywalker, at least he'd managed to get through it without throwing a punch at Pulaski, a temptation he'd succumbed to three years earlier. The target hadn't been Pulaski that time. It had been an A.D.A. in Brooklyn, an ex-cop named Jimmy Spagnelli, who'd accused Jaywalker of being overzealous in the way he'd gone after an arson investigator on the witness stand.

Jaywalker had ignored the insult, accepting it as a compliment in disguise. But Spagnelli hadn't wanted to let it go at that, and a moment later he called Jaywalker a "low-life shyster." Jaywalker's Jewish half had reacted by taking offense at that, and his Irish half had reacted by clocking Spagnelli with a right hook. Unfortunately, it had landed a bit high on the side of Spagnelli's head, clearly not a vital organ. For Jaywalker, the result had been a broken hand and a two-year suspension from practicing in Brooklyn.

Kind of like losing his driving privileges in Lithuania.

Over the course of the next three days, Jaywalker did precisely what Daniel Pulaski had left him no recourse but to do. He met in turn with each of Alonzo Barnett's three previous lawyers, collecting copies of court documents, motion papers and discovery materials. By the end of the week he'd put together the bare bones of a file. And during the course of amassing it, he'd gained a few insights into Barnett's reluctance to take a plea, but only a few. Among the highlights were "He's self-destructive," "He's a psycho," and "I dunno, beats the shit outa me."

The case appeared in court that Thursday, in Part 91. Part 91, located at the far end of the fifteenth floor of 100 Centre Street, was at that time designated as the L.T.D. Part, which stood for Long Term Detainees or, as one cynic suggested, Let Them Die. Its calendars were filled with cases of jailed defendants that were not only ripe for trial, but overripe. In a system that supposedly guaranteed an accused felon a speedy trial within six months of arraignment, every defendant in Part 91 had already been locked up for a year or more. And in a business that was evaluated largely on statistics, these aging cases were negatively skewing the average arrest-to-completion time that the administrative judge desperately needed to bring down in order to demonstrate efficiency and justify budget increases. So the word had gone out to get the cases disposed of by plea or, failing that, to get them tried.

Jaywalker had a couple of other cases besides Barnett's on that Thursday, involving defendants who were out on bail. So he stopped by Part 91 early in the morning and left word with the clerk that he'd be back. *Back* turned out to be just before eleven, and when he walked in, the judge was waiting for him.

Judges come in all shapes and sizes. Not all of them look like they were born to the bench like Learned Hand, say, whose iconic photograph—featuring his shock of white hair and bushy eyebrows, his black robe and his craggy face—has "judge" written all over it. Then again, it's entirely possible that Justice Hand may have looked like that at birth, only in miniature, seeing as his parents had pretty much *named* him to the bench, too. Still, we tend to think of judges as dignified, august father figures, peering down from the bench with an overabundance of firmness and just a hint of compassion. John Marshall comes to mind, as do Oliver Wendell Holmes, Benjamin Cardozo and William O. Douglas. Giants, all.

Shirley Levine hardly fit the mold.

Barely five feet tall and a hundred pounds if she was that, Levine was not what Jaywalker would have called a beautiful woman. Somewhere in her sixties, she was either cursed with a permanent bad hair day or simply unconcerned with her physical appearance. Her voice could charitably be called squeaky. She had no use for formality, having long ago dispensed with the trappings of the standard-issue black robe that came with the job.

Or perhaps she'd simply been unable to locate one small enough for her. She didn't expect people to rise to their feet when she entered her courtroom, and she quickly beckoned them to sit if they insisted on doing so. She needed no gavel to bring the room to order, and so far as Jaywalker knew, she'd never once raised her voice in anger.

Some judges maintain decorum through the volume of their voices or the sheer force of their personalities. Others develop a reputation from their willingness to toss troublemakers into the pens at the first hint of insubordination. A few make it their business to get even, taking out their frustrations on defendants in the rulings they make and the sentences they dispense.

Shirley Levine did none of those things.

She didn't have to.

She accomplished everything she needed to, and more, through her unfailing cheerfulness, her unquestioned fairness and her curious habit of treating people— all people—with uncommon decency. How she'd ever ended up as a judge was anyone's guess.

Not that she didn't have an interesting backstory. Rumor had it that in her early twenties she'd been involved in some sort of special operations in the War, and had been parachuted behind enemy lines in Nazi Germany. That she'd been good with a gun and better still with a knife. Jaywalker had tried to get her to open up once about the subject, offering to trade a few of his DEA stories in exchange. But she'd demurred. "Who can remember?" She'd laughed him off. Still, the rumors persisted, and in a place like 100 Centre Street, rumor was often as good as it got.

This would be Alonzo Barnett's trial judge, should he really insist on a trial. And though that would ensure a relatively pleasurable couple of weeks for Jaywalker, in the long run it would do absolutely nothing for Barnett. Save for the fact that after the jury had convicted him and the judge had sentenced him, her parting "Good luck" to him would be genuine instead of sarcastic.

"Ahh, Mr. Jaywalker," she said now as she spied him making his way up the aisle. "How nice to see you. And thank you for leaving us a note earlier." Then, turning to a court officer, she said, "Would you please bring out Mr. Barnett."

Would you please. Mister. From a *judge,* mind you.

Not that anything of substance went on that first day. The assistant D.A. in the part read off a note from Daniel Pulaski. The eight-to-life sentence was still being offered on a plea to an A-2, it said. But if the defendant didn't take it this time or next, it would be withdrawn. After that, he could have fifteen to life—or worse.

"How much time do you need?" the judge asked Jaywalker, once his client had been brought out from the pen.

"Two weeks would be good," he told her.

"Two weeks it is. See you then. Are you doing all right, Mr. Barnett?"

"Yes, ma'am."

It was stuff like that that confounded Jaywalker. Try as he might, he just couldn't picture Shirley Levine jumping out of a plane in the dark of the night, a gun stuck in her belt and a knife clenched in her teeth.

Back in the pens, Jaywalker had his second sit-down interview with Barnett. This one would take on a bit more urgency than the first, if only because of the ultimatum delivered by Daniel Pulaski's note. While threats to withdraw plea offers were often no more than that—threats—Jaywalker couldn't put it past Pulaski to follow through on his. What difference would it make to him if some defendant ended up with a fifteen-year minimum instead of an eight year one? So Jaywalker didn't mince words.

"If you ever want to take a plea, next time is the time to do it," he said. "I don't trust this D.A. to keep the offer open past then. I really don't."

Barnett seemed to think for a moment, and Jaywalker half expected him to say, "Okay, we'll do it next time." After all, he hadn't once said, "I'm not guilty" or "I didn't do it" or anything along those lines. In fact, at their first meeting, he'd made a point of admitting that the charges against him were true, every word of them. But what Jaywalker hadn't learned yet was that unlike most defendants, and for that matter most people, Alonzo Barnett was never quick to answer a question of any sort. Not that he stalled before replying or repeated the question aloud in order to buy time. No, Jaywalker would come to understand, it was simply a matter of Barnett's taking a moment to *think* before responding. A rare thing indeed.

"To tell you the truth," he finally said, "I don't intend to take a plea. If that's all right with you."

"Of course it's all right with me," said Jaywalker. "But it brings us to another issue."

"What's that?"

"Well," said Jaywalker, "you've been around long enough to know that the chances of beating a direct sale case aren't very good." A *direct sale* meant one in which the buyer was an undercover cop or agent, as opposed to an *observation* sale, where the authorities claimed to have witnessed a transaction between a seller and a buyer, both of whom were civilians.

Barnett nodded but didn't say anything. Not only had

he been around long enough to know that Jaywalker was speaking the truth, but his record of guilty pleas suggested he understood the odds.

"So," continued Jaywalker, "it might be a good idea if we spent a few minutes talking about the facts of your case."

"Fair enough," said Barnett.

"Why don't you tell me what happened." It wasn't a question on Jaywalker's part so much as an invitation. Nor was it something he always asked of a defendant, particularly in a sale case. Strange as it may sound, sometimes a lawyer and client talk about everything *but* the facts. There are times, for example, when they both know the defendant has done precisely what he's accused of but on the one hand doesn't want to lie to his lawyer *or* come right out and admit his guilt on the other. So without ever saying so, they agree to ignore it and spend their time dancing around it, the elephant in the room. Or, in this particular instance, the elephant in the cell.

Again, Barnett took his time before answering. When finally he did, he spoke only four little words. They added up to neither an admission of guilt nor a denial, but rather an explanation for his behavior. In no way did they amount to a legal defense, the way they might have had he said, for example, that he'd been forced into doing what he'd done, or coerced, or that he'd been insane at the time, or that he hadn't realized that it had actually been heroin he'd sold to the undercover agent.

Believe it or not, Jaywalker had once won a case on just such a theory. His client had been making a living by "beating" his customers, selling them supermarket-bought spices at marijuana prices. When the cops had examined the evidence they'd bought back at the station house, they'd realized they too had been victimized. So they'd simply sprinkled some of their own emergency stash into the ounce they'd bought, enough to convince the police chemist. But not the jury. Not once had Jaywalker insisted upon having an independent analysis conducted. The sample came back two percent cannabis, eighty percent oregano and eighteen percent basil. Highly aromatic stuff, perhaps, but hardly the kind to get high on.

No, Alonzo Barnett's four words of explanation fell far short of that standard. And when he uttered them, they initially struck Jaywalker as being not only legally worthless but pretty insignificant in terms of moral culpability, as well. Then again, he was at something of a disadvantage. For as he listened to them, he had yet to hear Alonzo Barnett's story. He had absolutely no way of knowing just how fertile with possibility the words were, or how in time they would germinate, take root, sprout and grow into a full-fledged defense, the likes of which Jaywalker would never have dared to even dream about, sitting there in the pens of 100 Centre Street, back on that Thursday morning in May of 1986.

"I did a favor," is all Alonzo Barnett said.

4

No good deed

The fact that he took a moment to think before answering a question in no way meant that Alonzo Barnett couldn't tell a story. He could, and for the next half hour he spoke almost without pause or interruption. So articulate was he and so riveting was his story that Jaywalker dared to break into it only once or twice, seeking some minor clarification here or amplification there. Other than that, it was Barnett's story, told in his own words and his own voice.

When he'd arrived at Green Haven in the mid-1970s to begin serving the latest of his prison sentences, Barnett had been accompanied, as all inmates were, by a *jacket*. A jacket, at least in prison parlance, isn't something you wear. It's your file, containing a certified copy of your conviction, your indictment, your presentence investigation report, your entire criminal record, your photograph and your fingerprint card. All of that is kept in a folder, or jacket, to keep it private and confidential.

But "private" and "confidential" are concepts that simply don't exist within prison walls. With guards on the take and inmates assigned to work as clerks in receiving, classification and records, every detail about an inmate's past is not only visible to prying eyes but is *currency*. And with respect to Alonzo Barnett, there were two details that stood out.

The first was that at age twenty-two, Barnett had been arrested and convicted for the felonious forcible rape of a fifteen-year-old girl. Never mind that the two of them had been in love and already had a child together, that there'd been absolutely no force involved or threatened, and that they would get legally married three years later. Or that in order to resolve the matter quickly and inexpensively, Barnett had waived his right to counsel, pleaded guilty to statutory rape as a misdemeanor and paid a twenty-five-dollar fine. If you'd opened Barnett's jacket, all you would have seen were the initial felony charge of forcible rape of a fifteen-year-old female and the fact that the arrest had resulted in a conviction.

The second thing you would have found, had you taken the trouble to read the indictment handed up in the case that had most recently landed Barnett in Green Haven, was that in addition to the usual counts of sale and possession, there was, way down at the very bottom of the list, a charge that had been added to the Penal Law only recently. "Sale of a Controlled Substance in the fourth degree upon school grounds" it read. Once again, the dire official language masked a far more innocent reality. The legislature, it turned out, had defined "school grounds" in such a way as to include "any area accessible to the public located within 2,500 feet of the boundary of any public or private elementary, parochial, intermediate, junior high, vocational or high school." In other words, anywhere within nearly *half a mile* of any such place. In Manhattan, that translated into a nearly ten-block radius, resulting in just about anyplace in the borough qualifying as school grounds. The law has since undergone several amendments, and the 2,500-foot zone is these days down to a slightly more reasonable 1,000. But labels being what they are, the charge made it look and sound as though Alonzo Barnett had set up shop in the playground and started handing out free samples of drugs to kindergarten kids.

Put that together with the forcible rape of a child charge, and Green Haven had a new arrival who might as well have had a bull's-eye painted on his back.

"Prison is a lot like the street," Barnett explained. "Only it's, like, *concentrated*. Out on the street, the strong gang up together and prey on the weak. But the weak have choices, at least. They can split. They can move out of the neighborhood. They can lock themselves indoors. And they can complain to the police. Inside, you don't have options like that. You can't move out just because you don't like the neighborhood. You can lock down in your cell, but only for so long. When it's mealtime, you got to come out and go to the mess hall. When it's rec hour, you got to go to the yard. You got a job—you got to go to work. As for the police, there are none. There are the COs, the corrections officers. But a lot of them are down with the gang members, and most of the others find it's easier to look away when trouble starts. And trouble is always starting."

"So what do you do?" Jaywalker asked, even though he pretty much knew the answer.

"You find safety in numbers," Barnett told him. "You join up with the Bloods or the Kings if you're Latino, or the Aryans if you're white. Me, I'm black. I joined up with the Muslims. I converted to Islam."

Jaywalker nodded. In the 1970s, it made sense. Today, in a post-9/11 world, it would have set off alarm bells. But back then, even if you didn't happen to be a big fan of

Malcolm X, hearing that someone was a Muslim didn't automatically make him a terrorist.

"And how did that work out?" Jaywalker wanted to know.

"Not so well," said Barnett. "At first, the brothers thought I was a plant, a snitch. Between the rape charge and the school-grounds thing, they figured I was looking to join up so I could spy on them and rat them out."

"To whom?"

Barnett laughed. "Funny, that's what I asked. But I never did get an answer. All I got was a contract put out on me, a price on my head. So I did the only thing I could. I found me a protector."

Jaywalker said nothing, but his stare must have said enough.

"No," said Barnett, "not the way you're thinking. I didn't become somebody's bitch, or anything like that. When I say I found a protector, I simply mean I allowed myself to be taken under the wing of an older con, a guy who'd been there long enough to have established a rep for himself. Someone the brothers trusted."

Jaywalker nodded.

"His name was Hightower. Clarence Hightower. He ran the prison barbershop, where the inmates went to get haircuts. He saw I was having a real hard time, and he'd heard about the contract on me. And for some reason he could tell I wasn't a snitch. So one day he offered me a job cutting hair. I told him I didn't know the first thing about it. He laughed and said, 'You think I did when I started? I was an enforcer for a numbers ring. All I knew was how to crack skulls and break kneecaps. You'll learn.'

"Still, I'd been in enough joints to know that, inside, nothing comes free. Nothing. So I ask him what it was going to cost me. I figured he'd tell me smokes or candy or commissary money, stuff like that. Instead he looks at me and asks what people called me on the outside. 'AB,' I tell him. He says, 'AB, what I'm doing for you is called a favor. Understand? It's the kinda thing you can't put a price tag on. But who knows. One day I may need me a favor myself. You just remember that, okay?' And I said 'Okay.'"

"And that was it?" Jaywalker asked.

"And that was it. I knew it might come home to haunt me someday," said Barnett. "But the way I looked at it, I had no choice. It was only a matter of how long it was going to take before I got a knife stuck into my gut or a razor pulled across my throat. Compared to owing a man a favor? What kind of choice was that?"

"Not much of one," Jaywalker had to admit.

Assigned to the barbershop, Barnett spent the first month sweeping up, sorting towels and linens, and keeping track of scissors, combs and Afro picks, which even though they were all plastic and round-tipped, had to be turned in each evening. There were no razors allowed in the shop. And bit by bit, simply by virtue of working for Clarence Hightower, Barnett managed to shed his reputation as a child rapist, school-yard drug dealer and snitch. And though no official word ever came down that the contract on him had been lifted, a time came when he felt safe. *Safe* being a relative word in prison, of course. After three months Hightower let Barnett start cutting hair himself, under his watchful eye. Before a year was up, he was an accomplished barber, at least to the extent one can become an accomplished barber with instruments designed for preschoolers.

Barnett was doing a four-and-a-half-to-nine at Green Haven, and he made parole on his second try, after five years. He'd lined up a bed in a halfway house and a job washing dishes in a restaurant, the New York Department of State having informed him that despite the qualifications spelled out in his written request, his felony convictions disqualified him from obtaining a barber's license. In his plan for parole, he'd listed among his goals reestablishing contact with his daughters and eventually getting them back from foster care.

His parole officer told him to get real.

Still, by the time of his release Barnett had won the trust of the brothers, earned his GED and kicked his heroin habit for good. He hadn't realized it at the time he'd signed up, but practicing Muslims didn't do drugs, drink alcohol, smoke cigarettes or curse their god. Had the Koran only thought to prohibit flying airplanes into buildings, it might be a different world we live in today. But this was 1981, a full two decades before that particular loss of innocence.

On the day of Barnett's release, Clarence Hightower was the last one in line to high-five him and wish him success on the outside. Hightower himself was doing a ten-to-twenty bit for aggravated assault and wouldn't be getting out for another three years. There was no mention of favors done or favors owed.

There'd be time for that later.

Barnett and Jaywalker were interrupted by a corrections officer, an old-timer known to Jaywalker by face, though not by name. Which was no surprise. Jaywalker had always been good at faces, while names and phone numbers eluded him. So the exchange of greetings became something of a guy thing.

"Hello, Counselor."

"Hey, big guy. Howya doon?"

Big Guy reached one hand through the bars and handed

Barnett a couple of sandwiches wrapped in paper, and a cardboard cup. Then, without asking, he did the same for Jaywalker. The COs all knew Jaywalker, knew he spent more time in the pens talking with his clients than all the other lawyers combined. Knew he worked straight through the lunch hour. And knew he never turned down a day-old cheese sandwich or a lukewarm cup of something that passed for coffee. They considered him one of their own, and they looked after him and, by extension, his clients.

"Thank you," Barnett and Jaywalker said as one.

"You got it," said Big Guy, moving on to the next pen.

They ate in silence for a few minutes, lawyer and defendant, separated by a dozen thick iron bars and the fact that one of them would be going home when the visit was over, while the other was already home, in a manner of speaking.

"So," said Jaywalker once they'd finished eating, "what happened next?"

As he always did, Barnett waited a few seconds before answering. And this time he took additional time to count on his fingers—backward, it would turn out. "Summer of 1984," he said after a while. "I've been out three years. Drug free. Have an apartment to call my own. Not much to brag about, but still…I'm working as a grill man at a different restaurant, a better one. Got visitation with my daughters. Haven't missed a single reporting date with my parole officer. Life is good."

Jaywalker nodded. These were significant accomplishments for anyone. For a recovering heroin addict and five-time felon, they defied all the odds.

"So who do you think shows up?"

Jaywalker didn't bother answering. He knew Barnett's

question was a rhetorical one. They'd both known who was going to show up.

"Catches me as I'm sitting on my stoop at the end of the day, minding my own business. Says he's been out a month and can't catch a break. Can I help him out?"

Jaywalker could only wince. He knew where this was going.

"So I reach into my pocket," said Barnett, "fish out whatever I've got on me and offer it to him. I think it was maybe eighteen dollars, something like that."

Reminded Jaywalker of some of his fees.

"'I don't want no charity,' Hightower tells me.

"I ask him what he does want.

"'You know,' he says. 'I been outa action all this time, I don' know who's doin' what, who to see, who to go to.'

"I ask him, 'For what?'

"'To get hooked up,' he tells me. 'I need to get back in the business.' The *bidness,* he called it. Which is right when I tell him he's got the wrong guy. I give him the eighteen dollars or whatever it was. I wish him luck. I stand up and I go inside. Lock the door behind me."

Oh, thought Jaywalker, what a wonderful ending to the story that would have been. An act of charity toward an old friend, a debt repaid. But of course it wasn't the end of the story. Jaywalker knew that every bit as well as Barnett did. Had it been the end of the story, the two of them wouldn't be sitting where they were today, talking through the bars.

No, Clarence Hightower would keep coming back. He'd come back five times, six times, each time with a slightly different story. Only they all had the same ending. "He needed to find a connection," Barnett explained. "He understood that I was finished with that stuff, and he said he was okay with that. But he also knew that I knew who was still around, who was still doing."

Doing.

"He kept saying that all he wanted was for me to hook him up, to put him together with someone who was in action. He had this customer, he said, a real live one who was looking to buy weight. Had all sorts of cash money. All I'd have to do was find somebody to cut him into. Once I'd done that, I could walk away from it. Keep a piece of the pie if I wanted to, turn it down if I didn't."

"And?"

"And I kept saying no."

"Until…" said Jaywalker.

"Until the seventh time, when he started crying like a baby and threatening to kill himself and all that. Until he played his hole card, and reminded me how he'd saved my life when no one else was going to. And telling me that because of that I owed him now. And you know what?"

"What?"

"He was right," said Barnett. "He *had* saved my life, and I *did* owe him. When it came right down to it, that was the truth. And it was a truth that no matter how hard I tried to look away from it, it kept looking me in the face."

"So…?"

"So I said okay. The next day I made a few phone calls and found out who was doing what. It wasn't hard. And I paid off the favor, just like he asked. Just like he told me I owed him."

They talked for another forty-five minutes about what had followed. Jaywalker jotted down some details on a yellow pad. But he hardly needed to. He knew the story. He'd known it before he'd become a lawyer ten years earlier. He'd known it from his undercover days as a DEA

agent. Unbeknownst to both Clarence Hightower and
Alonzo Barnett, the customer—the "real live one" with
all sorts of cash money, the one looking to buy weight—
was the Man. And the story wouldn't end until both men
had been arrested, Hightower for possession and Barnett
for sale.

As they say, no good deed goes unpunished.

Replaying the story in his mind that night, Jaywalker
was struck by the almost tragic aspect of it. Here was a
guy who'd done everything right. Given up drugs, found
a job and a place of his own, kept his nose clean, even
reestablished contact with his daughters. And then along
comes his past to catch up with him. He says no half a
dozen times, only to be told he has a debt to repay, a favor
owed. So he does it. And as a result, his whole world
comes crashing down.

Jaywalker could recite the various defenses to crimes
laid out in the Penal Law, as well as others mandated
by the Constitution, remembered from law school, or
grounded in case law or common law. He knew which
were complete defenses and which were partial ones,
which were primary defenses and which were affirmative ones.

There was alibi. There was justification, coercion and
duress. There was entrapment and agency. There was
infancy, along with insanity, incompetence, incapacity
and impossibility. There were abandonment, renunciation
and attenuation, lack of intent and lack of scienter. There
were misidentification and mistake, whether of fact or
law. Diplomatic immunity, transactional immunity and
use immunity, the statute of limitations and the statutory
right to a speedy trial. You had voluntary intoxication and
involuntary intoxication, ex post facto and post-traumatic

stress. Then you had extreme emotional disturbance, malicious prosecution, vindictive prosecution and selective prosecution. Also lack of jurisdiction and improper venue, double jeopardy and double punishment.

But nowhere, absolutely nowhere, was there a defense called "doing somebody a favor."

5

Grasping at straws

The average lawyer would have stopped right there, Jaywalker knew. Here was a client who was flat-out admitting his guilt to every single one of the charges against him. No ifs, ands or buts. The only explanation he could come up with for his actions—that he'd been doing somebody a favor—was no defense at all. Try killing someone and then telling the police it was just a favor you did for a friend, and see how far that gets you.

Yet, as Jaywalker and Barnett had continued to talk, Barnett had made it quite clear that he had no intention of pleading guilty. "Look," he'd said, "if I'm going to spend the rest of my life in prison—and it looks like I am—the last thing I want to do is put myself there. I may not have much of a chance at trial, but if I lose, at least I'll be able to say I went down swinging."

Much of a chance at trial?

Try *no chance at all,* Jaywalker had told him, though not quite in those words. But it hadn't seemed to matter. Alonzo Barnett was stone-cold guilty. The prosecution could prove it, and in spades. Without even a theoretical defense, Jaywalker had absolutely nowhere to go at trial. Yet a trial was exactly what Barnett was insisting on having.

Not that any of those things, or all of them added up, would have fazed most lawyers. Especially those working on the clock. To most of them, a trial simply meant a bigger payday. Not that you got rich back then on assigned counsel rates. But even at forty dollars an hour for in-court time and twenty-five for out-of-court, a two-week trial could generate a nice four-figure check. And since there was no chance of winning, there was also no pressure on the lawyer to knock himself out. If the defendant wanted to take the stand, fine. If he didn't, also fine. Either way, it was going to be his funeral.

The problem was, of course, that Jaywalker wasn't your average lawyer. Never had been, never would be. If Alonzo Barnett wanted a trial, then a trial he would get. But that didn't mean that Jaywalker was going to relax, sit back and listen to the meter click. Doing any of those things would have been constitutionally impossible for him, the functional equivalent of his donning a tuxedo, renting a stretch limo and going out dancing.

The problem was, where to begin?

A lawyer who comes into a case late finds himself at a serious disadvantage. Prior to his arrival, his adversary has been at work lining up witnesses, cementing and reconciling their stories, boning up on the law if necessary, and doing hundreds of other little things to maximize his head start. Which isn't to say that Jaywalker's predecessors on the defense side hadn't been doing some of those things, too. But occasionally there's a good reason—or even a number of good reasons—behind a client's dissatisfaction with his representation.

Jaywalker had come into Alonzo Barnett's case a full year and a half late, and had had not one predecessor, but three of them. The day after his second sit-down with Barnett, he took stock of what those lawyers had done, or failed to do, before his arrival.

First was the fact that none of them had made a serious attempt to get bail set in the case. While that might have made sense early on in the proceedings, at a time when Barnett had a parole violation detainer on him and couldn't have gotten out in any event, there'd soon come a time when the detainer had been lifted. Barnett had had so little time remaining on his parole that the authorities had simply terminated him, marking his file closed with the notation "unsatisfactory adjustment." Whether whoever was representing him at the time had noticed or not, or even bothered to check, was unclear. The result had been that on the new arrest, Barnett continued to be held in remand status. Jaywalker checked, of course, and when he discovered the omission, he went back in to see his client and bring him the news.

"Is there any amount of bail you could make?" he asked. "Anything at all?" He knew that even a defendant on a bad case with a bad record had a chance of getting a reasonable bail in Shirley Levine's courtroom. And in addition to knowing his client would much prefer to be out than in, Jaywalker had selfish reasons of his own in mind. It's much easier for the lawyer when he can meet with a defendant in his office than it is when he's got to visit him in jail. Even a jail around the corner from the courthouse, like the Tombs. And after all, Barnett had been caught selling heroin, and in pretty substantial amounts. It was only logical to figure he might have some money stashed away somewhere.

But Barnett surprised him.

"Don't get me bail," he said.

Which marked a first for Jaywalker. Because the thing

is, every detainee ever locked up in the history of the world wants to get out, with the possible exception of some homeless drunk in the middle of winter who's happy to have "three hots and a cot" while he sleeps things off.

But Alonzo Barnett was neither homeless nor drunk, and instead of it being midwinter, it was mid-May. So Jaywalker was forced to ask him why he didn't want to get out.

"It would be too hard on my daughters," Barnett said. "I've told them to give up on me, that I won't be coming out for a very long time, if ever. And it would be too hard on *me,* knowing I'd be living on borrowed time and would have to turn myself in sooner or later. I might decide to do something stupid, like run away. I couldn't do that to my girls. Although," he added, "I've got no place to run away *to.*"

In the end, Jaywalker convinced Barnett that it made sense to have a bail amount set, even if he had no intention of ever trying to post it, and the following day went before Judge Levine and had her set bail at $25,000. If nothing else, it downgraded Barnett's classification as a threat within the Tombs, freeing him up from having both his cell and his person subject to constant searches.

Another thing the trio of earlier lawyers had screwed up were the pretrial motions. They'd filed them—at least Lawyer Number 2 had—but done a pretty half-assed job. Long on paper but short on persuasion, they'd failed to recite sufficient grounds for the ordering of any evidentiary hearings prior to trial. The only thing that remained to be decided was how many of the defendant's convictions the prosecutor would be able to bring out if Barnett were to take the stand. As for discovery, a lot of things had been asked for, but Daniel Pulaski had successfully resisted turning over just about all of them. As a result, Jaywalker knew the dates and approximate times and locations of the three sales, as well as the amounts of heroin involved in each. That and the fact that the prosecution claimed to know of no exculpatory material that might in any way materially assist the defense.

Not much to work with.

But in addition to being a compulsive overpreparer, Jaywalker was a former investigator. Not all of his time at the Drug Enforcement Administration had been spent buying narcotics. When he hadn't been undercover, Jaywalker had been, like any other federal agent, an investigator. He knew how to slip a lock, tap a phone and bug a room. He could make a crime scene speak to him. He could walk into an apartment or pull over a car, and have a pretty good idea where the drugs were hidden. He was good with a camera and had a working knowledge of ballistics. He knew how to lift a fingerprint and match it to one on file. And he knew the back channels, the ins and outs of the criminal justice system.

It was that last piece of knowledge that he put to work now. And he began at the only place he could possibly think of.

Other than the cops and agents and state troopers who'd made the case against Alonzo Barnett and weren't about to speak with a defense lawyer, there was only one person who was in a position to know anything at all about the facts. His name was Clarence Hightower, and he was the guy who'd called in the favor. According to Barnett, Hightower had been arrested only minutes after Barnett himself, though for possession, rather than sale.

Finding Hightower's papers in the courthouse turned out to be a bit tricky, because they'd been sealed. The No Public Record stamp on the file could mean only one of three things, Jaywalker knew. First, that Hightower had been a juvenile or a youth, and Jaywalker knew he'd been neither. Second, that his case had ended with a dismissal or an acquittal. Or third, that he'd been convicted, but only of a *violation,* a minor noncriminal offense. Which struck Jaywalker as a bit unusual, seeing as Hightower's criminal record was in pretty much the same league as Barnett's, if not worse.

So he found a friendly clerk he'd known for years, gave him a sob story, and convinced the guy to look the other way for a few minutes. The clerk was taking a chance, but not all that much of one. Had they been caught, he knew Jaywalker would have taken the weight, explaining that he'd swiped the file without the clerk's knowledge. The clerk knew this because that's exactly the kind of thing Jaywalker had done in the past, whenever one of his little capers had been discovered. Even as it had led to a few of Jaywalker's overnights at Rikers Island, it explained his reputation as a stand-up guy who could be trusted if the shit were to hit the fan.

One of the things Jaywalker always looked for in a court file was a photograph of the defendant. He liked to put a face on things. When he found Hightower's mug shot, two things immediately jumped out at him. First, the guy wasn't much to look at. Second, he'd never win a best-dressed contest, not in his stained and ratty blue denim work shirt.

So much for first impressions.

According to the file, Hightower had indeed been arrested on October 5, 1984. It seemed that he'd walked right into the middle of things, not realizing that the three or four guys in plainclothes surrounding Barnett were handcuffing him and reading him his rights. Jaywalker already knew this, having heard it from Barnett, who'd explained that Hightower had walked over intending to hit Barnett up for some of the money left over from the transaction, just as he had after the second one. Hightower had been promptly rewarded for his greed by being stood up against a wall and searched, and the search had revealed a tinfoil packet containing a small amount of white powder.

Jaywalker continued combing through the file until he found the lab report. Unlike the drugs bought and seized from Barnett, which had been delivered to the United States Chemist for analysis, Hightower's tinfoil packet had been considered no big deal and had therefore been taken to the NYPD's lab. There, according to the report, it had been found to contain heroin, as well as lactose and dextrose—two sugars commonly used as additives—and quinine. Because the total weight had come to just under a tenth of an ounce, less than the eighth-of-an-ounce threshold required for a felony, Hightower had been charged with only a misdemeanor. Still, it could have cost him up to a year in jail, as well as a violation of his parole. But luckily for him, he'd been permitted to plead down to disorderly conduct, a violation, receiving the maximum permissible sentence of fifteen days, which by that time he'd already served. Jaywalker looked through the papers, hunting for the name of the judge who'd been so kind as to approve such a generous plea bargain: Robert H. Straub, Criminal Court Judge.

Now, if Shirley Levine was a plus fifteen on a scale of leniency, Ronald Straub was a minus twenty. Which explained why he'd handed out the longest sentence he possibly could, but not why he'd gone along with the plea arrangement in the first place. That, Jaywalker knew, could only have been due to the urging of whatever

A.D.A. had stood up on the case: Jonathan Hillebrand, Assistant District Attorney.

Jaywalker knew better than to question Judge Straub about the matter. He no doubt had been dealing with a calendar of over a hundred cases that day, and a year and a half later could hardly be expected to remember a plea that had probably taken two minutes at most. Besides, Straub might become curious about how Jaywalker had learned the disposition of a case that was supposed to have been sealed.

Jonathan Hillebrand was another matter. Jaywalker found him in one of the Criminal Court trial parts. He was a regular assistant, not in Special Narcotics like Daniel Pulaski. Which made sense, since Pulaski's office took only felonies, and Hightower's case had been a misdemeanor.

Not surprisingly, Hillebrand had no recollection of the matter. "It wasn't my case," he told Jaywalker, adding that he might have remembered the name had it been. "The way it works," he explained, "is that I get handed a bunch of files in the morning. Each one has a note on it from the assigned assistant, telling me to answer ready for trial or ask for an adjournment, and if there's an offer, what it is. The case you're asking me about must have had a note saying to offer the defendant a violation and fifteen days."

And the thing was, Jaywalker knew from experience that that was exactly how it worked.

Nor did he do any better when he tracked down the assistant whose case it *had* been, a young woman named Annie MacMurray. "Who remembers?" she told him. "I get hundreds of these things. We're told to get rid of the misdemeanors as fast as we can and pay attention to the felonies. I'm sure that's what I was doing."

"But the guy was on parole."

She shrugged her shoulders and said, "What can I tell you? I must not have noticed that. Or maybe he didn't have enough time left on his parole for it to matter."

In other words, Clarence Hightower had simply lucked out. He'd managed to slip through a small crack in a big system. It happened.

Still, Hightower was all Jaywalker had at this point. If Alonzo Barnett insisted on going to trial so that he could tell a jury he'd done someone a favor, the least Jaywalker could do was locate the guy he'd done the favor for, put him on the witness stand and have him corroborate the fact. It might not add up to a legal defense, but it might win some sympathy points with a jury. And from there, who knew? Stranger things had happened.

So Jaywalker put on his investigator's hat and spent the next three days trying to find Clarence Hightower.

And struck out.

The address listed on the court papers turned out to be a nonexistent one. Ditto the one Hightower had given the Department of Corrections at Rikers Island. Jaywalker tried the phone book, the unlisted directory, Social Security, Internal Revenue, the Motor Vehicle Bureau, the Department of Social Services. He even checked to see if by any chance Hightower had applied for a barber's license, as Barnett had tried to do. He hadn't. As a last resort, using a public phone, Jaywalker called the Division of Parole up in Albany.

"This is Detective Kelly," he told the woman who answered. "Manhattan North Homicide Squad, shield 5620."

"What can I do for you, Detective?"

So far, so good.

"I need to know who's supervising a particular parolee," he explained, furnishing her Hightower's full name and NYSIS number, which he'd made a point of copying down from the court papers.

"Hold, please."

It took a few minutes, during which Jaywalker kept an eye out. He knew all about call tracing and GPS technology, and he didn't want any real cops sneaking up on him and arresting him for criminal impersonation of a police officer. A felony was the last thing he needed on his record.

But no cops sneaked up.

"That supervision has been terminated," the woman told him.

"When?"

"December 12 of 1985. Last year."

Which struck Jaywalker as a bit strange. Hadn't Barnett told him that Hightower had been doing ten-to-twenty at Green Haven? Released in 1984, he would have still owed the state four or five years, at a minimum.

"Can you give me the name of the last PO who supervised him?" Jaywalker asked.

"I'm not supposed to," she told him. "Not on a closed case."

"Look," said Jaywalker gently, but not too gently. "I've got two dead kids I'm working on here, a four-year-old and a one-year-old. Both of them mutilated." Hey, if you were going to lie, might as well make it a big one.

"Anunziatta," she told him. "Ralph Anunziatta."

"Got a phone number, by any chance?"

"Try 212-555-2138."

"Thank you."

"I hope you find the perp. And, Detective?"

"Yes?"

"This conversation never happened."

Which was just fine with Jaywalker.

Not that Ralph Anunziatta turned out to be all that much help. "Yeah," he said, "I remember the guy. Sorta. I wanted to revoke him, but before I could do anything about it, they'd let him cop out to a disorderly conduct. Not even a crime. So the most I could do was to write him up for a technical violation and continue him on parole. Then, next thing I know, someone upstairs cuts him loose, fuckin' terminates him."

"Isn't that unusual?"

"A little," acknowledged Anunziatta. "But they say they gotta cut the numbers. Anyway, one less case for me."

What had been one less case for Parole Officer Anunziatta was the source of one more concern for defense lawyer Jaywalker. His wife caught him staring off into space that evening at the dinner table. Not that Jaywalker was any stranger to staring off into space. But his wife had an uncanny way of knowing just how many galaxies away he was at any particular moment and asked him what the problem was.

"I don't know," he said. "I'm representing this guy on a drug sale—several sales, in fact. And I don't know, I've just got a funny feeling…"

"Please don't tell me you've got another innocent defendant," his wife begged. Not too many years back, she'd lived through one of those with him. Or if not exactly with him, under the same roof. Jaywalker's obsession with trying to extricate a young man mistakenly accused of a series of knifepoint rapes had taken a tremendous toll on their marriage, their daughter and their bank account.

"No," he said. "Actually, he's as guilty as sin. But still…"

His wife said nothing. They'd been married long enough by that time for her to stay away from the *but still* part.

But still…

Later that night, his wife and daughter tucked into bed, Jaywalker sat at the kitchen table, scribbling thoughts on the back of an envelope. By the time he was finished, it might not have been the Gettysburg Address he'd composed, but he was looking at a fairly impressive list of pretty unusual developments in the way in which the criminal justice system had chosen to deal with Clarence Hightower.

First there was the fact that Hightower had never been charged in connection with the sales Alonzo Barnett had ended up making. According to Barnett, the guy he'd introduced Hightower to would deal with Hightower and his customer only through Barnett. This was hardly unusual. After all, the guy knew Barnett, not them, and this had been his way of insulating himself. But the acting-in-concert law being as broad as it was, surely Hightower could have been accused of sale, too. Only all they'd charged him with had been possession. Then again, he hadn't actually been present at the sales, and perhaps the cops hadn't known the full extent of his involvement. Maybe he'd just been lucky, was all.

Then there'd been the fact that despite his having been on parole, Hightower hadn't had a detainer lodged against him following his arrest. But stuff like that happened all the time, Jaywalker knew. It was a big system, and people messed up.

Next was the fact that they'd let him plead down from

a misdemeanor to a violation. Not that Jaywalker himself didn't get dispositions like that for his own clients every day. But usually not for those with horrendous records who owed parole time. Still, Jaywalker's conversations with the two assistant district attorneys who'd been involved had been unremarkable and hadn't left him with the feeling that either of them had singled Hightower out for special treatment. Maybe the stars had just aligned favorably for Clarence Hightower in court.

A bit more interesting was the fact that Hightower had never had his parole revoked for the possession arrest. True, he'd ended up pleading guilty to a violation, and a nondrug one at that. Which was exactly the sort of disposition Jaywalker would have tried to get him, had he been the lawyer. So once again, nothing too out of the ordinary.

But what about the early termination of Hightower's parole? Sure, Ralph Anunziatta had been happy to have one less guy to supervise. But hadn't he said he'd *wanted* to revoke Hightower, only to be overruled by some superior? So Anunziatta had had to settle for writing it up as a technical violation and continuing parole. Okay up to that point, arguably. But then the guy gets terminated *early?* Sure, it was just before Christmas, but no one had ever accused the Division of Parole of playing Santa Claus. And on top of everything else, now it seemed that Hightower had disappeared off the face of the earth.

Why did any and all of this matter to Jaywalker? Well, back in his DEA days, there'd been a couple of times when he and his team had arrested a midlevel dealer known to have an upper-level source of drugs. So what they'd done was offer the guy a deal right on the spot. "You promise to cooperate with us and give us your connection," they'd tell him, "and we'll cut you loose right now." If he agreed, they'd *un-arrest* him, a dubious enough legal procedure but a good way to enlist the guy's help in making a case against a higher-up. You traded a relative nobody for a somebody. And the beauty of it was that by skipping the arrest, processing and court appearance, you never alerted the big fish to the fact that the minnow had been caught and turned into bait.

Had the cops done just that with Clarence Hightower? Arrested him, "flipped" him and let him stay out on the street so he could help them make a case against Alonzo Barnett? And had they then added the wrinkle of arresting him for possession later on, in order to cover their tracks? It could explain everything. The lenient treatment in court, the early termination of parole, even the disappearance.

And it mattered. It mattered tremendously.

Because if Clarence Hightower had indeed been working as an informant when he prevailed upon Alonzo Barnett to hook him up with somebody, Jaywalker had at least the makings of a theoretical defense for Barnett. He could claim entrapment, arguing that but for Hightower's overbearing persistence, Barnett never would have committed the crimes he'd been arrested for. Criminals twist each other's arms all the time, trying to get accomplices for some illegal venture or other. But unless the twisting rises to the level of real physical force or a credible threat to use it, the *twistee* who ends up going along, however reluctantly, has nothing to complain about. If you don't believe that, ask Patty Hearst. On the other hand, if the arm-twisting is done by the police or someone working for them, it becomes a different story altogether.

Not that entrapment defenses ever really succeed. And the reason is pretty simple. In suggesting that a jury should acquit on entrapment, the defense lawyer is conceding guilt while asking for an acquittal based upon something that sounds very much like a technicality. He's essentially telling the jury, "Sure, my client did exactly what the prosecutor claims. But he did it only because the cops asked him really hard to do it." Might as well blame the Tooth Fairy, or claim "The Devil made me do it." In all the years he'd practiced and would continue to practice, Jaywalker would read of exactly one entrapment acquittal. It involved a money-laundering case made against a man named John Z. DeLorean, perhaps best known for supplying the wheels Michael J. Fox and Christopher Lloyd used to drive back to the future.

When a man's drowning, he's desperate enough to grab at any straw that comes drifting his way, however unlikely it is to keep him afloat. So as much as he hated to do it, the following day Jaywalker made it his business to pay another call on Daniel Pulaski, the assistant district attorney on Barnett's case. He did so unannounced, to make sure Pulaski wouldn't have time to prepare himself for whatever it was Jaywalker wanted. It was the same reason he went there in person, rather than making his request over the phone. He wanted to see Pulaski's reaction when he popped the question.

Pulaski rewarded him by making him wait forty-five minutes before seeing him. "So," he said, after they'd exchanged semipleasantries. "What can I do for you?"

"You can tell me," said Jaywalker, "what you know about Clarence Hightower."

"Who?"

If it wasn't a genuine expression of complete ignorance of the name, it sure came off as a damned good imitation of one.

"Clarence Hightower," Jaywalker repeated. "He was

arrested at the same time and place as Alonzo Barnett, and by the same cops."

"Never heard of him," said Pulaski.

"Do me a favor and check your file."

Pulaski looked at him as though he'd been asked for a personal loan. Jaywalker readied himself to hear "No," or some more profane form of it. But Pulaski surprised him. "Only for you, Jaywalker," he said. And got up, walked across the room and pulled a file out from under a stack of others.

"Why? Because I'm such a prince?"

"No," said Pulaski. "Because you're such a pain in the ass. And I know if I don't do it, you'll go over my head to my boss, or to the judge, or to the fucking mayor."

Which Jaywalker took as a compliment, or at least as much of a compliment as the man was capable of delivering. He sat and waited while Pulaski thumbed through the contents of the file.

"Okay, here we are," he said after a moment. "You're right." Then, reading from the file, "'Hightower, Clarence. Companion case. Misdemeanor possession of heroin.' No disposition shown."

"Pled to a discon," Jaywalker told him. "Time served. Never violated on his parole. Terminated early, in fact. And now he seems to have disappeared."

"So?"

"So I want to know if he's a CI," said Jaywalker. "Or was on this case." Purposely using the same initials that cops and prosecutors did for a confidential informer.

Pulaski searched the file further, until he found a pink sheet of paper. He pulled it out and studied it. Then he said, "Nope." And when Jaywalker said nothing, Pulaski slid the sheet across the desk that separated them.

Jaywalker looked at it. There was a heading, a case

number and the names of the officers involved, some of them detectives, others federal agents or state police investigators. Halfway down the page was a printed item that read "Confidential Informant," followed by a blank. The blank had been filled in in ink, in capital letters: NONE.

So much for grasping at straws.

If Hightower hadn't been an informant, linking his high-pressure tactics to law enforcement, then Alonzo Barnett's entrapment defense had just gone down the toilet.

6

The red-faced, two-fisted Irishman

With Alonzo Barnett stripped of his only plausible defense, Jaywalker could easily have considered himself off the hook. Here was a defendant, after all, who continued to insist upon a trial in spite of the overwhelming odds against him. And the irony of the situation was hardly lost on Jaywalker. Last time out he'd brushed aside a client's hesitation at rolling the dice, only to come up snake eyes. This time it was the client who was being reckless, not Jaywalker.

And the way the system was set up to work, it was Barnett's decision to make, not Jaywalker's. Every defendant, no matter how demonstrably guilty he may be, has an absolute right to a trial, guaranteed by the constitutions of both the United States and the State of New York. And Alonzo Barnett had made it clear that he intended to avail himself of that right. But it would be a trial in name only, an exercise in going through the motions. A *charade* of a trial. Over in civil court they actually have a term for it that they use when the defense literally doesn't show up and the plaintiff's case is permitted to come in unopposed.

An *inquest*, they call it.

Which is pretty much what Barnett's trial would have been, had Jaywalker not been the lawyer for the defense. Because going through the motions was something he simply didn't know how to do. In his world, there were no charades, no inquests. He would continue to treat Barnett's case as an absolutely must-win trial. The actual chances of winning were irrelevant. Even the fact that there was *no* chance of winning was irrelevant.

"Why?" his dumbfounded listener would ask him. "Why knock yourself out on behalf of some career criminal who's admitted his guilt, has absolutely no defense, but wants to go through with a trial out of nothing but sheer stubbornness?"

By way of an answer, Jaywalker would point out that the listener's problem wasn't really with the defendant's *right* to a trial, however doomed. "If he insisted on exercising that right, you wouldn't criticize me for sitting next to him and going through the motions, would you? After all, somebody's got to do it. So to fault me for being the one to sit there growing hair like some kind of Chia Pet would be the equivalent of blaming the Washington Generals just for showing up to be the designated losers to the Harlem Globetrotters, something they do night in and night out.

"You see," Jaywalker would explain, "it's only when I stop simply going through the motions and start to take my job seriously that you begin to have a problem. It's not until I really try my hardest to *win* that you begin asking me how can I possibly represent someone I know is guilty. And my answer to you is simple.

"How can I not?"

What he *wouldn't* say, and what he wouldn't even admit to himself at the time, was that in fighting his hardest to win Alonzo Barnett's case, Jaywalker was hoping to beat back some personal demons. The sting of that recent conviction still smarted, still kept him up at night. Suppose he could follow up losing a case he should have won—or better yet, should never have tried in the first place—by winning a dead-bang loser? Wouldn't pulling off something like that go a long way toward evening the score? Wouldn't it at least buy him some small measure of redemption?

All that said, without an entrapment defense, Alonzo Barnett was pretty much left with no defense at all. Jaywalker would have to settle for attacking the testimony of the prosecution's witnesses and combing their reports—once he finally got them from Pulaski—for inconsistencies. He'd have a sample of the drugs tested by an independent chemist to make sure it was really heroin. He'd even try to line up character witnesses for Barnett, although putting them on the stand would open them up to all sorts of damaging cross-examinations.

"Tell me. Is your opinion of the defendant's reputation affected in any way by the fact that he's been selling heroin for the past twenty years? Or that he has five felony convictions?"

Okay, maybe no character witnesses.

But how about Barnett's boss, the restaurant owner he'd been working for at the time of his arrest? But Pulaski would no doubt use Barnett's employment to show he hadn't needed to deal in drugs but had made a conscious choice born out of greed. Maybe there was some way to put the defendant's two daughters on the stand, to show what a loving father he was?

"I see," Pulaski would say. *"And perhaps you can tell*

us, young lady, just why it was that your sister and you were removed from your home and placed in foster care, even before your father's latest arrest?"

It seemed that every idea Jaywalker came up with had a downside to it, a downside that far outweighed its upside. Well, he decided, there was still Clarence Hightower. Put on the witness stand by the defense, he might be able to show the jury how reluctant Barnett had been to get back into the business of dealing. While that might have no true legal significance, it was at least something. Yet Jaywalker had already struck out trying to find Hightower. And since it turned out that the man hadn't been working as a CI, it meant law enforcement wasn't responsible for knowing his whereabouts or duty-bound to make him available to the defense.

Although Jaywalker prided himself on doing his own investigative work, he also recognized that there were limitations to the practice. The first was when he needed to call an investigator to the stand as a witness. The second was when he needed someone who could go to a neighborhood and blend in better than he himself could.

Jaywalker was white. Alonzo Barnett and Clarence Hightower were both black. Yes, today they'd be African-American, but this was 1986, and back then they were black. So Jaywalker picked up the phone and dialed Kenny Smith's number.

Kenny wasn't exactly an investigator. Not in the sense that he was licensed or had a carry permit, or would make much of an impression if ever called to testify. What Kenny was, was a former client of Jaywalker's and a friend. And Kenny was not only black but lived up in Harlem, as had Alonzo Barnett until his arrest, and Clarence Hightower until his vanishing act.

* * *

Kenny showed up at Jaywalker's office an hour later. Standing a full six foot five inches, at forty he still looked like the professional basketball prospect he'd once been until good friends and bad decisions had combined to derail his dreams, even if they'd failed to wipe the broad smile off his face. Kenny said he'd never heard of Clarence Hightower, but he'd be more than happy to see if he could find him.

Jaywalker handed him a subpoena, just in case Kenny were to get lucky. It wasn't a judicial subpoena, the kind that had to be signed by a judge. Jaywalker was concerned that if he went to Levine, Pulaski might find out about it. So he'd used an attorney's subpoena, which was just as good. Well, almost kinda sorta.

"I'm afraid the most I can pay you is a couple hundred bucks," he told Smith, knowing that only investigators whose names were on an approved list could submit their hours and get reimbursed through the system. "But I'll pad my voucher, make it look like I was out looking for him myself."

"Don't worry about it," said Kenny. "I owe you."

Which was true, Jaywalker would have had to admit. He'd gotten Kenny out of more than a few jams over the years. But still, didn't Smith's comment have an awfully familiar ring to it?

A few days later, more out of frustration than anything else, Jaywalker sat down at his desk—he'd had one in those days—and knocked out what he called a Demand for a Supplemental Bill of Particulars. In it, he asked that the prosecution be directed to furnish him a laundry list of things, including the names of trial witnesses, all reports they'd prepared and any past disciplinary actions taken against them. He wanted not only the lab reports and chemists' notes, but the right to an independent analysis of the drugs by his own expert. He requested more specificity regarding the precise times and locations of the various sales. And then, even though he'd seen the answer with his own eyes, he asked whether any confidential informers had been involved in any way with the case. Did he distrust Daniel Pulaski? Yes, as a matter of fact. But that wasn't the point. Pulaski was only the assistant district attorney. He'd caught the case after it had already been made by New York City detectives, New York State Police investigators and federal agents. Maybe he didn't really know if there'd been a CI involved. Maybe that pink sheet of paper with *NONE* inked on it didn't know, either.

Besides, a part of him wanted to send Pulaski a message, to put him on notice that unlike Alonzo Barnett's three previous lawyers, this one wasn't going to roll over and play dead. With nothing to work with, Jaywalker might not be able to win the case, but he sure was going to give it his best shot.

He received Pulaski's response in the mail four days later. It argued that motions had already been made within the statutory forty-five-day period allowed following arraignment, responded to in a timely fashion by the People and decided by the court. Mr. Jaywalker, Pulaski pointed out, was exactly 195 days late in asking for the relief he sought.

And despite her good nature and sense of fairness, Judge Levine found herself compelled to agree the next time the case came up in front of her. But even as she denied Jaywalker's demand as untimely, she turned to

Pulaski and said, "Surely you can give him the lab reports, and the times and places of the sales, can't you?"

"I'll send him the lab reports," Pulaski grunted. "The rest of the stuff he gets after we pick a jury. Just like the law requires."

"And how about the confidential informer business?" she asked him.

"I already showed him the form that indicates there was no CI."

"So how did this case ever get initiated?" Jaywalker asked, hoping to pique the judge's curiosity and enlist her help. The usual route, they all knew, began with an informer telling his handlers that he knew a dealer he might be able to introduce an undercover to.

"That's evidence," Pulaski snapped. "You'll find out at trial."

"Ahh," said Jaywalker. "The old *trial-by-ambush* strategy."

"Boys, boys," the judge scolded. Then, knowing that Pulaski was correct that he could withhold the information, but only in a technical sense, she suggested he might want to give them a clue. "Come on," she prodded him. "How about at least a hint or two?"

"Fine," the A.D.A. snapped. "The case began with an anonymous tip."

"There," said Levine. "That wasn't so hard, was it?"

Pulaski said nothing. Evidently it *had* been.

"Now," said the judge. "Are you gentlemen sure we can't dispose of the case?"

"I've offered counsel the minimum," Pulaski was quick to point out. "Eight-to-life on an A-2."

"And while my client appreciates the prosecution's generosity," said Jaywalker, "he prefers to take his chances at trial."

"Then a trial he shall have," said Levine. "When can you gentlemen be ready to begin? This thing's getting almost as old as I am."

They agreed on a date three weeks away. It actually wasn't all that long an adjournment, considering the fact that Jaywalker had been on the case less than two months. Then again, with no defense to raise and no witnesses to call other than the defendant himself, there wasn't all that much for him to do between now and then, either.

Not that he wouldn't come up with enough to keep himself busy.

He spent the better part of three straight days in the Tombs with Alonzo Barnett. What began as preparation for testifying gradually turned into an extended conversation. Barnett, Jaywalker decided, would make an excellent witness. He was a good listener and an excellent storyteller. He had a nice self-effacing quality about him, an attribute that was bound to come in handy when he was forced to describe his career as a drug dealer.

No longer a young man, Barnett had no rough edges to him and no anger seething within him. He came across as nonthreatening. He wasn't handsome, at least not in a Hollywood way, but he was nice to look at. And he had a deep, almost melodic voice. Most of all, he was intelligent. He used three- and four-syllable words, but for precision rather than show. His habit of pausing before answering a question made him seem thoughtful instead of glib. And there was an undercurrent of sadness to just about everything he said—until he got to the subject of his daughters. Then his eyes would light up, the skin at the outer corners would crinkle, and a broad smile would spread across his face, only to be replaced a moment later by a grimace, as he remembered how his most recent transgression had betrayed them and separated him from them once again, this time probably for good.

Yes, Jaywalker decided, Barnett would make a terrific witness, even a game-changing one—in some other case. In this one, all of his listening skills and storytelling ability would be for naught. His self-effacing, nonthreatening demeanor might win him points with the jurors, but in the end, it wouldn't be enough to win him their votes. His pleasant looks, melodic voice and palpable intelligence simply weren't going to be enough. Not even his obvious devotion to his daughters would translate into an acquittal. It was going to be one of those cases that ended in a conviction punctuated by a bit of muffled sobbing in the jury box, perhaps even accompanied by a recommendation of leniency. A recommendation that Shirley Levine would be happy to bow to, if only the legislature had seen fit to allow her.

And for Jaywalker, the worst part of it was that over the course of those three days, he became genuinely fond of Barnett. Not that he didn't eventually come to like almost all of clients; he did. But that was more a reflection of how Jaywalker treated them, especially when viewed in the context of how the rest of the world had treated them up to that point. With Barnett, it was different. Here was a man who, in spite of his past history and his present charges, was so thoroughly engaging that there were times—especially back home, late at night—when Jaywalker would worry if he wasn't getting *too* close to his client and running something of the same risk a physician ran when he undertook to operate on a member of his own immediate family. In a world filled with lawyers who cared too little about their clients, leave it to Jaywalker to lose sleep over the possibility that he was beginning to care too much.

* * *

And then, a week before the trial was scheduled to begin, Daniel Pulaski phoned. "Well," he told Jaywalker, "you lucked out."

"Oh? How's that?"

"I've been promoted to the Investigations Division," he said. "I'm going to have to reassign almost all of my trial cases."

"Congratulations," said Jaywalker. "But why not keep this one?" By that time he'd convinced himself that as much as he disliked Pulaski, the man's sarcasm and sneakiness could actually end up working to the defense's advantage. What better way to highlight Alonzo Barnett's likableness, after all, than to pit him against a slimeball, a thoroughly unlikable cross-examiner?

"Don't take offense," said Pulaski, immediately ensuring that Jaywalker would. "But from the People's point of view, this case pretty much tries itself, even with you at the defense table. Anyway, it's not like I'm handing it off to some loser. I'm giving it to a rising young star in the office."

"And who might that be?"

Pulaski had asked if he happened to know Mickey Shaughnessey.

"Never heard the name," confessed Jaywalker.

"Well, you will," Pulaski assured him. "You and the rest of the do-gooders on the defense side. I'm only sorry I won't be there to watch the sparks fly."

"A street fighter, huh?"

"You might say that." Pulaski laughed. "Well, you two have fun." Followed by a click.

So the slimeball had been replaced by a brawler. Fair enough, Jaywalker decided. Alonzo Barnett's thoughtful, quiet intelligence might come off even better against a red-faced, two-fisted Irishman.

Although it was far from the top of his list of favorite things to do, Jaywalker spent the next day hitting the books. He wanted to check out a seldom-used defense called *agency*. At least that was its short name, sort of how Jaywalker was short for Harrison J. Walker. Technically termed "agent of the buyer," it went something like this.

A drug deal often involves more than just two people. There are the hand-to-hand participants, the seller and the buyer. But frequently there's a cast of supporting characters. There can be a broker, the guy who puts the seller and buyer together, and in that respect acts not all that differently from a real estate broker. There can be a middleman, somebody who positions himself between the seller and the buyer. For a piece of the action, whether that turns out to be cash, drugs or both, he serves to insulate the principals from each other, lest one be looking to either rip off or arrest the other. Then there's the connection, the seller's immediate source of supply, and *his* connection, on up the ladder. There may be a moneyman, separate and distinct from the seller. There may be a stash man, who sits on the drugs, a re-up man to replenish the supply, a lookout to watch out for the Man and even a gofer or two.

Under the law of "acting in concert," all these individuals are equally guilty of participating in the sale. With one exception, of course, and that's the buyer. Not even the vast breadth of the acting-in-concert law can ignore the fact that since he's the one who's purchasing the drugs, the buyer can't at the same time be selling them.

From that necessary distinction has grown an arcane

and almost unheard of defense. Borrowing from the principles of contract law, some clever defense lawyer postulated years back that if someone aids a transaction by helping the buyer rather than the seller, it follows that he can be no more guilty of sale than the buyer is. Take, for example, a buyer who speaks only English, who's going to purchase drugs from a seller known to speak only Spanish. To protect himself from being overcharged or short-weighted, the buyer enlists a bilingual friend to come along and act as an interpreter, either as a favor or for a fee. The friend's only role is to translate for the buyer; he's never even met the seller. In theory, the friend, should he be arrested, can argue that he acted solely as the agent of the buyer and therefore can't be convicted of sale. Criminal facilitation, perhaps, for having assisted in the overall transaction, but not sale. And while Alonzo Barnett was facing multiple counts of sale, nowhere in the indictment was there a count charging him with criminal facilitation, an oversight that left Jaywalker free to argue that his client had merely been acting as an agent for the buyer.

In theory, at least.

In practice, it never seemed to work out that way. Despite spending an entire day searching the case law, Jaywalker was unable to find a single case where a defendant had actually been acquitted on agency, or a single instance where a judge had been reversed for refusing to instruct the jury on the defense.

Still, he tucked the idea away in the back of his head, in a subfile he labeled Hail Mary Plays.

The following day Jaywalker got a call from the red-faced, two-fisted Irishman who'd be taking over the case from Daniel Pulaski.

"Hi," she said, sounding neither red-faced, two-fisted, nor even particularly Irish, for that matter. "My name's Miki Shaughnessey, and I'm the new assistant on the Alonzo Barnett case."

Jaywalker found himself momentarily speechless.

"Are you there?" he heard her asking.

"Yes, I'm here. It's just that I was expecting someone more…more—never mind."

"I've got some lab reports for you," said Shaughnessey. "I can send them out to you, if you like. Or you can stop by and pick them up."

He was at her 80 Centre Street office twenty minutes later. Miki Shaughnessey was as different as could be from what he'd expected, right down to the spelling of her first name, which Jaywalker read off a piece of paper taped to her door, the permanent plaque having not yet arrived. She was also as different as could be from Daniel Pulaski. And not just because she was strawberry blonde, petite and cute. While those things made her good to look at, this was 1986. Jaywalker's wife was very much alive back then, and he was very much in love with her. It would only be after her death that he would look elsewhere for consolation, first to the confines of his bed, then to the bottle, and eventually to other members of the female persuasion.

No, the reason Miki Shaughnessey was an improvement over Daniel Pulaski had less to do with her looks than it did with her openness. Jaywalker had sensed as much from the moment of her initial phone call. Pulaski would have held on to the lab reports for as long as possible. Hell, he'd done just that for twenty months so far. Then, at the last possible moment, he'd have sent them to Jaywalker by Third Class Mail. Shaughnessey had not only called him to say she had them, but had actually invited him to come over to pick them up. And while part of Jaywalker would miss doing battle against the likes of Pulaski, right now he'd settle for Shaughnessey's openness.

"So," she was telling him now, "I understand that I'm about to go up against one of the best."

"Don't believe everything you hear." He brushed her off with characteristic modesty. "And you must be good, or Pulaski wouldn't have picked you to try this case. I hear he's a big shot over in Investigations now."

"Not yet. His transfer doesn't actually take place for another six weeks. And while I appreciate his vote of confidence in me, I feel like I'm being thrown to the wolves. Not only does he give me an A-1 felony for my first trial here, he puts me up against you."

"Don't worry," Jaywalker told her. "I'm sure you'll do just fine." And it was true, he knew. Because while he would have pulled no punches against a prick like Pulaski, he'd never take advantage of a novice. Sure, once the opening bell rang, he'd do everything he could for Alonzo Barnett, but that everything wouldn't include playing dirty. And he knew that Shirley Levine would go out of her way to make Shaughnessey's first trial a fair one, too.

But even as he was telling Miki Shaughnessey not to worry, Jaywalker had already begun to. Because tucked into her little speech were several things that immediately raised red flags for him. First was the revelation that Daniel Pulaski's transfer wouldn't take place for another six weeks. The Barnett trial was only two weeks away and would last two weeks at most. Had Pulaski wanted to, he could easily have tried it himself before going over to Investigations. Then there was the fact that

Miki Shaughnessey was being entrusted with an A-1
felony as her very first trial in the office. Sure, it was a
winner from the prosecution's point of view. But still, it
was kind of like handing a brand-new assistant a murder
case first time up to the plate. Why would Pulaski take
a chance doing something like that, especially when he
himself knew the case inside out? Why not let Shaughnessey second-seat him and learn by watching how it was
done? Or, if he really wanted to give her some on-the-job
training, have her try it with *him* in the second seat?

Why was Pulaski bailing out?

And what was he himself missing?

Don't be paranoid, Jaywalker told himself. But it was
hard for him to take his own advice. Paranoia wasn't exactly a prerequisite for being a good defense lawyer, but
it sure came in handy from time to time.

They talked for another twenty minutes. Jaywalker assured Shaughnessey that he wouldn't oppose an adjournment of the trial if she felt she needed one. She agreed to
let him know what witnesses she intended to call, along
with the order in which she planned on calling them, as
soon as she figured those things out.

"So why *is* your guy going to trial?" she asked at one
point. "I mean…" Her voice trailed off, leaving the obvious unsaid, that it seemed futile on the defendant's part,
futile and self-destructive.

Jaywalker answered her with a shrug. "It happens," he
said.

She nodded as though she understood. She might be
inexperienced, Jaywalker decided, but she seemed like a
quick learner and a straight shooter. Shirley Levine was
a good judge and Alonzo Barnett a nice man. Together
they would have a good trial, the four of them. And when
it was over, Barnett would shake Jaywalker's hand, thank

him for doing his best, and go off someplace upstate to spend the rest of his life sitting in a cage. For doing a guy a favor. All so a bunch of politicians up in Albany could outshout each other over which of them was toughest on crime.

Even back as early as 1986, Jaywalker knew he could keep doing this work only so long before it would drive him totally nuts, before it would send him rummaging through the bottom of his closet and digging out his gun from his DEA days. Before it would make him want to blow away the sheer insanity of these stupid drug cases, for once and for all.

7

The anonymous caller

"Alonzo Barnett is sitting here at the defense table today for one reason, and one reason only," Jaywalker told the jury. "And that's because against his own self-interest and at his own peril, he did what he thought was the right thing to do. He returned a favor. He repaid a debt. In Alonzo Barnett's eyes, another man had quite literally saved his life several years earlier. And when that man came calling and begging for help, Mr. Barnett at first said no, he couldn't help him. He said that over and over again, in fact. He said it on six different occasions. Until the other man put it a different way. 'You owe me,' is how he put it. And as Mr. Barnett thought about it, he realized that the other man was right, that Mr. Barnett *did* in fact owe him. So he relented, and he did the favor. And because he did the favor, he was arrested and charged with a series of very serious crimes.

"That's why he sits here today. And that's why you sit where *you* sit today, to render judgment on what Mr. Barnett did almost twenty-one months ago."

It was one of the shortest opening statements Jaywalker had ever made or, for that matter, would ever make. It was shorter than Shirley Levine's preliminary explanation of the rules that govern criminal trials, shorter by almost ten minutes than Miki Shaughnessey's opening, shorter by a full two days than the time it had taken them to pick a jury of twelve regular jurors and four alternates.

Because there was simply nothing else for Jaywalker to say. He couldn't talk about entrapment, because Clarence Hightower hadn't been an informer working for law enforcement. He couldn't talk about agency, because if you were to really analyze Barnett's role in the transactions, the principal he'd been working for had been Hightower. And Hightower had wanted to obtain drugs in order to sell them to a buyer. A buyer who'd turned out to be an undercover agent.

"Call your first witness," Judge Levine told Miki Shaughnessey.

Jaywalker reached across the defense table and retrieved a subfile marked Pascarella. True to her word, days earlier Shaughnessey had told him the names of the witnesses she was going to call and the order in which she expected to do so. His initial impression of her had been borne out by everything that had happened since. Where Daniel Pulaski had been two-faced and closefisted at every turn of events, Shaughnessey was open, honest and aboveboard. If she truly represented the next generation of prosecutors at Special Narcotics, the office would soon be rivaling the New York County District Attorney's in terms of the integrity of its staff. Furthermore, over the past two days Shaughnessey had demonstrated that she was more than just a pretty face. Despite her inexperience, she'd held her own during jury selection, displaying a quick wit and a level of comfort that a lot of seasoned lawyers never achieve. For two full days she'd matched Jaywalker challenge for challenge as they whittled an initial pool of a hundred and twenty jurors down to a final sixteen. If the jurors seemed to like Jaywalker and his client—and he always made it his business to see that they did—they seemed to like Miki Shaughnessey every bit as much.

The jury they ended up with struck Jaywalker as a pretty middle-of-the-road group, neither lockstep pro-prosecution nor bleeding-heart pro-defense. Which, as far as he was concerned, meant that he'd already lost round one. A fair and unbiased jury was great if you happened to have the facts and the law on your side. If you didn't, those same qualities were likely to work against you.

"The People," Shaughnessey said now, "call Lieutenant Dino Pascarella."

Direct sale trials, Jaywalker knew from experience, follow a very predictable pattern. The prosecution usually begins with a team leader who supervised the cops or agents in the field. Then comes the undercover officer, explaining when, where and how he bought the drugs, and who he bought them from. After that, a member or two from the backup team describes the corroborating surveillance they conducted during the buy or buys, and the eventual arrest of the seller or sellers.

Even had Miki Shaughnessey not laid out the structure of her case to Jaywalker in advance, the "Lieutenant" that preceded Dino Pascarella's name would have been enough of a hint that in this particular operation, he'd been the team leader. Entering the courtroom now through a side door, Pascarella made his way to the witness stand with practiced self-assurance. He was a dark-haired man who looked to be in his late thirties, dressed in what might have passed as a conservative blue business suit, had it not been just a bit on the shiny side.

Shaughnessey began by establishing her witness's twelve years of experience, first as a New York City police officer, then a detective, and for the past two years as a lieutenant in narcotics. The present case, he estimated, was the five hundredth he'd worked on, and perhaps the twentieth he himself had supervised.

SHAUGHNESSEY: Did there come a time, Lieutenant, back in September of 1984, when you had a telephone conversation with a civilian?

PASCARELLA: Yes, there did.

SHAUGHNESSEY: And as a result of that conversation—

JAYWALKER: Objection.

Because the content of the conversation was hearsay and therefore inadmissible, the phrase "as a result of" improperly asked the jurors to infer the nature of the conversation. Not that they wouldn't anyway, Jaywalker knew. But he wanted to see how Miki Shaughnessey reacted to being thrown off her rhythm. Unfortunately, Judge Levine, even while sustaining Jaywalker's objection, proceded to coach Shaughnessey on how to cure the defect.

THE COURT: Yes, sustained. The proper way to phrase the question, Miss Shaughnessey, is "*Following* that conversation…"

SHAUGHNESSEY: I'm sorry. Following that telephone conversation, did you do something?

PASCARELLA: Yes, I did.

SHAUGHNESSEY: Please tell us what you did.

With that open-ended invitation, Lieutenant Pascarella proceeded to recount how he'd opened an investigation under the authority of the Joint City, State and Federal Task Force into the suspected drug dealings of a subject known up to that point only as John Doe "Gramps."

SHAUGHNESSEY: Why John Doe "Gramps"?

PASCARELLA: The "John Doe" was because we didn't know his real name yet. The "Gramps" was because he was an older gentleman who'd been seen with a couple of children, both girls, who we assumed were his granddaughters.

SHAUGHNESSEY: Did you later learn that your assumption was incorrect?

PASCARELLA: Yes. We found out at some point that they were actually his daughters.

The investigation had begun with surveillance of "Gramps." A total of eleven men and one woman had participated. In short order, according to Lieutenant Pascarella, members of the task force succeeded in "taking the subject home."

SHAUGHNESSEY: What do you mean by that?

PASCARELLA: I mean we established where he was living, at 562 St. Nicholas Avenue. That in turn allowed us to check telephone listings and utility records. And although it turned out the subject had no phone, we were able to identify him through Con Edison records.

SHAUGHNESSEY: Did you learn his true name?

PASCARELLA: Yes, we learned that his name was
    Alonzo Barnett. From that we were able to obtain a
    photograph of him from NYPD files.

Which normally would have had Jaywalker on his feet
objecting and even moving for a mistrial. To anyone with
half a brain, implicit in the witness's answer was the fact
that the defendant had a prior record, something the prosecution is normally prohibited from revealing, unless and
until the defendant takes the stand.

But Jaywalker had long ago decided that this was one
of those trials in which the defendant *had* to take the
stand. Knowing that, he'd spent a good portion of jury selection laying out Barnett's record in considerable detail,
complete with his many convictions for sale and possession of drugs. So now, as Miki Shaughnessey began
asking her witness about those convictions, Jaywalker
kept his silence. That said, he did nod once or twice, his
way of reminding the jurors that he'd told them so, and
that they, for their part, had assured him they'd still be
able to decide the case on the basis of the evidence.

SHAUGHNESSEY: Did you learn anything else from
    the NYPD records?

PASCARELLA: Yes. We learned that Mr. Barnett had a
    number of prior convictions for selling drugs in fairly
    substantial quantities.

SHAUGHNESSEY: How was your surveillance of the
    defendant conducted?

PASCARELLA: Several ways. By having plainclothes officers follow him on foot, and by using unmarked vehicles. Also watching him through high-powered binoculars from an outpost in a building directly across the street.

SHAUGHNESSEY: And was the surveillance successful?

PASCARELLA: Up to a point, it was. We succeeded in observing Mr. Barnett go to various places and meet with different individuals. But he was extremely wary. It was almost as if he knew he was being watched and had constructed an elaborate cover to hide his illegal activities. He'd adopted what appeared to be a very simple lifestyle, and he made it a point to conduct whatever business he was engaged in in a way that we were never able to observe an actual drug deal or anything like that.

SHAUGHNESSEY: So what, if anything, did you do?

PASCARELLA: We—*I* made a decision to enlist the services of an undercover officer in order to attempt to make a direct purchase of drugs from Mr. Barnett.

SHAUGHNESSEY: Whom did you select for that role?

PASCARELLA: Because Mr. Barnett had operated off and on in the area for so many years and with so many individuals, I felt it would be best if we brought in someone from another city altogether, someone who could pose as an out-of-town dealer. We selected a DEA agent stationed in Philadelphia, a man with extensive undercover skills and experience. He also happened to be a black man, like Mr. Barnett.

With that, Miki Shaughnessey announced that she had no further questions, walked to the prosecution table and sat down.

Jaywalker didn't have a lot of cross-examination for Lieutenant Pascarella, but there were a few things he wanted to establish. He began with the September, 1984, phone conversation the witness had said he'd had with a civilian.

JAYWALKER: What was the individual's name?

PASCARELLA: I don't know. He refused to give it to me.

JAYWALKER: But it was a male?

PASCARELLA: It certainly sounded like a male.

JAYWALKER: Did you ever learn how he'd known to ask for you?

PASCARELLA: He hadn't known. The call came in to our main number. A secretary routed it to me.

JAYWALKER: What did the caller tell you?

It was the kind of question most lawyers would never have asked, because it was begging for trouble. But Jaywalker wasn't most lawyers, and he'd long ago decided to throw caution to the wind in this particular case. When you're ahead, it's fine to be careful and play conservatively. When you're not, the only thing that playing conservatively guarantees you is a conviction. And Jaywalker was anything but ahead in this trial.

PASCARELLA: He told me there was this guy dealing drugs, specifically heroin, in large amounts. And that he could often be seen hanging out with a couple of young girls on the stoop of a particular address, 562 St. Nicholas Avenue, in Harlem. That he was a black male, about fifty years old, with graying hair.

JAYWALKER: That was it?

PASCARELLA: That was it.

And Jaywalker knew it was, having examined the note Pascarella had made of the conversation even while the anonymous caller had still been on the line. Though that fact didn't stop Jaywalker from bringing out now what the caller *hadn't* said then.

JAYWALKER: So he never identified himself in any way? Never told you he was a friend of the guy, for example, or a neighbor, or a customer or a competitor?

PASCARELLA: No.

JAYWALKER: Did you ask him?

PASCARELLA: I tried, but he didn't give me time. He hung up the phone.

JAYWALKER: Were you able to trace the call, to learn the number and location it came from?

PASCARELLA: Only that it came from a pay phone.

JAYWALKER: Was the conversation taped?

PASCARELLA: Taped? No.

JAYWALKER: Why not?

PASCARELLA: Happened too fast.

JAYWALKER: I see. Can you tell us how long your team conducted surveillance of Mr. Barnett?

PASCARELLA: All told?

JAYWALKER: Yes.

PASCARELLA: I'd say a good hundred hours, maybe, spread out over a week.

JAYWALKER: And in all of that time, how many sales were the surveillance team members able to observe?

PASCARELLA: The surveillance team members?

JAYWALKER: Yes, the eleven men and one woman who conducted the surveillance on foot, in cars and through high-powered binoculars from an outpost.

PASCARELLA: None.

JAYWALKER: So these dozen surveillance officers from three different agencies spent a hundred hours over an entire week. Yet never once did even one of them see what some anonymous civilian caller had claimed to have seen with his naked eye?

Shaughnessey's objection was sustained, and rightfully so. Technically speaking, the caller had never claimed to have seen an actual sale take place. *And* the question was argumentative.

JAYWALKER: But you say the surveillance officers were successful up to a point. Right?

PASCARELLA: I'd say so.

JAYWALKER: After all, they did manage to figure out that Mr. Barnett lived at the same address as the stoop he occasionally sat on?

PASCARELLA: *[No response]*

JAYWALKER: And that the two girls were his own daughters?

PASCARELLA: Yes.

JAYWALKER: Did they also discover, by any chance, that he worked for a living, at a legitimate job?

PASCARELLA: Yes.

JAYWALKER: As a cook at a restaurant?

PASCARELLA: Yes.

JAYWALKER: That he occasionally took his daughters to the park or to a museum?

PASCARELLA: Yes.

JAYWALKER: That he attended Friday religious services?

PASCARELLA: Yes.

JAYWALKER: Tell me, Lieutenant. You ascribed
Mr. Barnett's refraining from conducting his drug
business in open view to his being "wary." Did it ever
occur to you that it could be more simply and accu-
rately attributed to the fact that he wasn't conducting
any drug business at all?

PASCARELLA: I'm convinced he was dealing.

JAYWALKER: That's nice, I'm sure, but it's not what I
asked you. My question was, did it ever—even once—
occur to you that maybe Mr. Barnett *wasn't* dealing?
That the reason you weren't seeing anything was because there was nothing to see?

PASCARELLA: No.

JAYWALKER: How about Mr. Barnett's simple lifestyle?
You say that was an elaborate cover. Did it ever occur
to you that it wasn't a cover at all? That in fact it was
nothing more than the manifestation of a very simple
life lived on a very modest income?

PASCARELLA: No.

JAYWALKER: What's a "CI," Lieutenant?

PASCARELLA: A confidential informer.

JAYWALKER: Did you ever attempt to enlist the services of a CI in this case? You know, have an informer approach Mr. Barnett and either try to buy drugs from him or try to introduce an undercover officer to him for the purpose of buying drugs?

PASCARELLA: With a CI? No.

JAYWALKER: Yet isn't that how it's usually done?

PASCARELLA: Sometimes. I don't know about "usually."

JAYWALKER: *[Holding up a sheet of paper]* How about, let me see, how about in 97.3 percent of all direct sale cases made in New York County over the past forty-eight months?

PASCARELLA: If you say so.

JAYWALKER: I just did. What I'm asking is, do you agree with what I just said, or do you disagree? *[Waves sheet of paper]*

PASCARELLA: I agree, I guess.

JAYWALKER: But that's not how it was done in this particular case.

PASCARELLA: No.

JAYWALKER: This was one of those…let's see, 2.7 percent of cases where you decided to skip the use of a confidential informer altogether. Right?

PASCARELLA: I guess so.

JAYWALKER: And why was that?

PASCARELLA: Because the subject was too *hinky,* too careful. I was afraid that if we used a CI, it might scare him off.

JAYWALKER: I see. And yet this is the same subject who the anonymous caller told you he could tell was dealing heroin, the same subject who could be found right out in the open on the front stoop of what turned out to be his own apartment building, sitting there with two girls who turned out to be his own daughters. Is that—

The rest of the little speech was drowned out by Miki Shaughnessey's objection and Judge Levine's sustaining it. But that was okay. By that time Jaywalker had spent twenty minutes with Dino Pascarella, flirting with fire without getting burned too badly. Not that he'd ever quite demonstrated that anything the witness had said was untrue. But if Jaywalker was lucky, maybe he'd piqued the interest of someone in the jury box. Someone who was open to the possibility that a cop—even a cop with the word *Lieutenant* plunked in front of his name—was capable of stretching things to the breaking point and beyond.

As soon as Pascarella left the courtroom, Judge Levine declared a recess and excused the jury for lunch. Including opening statements, they'd been working for close to two hours already. But before the judge could leave the bench, Miki Shaughnessey was on her feet asking for an opportunity to examine the statistic sheet.

"The what?"

"The piece of paper Mr. Jaywalker read from," said Shaughnessey. "You know, when he recited the statistics about the use of confidential informants. I think I have a right to see it, and even have a copy of it."

"Mr. Jaywalker?" said the judge, looking his way.

Without objection he handed Shaughnessey the sheet he'd held aloft and then waved in the witness's direction moments earlier. She took it from him and stared at it, turning it over several times before looking up and complaining that there must be some mistake, that what she'd been given was nothing but a blank piece of paper.

"Why am I not surprised?" sighed Judge Levine. "As the trial progresses, Miss Shaughnessey, I think you'll find yourself getting used to Mr. Jaywalker and his, shall we say, unorthodox way of doing things."

Shaughnessey's reaction was to shoot Jaywalker a dirty look before turning and storming out of the courtroom.

That afternoon, after finally calming down, she accused him of taking advantage of her. But as he pointed out, that had hardly been the case. If anyone had been taken advantage of, it had been the witness. And with respect to him, all Jaywalker had done was to trick him into admitting the truth, that the vast majority of direct sale cases did in fact depend upon the use of an informer for an initial introduction. The phantom-statistic tactic had been no different, say, from encouraging a witness to believe you had a video recording of his actions, so that he'd be less tempted to lie about them. Clever? Sure. Devious? A bit. But unethical or improper? Hardly. Like any other witness, Lieutenant Pascarella had been called to the stand with the expectation that he would tell the truth. Jaywalker had simply made sure he did so.

Still, even allowing for the points he'd scored on cross-examination, Jaywalker would have been lying if he told himself that Pascarella hadn't hurt the defense. In not objecting to the testimony about the anonymous call, he'd allowed the jury to hear that at least one person besides the police had reason to conclude that Alonzo Barnett was selling heroin. And Jaywalker's decision to call his client as a witness had opened the door for Shaughnessey to remind the jury of the details of Barnett's criminal record, including his multiple past convictions for the exact same crime on which he was now standing trial.

The fact that precious few jurors tend to be heroin dealers themselves means that the drug sale defendant starts with one strike against him before he even comes up to bat. Throw in an anonymous observation that he's been dealing, and you may as well call that strike two. Add the fact that he's been caught doing the same thing over and over again for just about his entire adult life and, well, you get the picture. So what if Dino Pascarella hadn't been the best witness of all time? How good did he really have to be? Especially with the undercover agent coming up next, with all of his "extensive skills and experience."

8

The man from Philadelphia

"The People call Trevor St. James," Miki Shaughnessey announced when the trial reconvened that afternoon.

All eyes turned as a court officer led a large black man into the courtroom through a side door. He was wearing a dark suit over a brown turtleneck sweater, and—best of all—he sported a pair of mirrored sunglasses.

Somewhere, no doubt, there's a courtroom lit brightly enough, whether by Mother Nature or General Electric, that eye protection is advisable. Most likely that courtroom is in Southern California, Florida or someplace even closer to the Equator. As for the fifteenth floor of 100 Centre Street, anyone wearing sunglasses there is either legally blind or hiding behind them.

Keep them on, Jaywalker telepathically begged the witness. He'd actually heard lawyers object that they couldn't see a witness's eyes through a pair of dark lenses and succeeded in getting a judge to order them removed. It was something he himself would never do, especially with *mirrored* sunglasses. Never mind that they added a little something to the undercover mystique that enveloped the witness as he made his way to the stand. Sooner or later the jurors would get over that and begin to think of the shades as a prop, and the wearer as having something to hide besides his eyes.

And then, as though on cue, as soon as Trevor St. James had finished swearing to tell the truth, the whole truth and nothing but the truth, he removed the sunglasses, folded them and slipped them into the outer pocket of his suit jacket as he took his seat. So before he'd even begun his testimony, the guy had treated the jurors to a glimpse of his street image and then unmasked himself as one of them. Nice touch, thought Jaywalker, wondering if St. James had scripted it, or Shaughnessey.

SHAUGHNESSEY: By whom are you employed, Mr. St. James?

It would be the only time in the entire trial that she addressed or referred to him as "Mr."

ST. JAMES: I'm employed by the Drug Enforcement Administration, which is a division of the United States Department of Justice.

SHAUGHNESSEY: In what capacity?

ST. JAMES: As a drug enforcement agent.

SHAUGHNESSEY: How long have you been so employed?

ST. JAMES: Nine and a half years.

SHAUGHNESSEY: And as a DEA agent, is part of your work performed in an undercover capacity?

ST. JAMES: Yes. It's actually a fairly large part of my work.

Shaughnessey had the witness describe what undercover work entailed. His explanation couldn't have been news to anyone in the courtroom by this time, seeing as both lawyers had discussed the subject at some length during jury selection, and Shaughnessey had gone into it again in her opening statement. Still, it made for pretty good listening. Jaywalker had discovered long ago that jurors tend to be fascinated by everything about the world of bad guys. And here they were, about to be treated to an inside tour of that world from a bad guy who was really one of the good guys. What could possibly be better for the prosecution—and worse for the defense?

SHAUGHNESSEY: Did there come a time in September of 1984 that you were asked to participate in a narcotics investigation in Harlem?

ST. JAMES: Yes, there did.

SHAUGHNESSEY: Can you tell us how that came about?

ST. JAMES: Yes. I was assigned to the Philadelphia office at the time. But I'd grown up in Harlem and was familiar with the area. So somebody must have decided that I was well suited to impersonate an out-of-town dealer looking to buy large quantities of heroin to resell out of state.

SHAUGHNESSEY: And what did you do upon your arrival?

ST. JAMES: I met with the team leader, Lieutenant Pascarella, and the various members of the backup team.

I learned that an individual initially known only as John Doe "Gramps" had been positively identified as Alonzo Barnett, and that he was the subject of intensive ongoing surveillance. I was told—

THE COURT: Mr. Jaywalker?

It was Judge Levine's way of checking to make sure he was awake. But she needn't have bothered. Jaywalker does a lot of things during the course of a trial, but falling asleep has never been among them. His decision not to object to what was obviously going to be hearsay testimony was therefore a calculated one. He wanted to hear what Trevor St. James had been told, and he wanted the jurors to hear it, too. So when he stood to say "No objection," he threw in an exaggerated shrug, his way of saying, *Hey, we've got nothing to hide here.*

What Agent St. James had been told, it turned out, was pretty much what Jaywalker had expected, that up until that point in the investigation, the surveillance of Alonzo Barnett had failed to bear fruit. St. James's job would be to figure out a way to approach Barnett, gain his confidence and attempt to buy drugs from him.

SHAUGHNESSEY: And how did you go about trying to do those things?

ST. JAMES: Well, surveillance had established that Mr. Barnett had several associates, individuals he hung out with. One of those associates in particular interested the team. They'd tentatively identified him as John Doe "Stump," because he was short and heavyset. And they'd observed him in Mr. Barnett's company on a number of occasions. So what I did was try to strike up a conversation with Stump one day, approaching him a few blocks away after he'd been seen meeting with Mr. Barnett.

SHAUGHNESSEY: Did you ever learn Stump's true name?

ST. JAMES: Yeah, I think I heard it. I believe the backup team found it out at some point, but I honestly don't remember it.

Agent St. James described how he'd called to a couple of people within earshot of Stump and asked them if they knew how to get to Big Wilt's Small's Paradise. Small's was a Harlem institution that had opened way back in the 1920s. At some point the basketball legend Wilt Chamberlain had bought into it, hence the name. Everyone in Harlem had heard of it, but none of the people St. James asked knew exactly where it was. Except Stump.

"It's up on 135th Street," he told the stranger. "Over on 7th Avenue."

"Which way is that?" St. James had asked him.

"Where you from, man?"

"Philly," St. James had replied.

"Ain't got no cheese steaks at Small's, you know."

"Ain't lookin' for no cheese steaks," St. James had laughed, before rubbing both nostrils and sniffing in loudly.

The gesture hadn't been lost on Stump. "What is it you might be lookin' for?" he'd asked. "Little bit a blow?"

"Nah," St. James had said. "Blow I can find any ole place. I be lookin' for some *shit,* brotha. Some *weight.*"

Here Miki Shaughnessey stopped her witness and had

him explain a few of his terms. *Blow* was cocaine, *shit* was heroin, and *weight* was a lot of it.

"How long you in town?" Stump had asked St. James.

"A few days. A week if I gotta be."

"Do yourself a favor," Stump had told him, "and stay away from Small's. Place be crawling with the *po*-leece."

"Good to know," St. James had said.

"Tell you what," Stump had offered. "You be back here this same time tomorrow. I see if I can't hook you up with my man. He jus' might be able to help you out with what you lookin' for."

St. James had said, "Bet," meaning he'd be there.

But before Stump had walked off, he'd issued a warning of sorts to St. James. "'Tween now an' then," he'd said, "I be checkin' you out, makin' sure you ain't the Man."

The Man, Shaughnessey had St. James explain, was another term for the *po*-leece, and was definitely not to be confused with *my man.*

Several jurors laughed loudly at the distinction, until Jaywalker stared them down. *This isn't funny,* he wanted them to know. *There's a man's freedom on the line here.*

As for Stump's threat to check out the stranger, it was just that, a threat. Jaywalker knew that from his own undercover days. The same dealer who'd accuse him of being the Man one minute would sell to him the next one. The truth was, nobody ever really bothered to check out anybody. In the world of buying and selling drugs, caution got trumped by greed. Every time out.

SHAUGHNESSEY: What happened after that?

ST. JAMES: I met Stump the next day, like he'd suggested. But he said there was a problem. His man was spooked, he told me, and didn't want to meet me.

SHAUGHNESSEY: What did you take him to mean when
    he said "spooked"?

ST. JAMES: *Spooked* means nervous like, afraid.

Interesting, thought Jaywalker. If he had the timing
down right, this conversation would have taken place at
the point where Alonzo Barnett had been telling Clarence Hightower that he couldn't help him. Not because
he was nervous, though, but because he'd given up selling drugs and had no interest in getting back in business.
So either Hightower had been deliberately stringing his
customer along with a story while he tried to break down
Barnett's resistance, or Agent St. James was now putting
his own spin on what Stump had told him. One of them
was fudging. But which one? And why?

SHAUGHNESSEY: What happened after that?

ST. JAMES: Me and Stump set up another meet for a
    couple days later. And at that meet, he told me it was a
    go, that his man AB—that's what he called him—had
    agreed to meet me. So the two of us, me and Stump,
    we went back to the stoop that evening. He introduced
    me to AB, and then he left the set.

SHAUGHNESSEY: He left the set?

ST. JAMES: Stump. He split. Walked away.

SHAUGHNESSEY: I see. And the man Stump intro-
    duced to you as AB. Do you see him in the court-
    room today?

ST. JAMES: Yes, he's sitting right over there. *[Points]*

THE COURT: Indicating the defendant, Alonzo Barnett. Correct, Mr. Jaywalker?

JAYWALKER: Absolutely.

It was always a good idea to concede what you couldn't contest. It bought you credibility in the eyes of the jury. That way, when you fought over something, the jurors were more likely to take your side.

SHAUGHNESSEY: Did you and the defendant then have a conversation?

ST. JAMES: Yes. I told him I was up from Philly and looking to score some high-quality heroin. I said I was prepared to buy as much as a kilo, but that I wanted to start small, with a sample, to check out the purity.

SHAUGHNESSEY: When you said a kilo, what did you mean?

ST. JAMES: A kilo is a kilogram, a little over two point two pounds, or about thirty-five ounces. It's a lot of weight, and it can go for as much as forty thousand dollars if it's uncut.

SHAUGHNESSEY: What happened next?

ST. JAMES: The defendant told me to come back the next evening. In the meantime, he said, he was going to talk to his connection.

SHAUGHNESSEY: What's a connection?

ST. JAMES: A source of supply. The guy he was get-
    ting it from.

SHAUGHNESSEY: And the following evening, did you
    do as he instructed you to?

ST. JAMES: Yes, I did.

SHAUGHNESSEY: How did you get there?

ST. JAMES: I drove an unmarked government vehicle, a
    late-model Cadillac.

Jaywalker looked up from his note-scribbling, sup-
pressing a grin. Just as they had back in his day, DEA
agents still seized cars that had been used to facilitate drug
deals. Then, after conducting civil forfeiture proceedings,
they put the cars into service to use during undercover
and surveillance operations. Which was how Jaywalker
had once ended up in an almost-brand-new five-speed
Corvette, trying to see how fast it would go early one
morning on the Harlem River Drive. He'd opened it up
pretty good before being flagged over by a motorcycle
patrolman, one of those guys in the storm trooper outfits,
with the squashed down cap and knee-high boots. "I'll
give you a choice," the cop had said. "Two tickets for exceeding sixty, or one for going a hundred and twenty."
Sorry, Jaywalker had told him, but he was *on the job.* An
insider's way of saying he was the Man.

SHAUGHNESSEY: What happened when you arrived
    there?

ST. JAMES: The defendant got in and told me to drive to a particular corner, 127th Street and Broadway.

SHAUGHNESSEY: What happened there?

ST. JAMES: He told me to wait while he got out. He walked around the corner and out of my sight. He was gone about twenty minutes. When he came back, he told me that his man refused to meet with me, that he'd deal only with him. So I took a chance. I fronted the defendant a hundred dollars and told him to bring me back a sample.

SHAUGHNESSEY: Fronted?

ST. JAMES: Gave him the money up front, in advance.

SHAUGHNESSEY: Was there anything special about the money?

ST. JAMES: Yes, it was what we call Official Advance Funds. Meaning the bills had been photocopied to show the serial numbers. That way, if the backup team recovers any money at the time of an arrest, they can compare the bills to the photocopy for evidentiary purposes.

SHAUGHNESSEY: Did there come a time when the defendant returned to your car?

ST. JAMES: Yes. After about another twenty minutes, he came back, got in and told me to drive. When we'd gone a few blocks he handed me an amber-colored glass vial containing a white powder. I thanked him

and said I'd be checking it out, and would want more
if it was good. We agreed to meet again in two days. I
drove him back to his building and dropped him off.

From there Agent St. James had proceeded to a pre-
arranged location, where he met with the backup team.
There he field-tested the contents of the vial, watching the
re-agent turn a telltale red, indicating a positive reaction
for the presence of an opiate. He then turned the evidence
over to one of the backup team members for vouchering
and a more sophisticated chemical analysis.

The second of the three buys, according to Agent
St. James, followed much the same pattern. The United
States chemist had reported that the sample tested out as
eighty-one percent heroin, pretty close to pure, and strong
enough to drop a user in his tracks were he to cook it and
shoot it up uncut. St. James met with Barnett as scheduled
and ordered an ounce, which Barnett told him would cost
fifteen hundred dollars. A day later they drove back to the
same corner, where St. James handed Barnett the money
and watched him walk out of view. Twenty minutes later
Barnett returned with a small paper bag. Inside the bag
was a glassine envelope containing a white powder that
turned out to be just over an ounce of eighty percent pure
heroin.

The third buy had taken a little longer to set up. Agent
St. James had said he wanted an eighth of a kilo this time.
Jaywalker knew the amount arrived at had been no accident. Since an eighth of a kilogram translated to a little
more than four ounces, it would bump the case up into
the first-degree category, not only for sale but possession, with the mandatory life sentence that an A-1 felony
carried.

After checking with his source, Barnett had reported

that an eighth would cost five thousand dollars. St. James said he'd have to go down to Philadelphia to get the money. By the time he "returned" and was ready to make the buy, it was October 5.

Again St. James picked Barnett up in the Cadillac and drove to 127th Street, where this time he handed Barnett five thousand dollars in prerecorded bills. Again Barnett took the money and disappeared from view. Twenty minutes later—and Jaywalker knew it was no coincidence that it seemed to take twenty minutes each time, since claiming that it had made it easier for the witness to remember—Barnett reappeared. Only this time he never made it to the Cadillac. As Agent St. James watched from behind the wheel, members of the backup team swooped in and made the arrest. St. James, satisfied they had the right man, pulled away from the curb and drove off, just as he would have done had he been a real buyer.

Shaughnessey had him identify the glass vial from the first sale, and the paper bag and glassine envelope from the second one. The third package, the eighth of a kilo, he'd never seen, of course. Not that Alonzo Barnett hadn't been charged with selling that, too. The Penal Law conveniently defines sale to mean "sell, exchange, give or dispose of to another, or to offer or agree to do the same." Next time you share some of your marijuana with a friend or pass him a half-smoked joint, think about it. It's a sale.

With that, Shaughnessey announced that she had no further questions and resumed her seat at the prosecution table. Miki Shaughnessey had certainly done her job well, just as Trevor St. James had done his. Okay, so maybe he'd put a bit of a spin on whatever Stump had told him about Barnett's initial reluctance to deal with him. And perhaps he'd made all of the intervals twenty minutes in order to make things easier to remember on the witness stand. But the bottom line was, the three transactions had gone down pretty much as he described them. Alonzo Barnett had indeed sold him heroin, not just once but three times, if you wanted to count the aborted third sale. And even if you didn't count it, the backup team witnesses would soon enough testify to Barnett's possession of the eighth of a kilo, a crime every bit as serious as its sale, and one that carried the identical punishment.

So no matter how you chose to look at things, Alonzo Barnett had done precisely what the indictment accused him of. And what the indictment accused him of was repeatedly selling fairly substantial amounts of heroin. Not only was that serious stuff, it was *bad* stuff. But as Jaywalker rose now to begin his cross-examination, he couldn't afford to think about that, or to ask himself how he could possibly represent someone at trial whom he knew was guilty. Jaywalker had a job to do, and he knew only one way to do it. And that was to pretend that the man sitting next to him at the defense table was his own brother or his own son. Did the fact that he happened to be neither mean that he deserved any less than Jaywalker's best?

9

Tilting at windmills

"So help me out here, Agent St. James. You were brought
up here from Philadelphia because the surveillance team
was unable to observe Mr. Barnett making any sales. Is
that correct?"

The witness shifted slightly in his seat before answering, "Only if you want to put it that way."

"Well," said Jaywalker, "you were brought up from
Philadelphia, right?"

"Right."

"And the surveillance team had been watching
Mr. Barnett. Or, in your words, conducting *intensive ongoing surveillance*. Right?"

"Right," St. James agreed.

"All twelve of them?"

"I'm not sure exactly how many—"

"With binoculars, unmarked cars and secret outposts,
no?"

"If you say so."

"How about if Lieutenant Pascarella says so?"

Miki Shaughnessey's objection was sustained.
Which was just as well, because Jaywalker was ready to
move on.

JAYWALKER: Now, this guy "Stump." You say you don't remember his name?

ST. JAMES: That's right.

JAYWALKER: Does the name Clarence Hightower refresh your recollection?

ST. JAMES: That sounds like it might be it. But remember, I only saw him and spoke to him a couple times.

JAYWALKER: Know anything about his six-page criminal record?

SHAUGHNESSEY: Objection.

ST. JAMES: No.

THE COURT: Well, he's answered the question. He doesn't know.

JAYWALKER: In fact, you don't know much of anything about him. True?

ST. JAMES: True.

JAYWALKER: And yet, when Stump told you that Mr. Barnett was "spooked" and didn't want to meet you, you chose to accept that at face value—

ST. JAMES: Yes.

JAYWALKER: —rather than wondering if perhaps Mr. Barnett simply wasn't interested in helping anyone buy drugs. Correct?

ST. JAMES: Yes, I believed Stump.

JAYWALKER: This man you knew nothing about, not even his name?

ST. JAMES: I believed him.

Jaywalker moved on to the three transactions themselves. He had no interest in getting the witness to repeat everything he'd said about them on direct. But he did have a point or two he wanted to make. First he wanted to ascertain whether St. James had been the sole undercover operative in the case, or if he'd had a second officer nearby, shadowing his every move. That officer, had there been one, would have been referred to with a highly appropriate designation.

JAYWALKER: Were you working alone in this case, or did you have a "ghost"?

ST. JAMES: I was working alone.

JAYWALKER: No one close by, blending in?

ST. JAMES: No.

JAYWALKER: Either for your safety—

ST. JAMES: No.

JAYWALKER: —or to confirm that everything you're telling us is true?

ST. JAMES: No.

JAYWALKER: Now, I notice that the third time you wanted to buy heroin, you ordered an eighth of a kilogram.

ST. JAMES: That's correct.

JAYWALKER: Which is just over four ounces and therefore constitutes A-1 felony weight, for both sale and possession. Right?

SHAUGHNESSEY: Objection.

THE COURT: Overruled. The witness may answer the question, and then we'll move to another subject.

Meaning, no questions about the severity of the sentences involved, which might affect the jurors' decision.

ST. JAMES: I don't know much about A-1 felony weight. I'm a federal agent, and we don't deal with New York law much. Maybe the NYPD worries about those things. I don't know.

JAYWALKER: I see. Well, whose idea was it that you order an eighth of a kilo?

ST. JAMES: Lieutenant Pascarella's.

JAYWALKER: And who does he work for again?
ST. JAMES: The NYPD.

JAYWALKER: So you just did what you were told to do?

ST. JAMES: Yes and no.

JAYWALKER: What does that mean?

It was the kind of question that gave the witness a chance to bury you, and hence the kind they told cross-examiners never to ask. Which didn't stop Jaywalker.

ST. JAMES: I always try to buy as much as I can.

JAYWALKER: Because it makes it worse for the guy who's selling to you?

ST. JAMES: No.

JAYWALKER: Because it makes you look better?

ST. JAMES: No, not at all.

JAYWALKER: Why, then?

ST. JAMES: Because it gets more narcotics off the streets and out of the hands of kids.

Not bad, thought Jaywalker. But even as he smiled at the witness for scoring a jab, he was ready with a counterpunch.

JAYWALKER: So you say your idea is to buy as much as possible?

ST. JAMES: Yes.

JAYWALKER: At the taxpayers' expense?

ST. JAMES: *[No response]*

JAYWALKER: Until the world's supply is exhausted or we're all broke? Whichever happens first?

ST. JAMES: When we make seizures of drugs, we often recover a lot of the money we've spent. Many times we even come out ahead.

JAYWALKER: I see. How much money was recovered in this case?

ST. JAMES: If I'm not mistaken, I believe your client had five hundred dollars on him when he was arrested.

JAYWALKER: Out of the five thousand you'd given him. And that's not counting the sixteen hundred you'd given him previously.

ST. JAMES: *[No response]*

JAYWALKER: Do you consider that a good return on the government's investment?

ST. JAMES: *[No response]*

JAYWALKER: And in terms of seizing drugs, how much was seized in this case, if you know? Not counting what Mr. Barnett had on him when he was arrested.

ST. JAMES: Not counting that? None.

JAYWALKER: Am I confused, or isn't the goal of an undercover operation to buy a little in order to seize a lot?

ST. JAMES: Sure, that's the goal. In the real world, it doesn't always work out that way.

JAYWALKER: I see. And there's another goal to buying drugs undercover, isn't there?

ST. JAMES: I'm not sure I follow you.

JAYWALKER: Have you ever heard the expression *moving up the ladder?*

ST. JAMES: If it's the same as *moving up the food chain,* yes.

JAYWALKER: Forgive me for dating myself. What does *moving up the food chain* mean?

ST. JAMES: It means trying to make a case not just against the subject you're buying from but against his connection, as well.

JAYWALKER: And his connection's connection—

ST. JAMES: Yes.

JAYWALKER: —on up the line?

ST. JAMES: Yes.

JAYWALKER: Hence the terms *up the food chain* or *up the ladder?*

ST. JAMES: Right.

JAYWALKER: And did any of that happen in this case?

ST. JAMES: No, it didn't.

JAYWALKER: One month, three government agencies, fourteen officers, six thousand six hundred dollars. And you didn't move up a single rung of the ladder. Or, as you might say, a single link in the food chain. Not one, right?

ST. JAMES: Happens.

JAYWALKER: Especially if you're not trying.

Miki Shaughnessey jumped up, asking that the comment be stricken, a request that Shirley Levine quickly granted. And although Jaywalker knew the judge never really got angry with him—they liked each other too much for that—sometimes she did a pretty good imitation, and this was one of those times. "Ask questions," she snapped at him, right in front of the jurors. "Don't make statements."

He could have simply said "Sorry" and moved his questioning on to some other subject. But with his "especially if you're not trying" comment now stricken from the record, the agent's rather glib "Happens" would become the last word spoken on the matter, and the last to show up in the printed transcript. So Jaywalker decided to rephrase what he'd said, only in question form.

JAYWALKER: Would you agree, Agent St. James, that as a general rule, working your way higher up in the distribution chain happens only when you're making a serious effort to make it happen?

SHAUGHNESSEY: Objection.

THE COURT: Overruled. The witness may answer.

ST. JAMES: The truth is, every once in a while you try as hard as you can, but in spite of everything you do, you just can't make a case against a seller's connection. At least not without jeopardizing your safety, the safety of your fellow officers, or both.

Jaywalker smiled wryly. This guy was good, he had to admit.

JAYWALKER: Was there even the remotest suggestion of violence or weapons in this particular case, at any point?

ST. JAMES: Counselor, in my line of business, violence and weapons are everyday things.

This guy was better than good. He was taking Jaywalker's best shots and not only parrying them, but counterpunching effectively.

JAYWALKER: Which is why I asked you about this particular case. Any violence in this one?

ST. JAMES: No.

JAYWALKER: Any guns—used, threatened to be used, displayed, or even hinted at?

ST. JAMES: No.

JAYWALKER: Still, this turned out to be one of those *every once in a while* cases where in spite of everything you tried, you never could make it even one step up the ladder?

ST. JAMES: That's correct, Counselor.

JAYWALKER: By the way, do you see now why we call it a ladder? You have to actually do some work in order to get yourself up to the next level.

This time he did apologize, though it didn't stop Judge Levine from striking the comment, instructing the jury to disregard it, and wagging a *this-is-your-last-warning* finger in Jaywalker's direction. But he'd made the comment because he was done and knew he couldn't get into any more trouble, at least for the moment. Turning from the witness, he said "No more questions," and sat down.

By that time it was quarter of five, and rather than begin with another witness, the judge broke for the day. Only when the last juror had filed out of the courtroom and the court officers had led Alonzo Barnett back into the pens did she turn her attention to the lawyers.

"Mr. Jaywalker—" she began.

Here it comes, he thought. Apparently the final warning had been the one *before* the finger-wagging. So even Shirley Levine had finally had enough of his antics and was about to hold him in contempt, maybe even give him a night on Rikers Island to think things over.

"—why are we trying this case?"

Which caught Jaywalker so off guard that he laughed out loud. But as relieved as he was at avoiding jail time, he knew the judge hadn't asked her question out of idle curiosity. The truth was, there'd been a time when he'd thought about waiving a jury and opting for a bench trial. Judging from Levine's question, he now knew what a mistake that would have been. But it was even worse than that. What Shirley Levine was implying—hell, she wasn't implying it, she was coming right out and saying it—was that two witnesses into the case, it was already clear that there was no theory under which a rational jury could possibly acquit his client.

A lot of lawyers would have answered her by deflecting the blame onto the defendant. "What can I tell you?" they would have said with a helpless shrug of the shoulders. "My client's an absolute psycho who refuses to take a plea." But Jaywalker was decidedly old-school when it came to placing blame. He could still remember hearing his father tell him that a good carpenter never complains about his tools. Jaywalker had always figured that the same advice has to apply to pretty much every trade, including the one he'd ended up practicing. A good lawyer doesn't complain about his client. You take what you're given, and you do the best you possibly can with it. And if you lose, *you* lose. Not just that guy sitting next to you.

"Why are you tilting at windmills here?" the judge was asking him now. "Fighting against impossible odds?" Here he'd thought her earlier question had been nothing but a rhetorical one, a not-so-subtle suggestion that he sit down with Mr. Barnett and explain the odds to him. No, it seemed she really expected an answer from him as to why there hadn't been a guilty plea.

"Because…" he began. But one word into his response, he realized he had absolutely no follow-up. There *was* no reason, when it came right down to it, except that Alonzo Barnett wanted a trial. He'd said that to his first lawyer, his second lawyer and his third. Their reactions had been simple. They'd walked away from him as quickly as they could.

Jaywalker didn't walk away from his clients. Not even when they continued to make the same sort of self-destructive choices that had gotten them into trouble in the first place. But with Barnett, it was more than that. Here was a guy who'd defied the odds and turned everything around. It might have taken him fifty years, but look at what he'd done. Stopped not only using drugs but selling them, as well. Cut out drinking. Never missed an appointment with his parole officer. Found himself a decent job and an apartment to call his own. And the time he'd had left over after those endeavors? Had he spent it hanging out with a bunch of junkies and ex-cons? No, he'd devoted it to the two loves of his life, his daughters. In a word, here was a man who'd done nothing less than completely redeem himself. And Jaywalker, who'd be the first to tell you that he had no place in his heart for organized religion and no room in his thinking for the existence of a higher power, was nevertheless a believer in redemption.

A huge believer.

Then something had happened. Barnett's overblown, misguided sense of loyalty had betrayed him into believing he owed someone a favor, a favor that carried with it huge personal risk for him. That favor now threatened to undo everything he'd accomplished and send him back to prison for the rest of his life. So what was Jaywalker supposed to do? Twist the poor man's arm to the breaking point until he hollered uncle and agreed to a slightly shorter sentence before kissing his daughters goodbye for the last time? No, he couldn't do that. Not if Barnett wanted to fight. What Jaywalker *could* do—in fact, the *only* thing he could do under the circumstances—was go to war with him and fight like an absolute madman until the last drop of fight was drained out of him.

"Because…" He struggled to answer the judge again. "Because I'm a lunatic, okay? Tilting at windmills? That's what I do for a living. Fighting against impossible odds? That happens to be my job description."

Any other judge would have turned sarcastic on him, agreeing with the lunatic part and ridiculing the rest of his little speech. Not Shirley Levine. Shaking her head sadly from side to side, she said, "God bless you, Mr. Jaywalker." She said it in a voice so soft that the words had to have been meant for only him to hear. And in the often strange and lonely world that Jaywalker inhabited, those words fell on his ears like pure music.

10

The encyclopedia salesman

Thursday's witnesses were members of the backup team, the task force officers who'd conducted surveillance during the buys and arrested Alonzo Barnett. First up was a veteran DEA agent by the name of Angel Cruz. Cruz was a short, medium-complexioned Hispanic. Today, he'd be a Latino. In his younger days he'd done his share of undercover work, and Jaywalker had cross-examined him some years back in a federal trial down in Foley Square. That one had turned out well for Cruz and the government. For Jaywalker and his client, not so well.

Miki Shaughnessey wasted little time with preliminaries. Jaywalker had half expected her to begin with the time period prior to Agent St. James's entry into the case, back when the surveillance team watching the defendant had had no luck in observing anything resembling a narcotics transaction. But apparently Shaughnessey had decided to leave that time period to Jaywalker, preferring instead to get right to the sales themselves. And it was a smart decision on her part, Jaywalker had to admit. By zeroing in on the charges in the indictment, Shaughnessey would come off as focused and relevant in the eyes of the jury. Jaywalker, if he chose to backtrack into the period before the first sale took place—as he'd done already to some extent with St. James—would run the risk of looking as though he was trying to divert the jurors' attention and, worse yet, waste their time.

As a result, Agent Cruz's direct testimony took less than an hour. He described a team meeting conducted prior to the first buy, at which Agent St. James had been supplied with prerecorded bills. Then, keeping back a discreet distance, two teams of officers in unmarked cars had followed St. James and his Cadillac. At 125th Street they'd seen him meet a short, stocky, black man known at that time only as John Doe "Stump." Stump had joined St. James in the Cadillac, and together they'd driven to 562 St. Nicholas Avenue, known from earlier surveillance to be the building in which Alonzo Barnett, also known as John Doe "Gramps," lived. Both men had gotten out of the car then, although in cop-speak that came out as "At that particular location and point in time, I did surreptitiously observe Agent St. James and John Doe 'Stump' proceed to exit from the official government vehicle in which they had previously been present."

SHAUGHNESSEY: What, if anything, did you see?

CRUZ: I observed Stump walk over to another black male who was sitting on the stoop and engage him in conversation.

SHAUGHNESSEY: Do you know that man's name?

CRUZ: Yes. I've since learned his name is Alonzo Barnett.

SHAUGHNESSEY: Do you think you would recognize that man if you were to see him today?

CRUZ: Yes. That's him sitting right over there.

Jaywalker conceded that sitting right over there was the defendant. Shaughnessey asked her witness what had happened next.

CRUZ: After a minute or so, Stump motioned Agent St. James over and appeared to introduce him to Mr. Barnett. Then Stump walked away, out of my sight. After speaking together for a minute or so, Agent St. James and Mr. Barnett walked to the Cadillac and got in, Agent St. James behind the wheel and Mr. Barnett in the front passenger seat.

SHAUGHNESSEY: What happened next?

CRUZ: They started moving, and I followed them, a few cars back.

The Cadillac had continued to the corner of 127th Street and Broadway. There Barnett had gotten out and walked around the corner and out of sight, while Agent St. James had remained behind the wheel.

SHAUGHNESSEY: What did you do?

CRUZ: I remained in my vehicle and continued to watch the Cadillac.

SHAUGHNESSEY: Why did you do that?

Jaywalker knew the answer by heart from his DEA days, could have recited it in his sleep if called upon to do so.

CRUZ: Because the safety of the undercover agent is always my paramount concern.

Well, that and the money, Jaywalker knew. Although that particular consideration didn't seem to get mentioned quite as often in court. In any event, Agent Cruz explained that another officer had gotten out of the vehicle and followed Barnett on foot.

About twenty minutes later, Barnett reappeared and got back into the Cadillac. Five minutes passed, and then Barnett got out again and, as before, walked around the corner, while Agent St. James stayed behind the wheel.

Another twenty minutes went by. Funny how that happened, noted Jaywalker. Again Barnett appeared, walked to the Cadillac and got back in. Agent St. James pulled away from the curb and drove back to 562 St. Nicholas Avenue. There he dropped Barnett off and drove away.

The members of the team met up at the same location as before. There Agent St. James produced a small glass vial. A field test for the presence of opiates proved positive, indicating that the white powder inside it was heroin. Agent Cruz took custody of the evidence and later delivered it to the United States Chemist for a more sophisticated analysis.

The second and third buys pretty much followed the same script, according to Agent Cruz's observations and testimony. Again, Agent St. James had waited in his Cadillac while Alonzo Barnett had gotten out and walked around the corner. It wasn't until the third and final transaction that Agent Cruz and five other members of the backup team had intercepted Barnett and arrested him as he was walking back to the Cadillac.

SHAUGHNESSEY: Was a search conducted of Mr. Barnett at that point?

CRUZ: Yes, it was.

SHAUGHNESSEY: By whom?

CRUZ: By me, in the presence of other members of the team.

SHAUGHNESSEY: What, if anything, was recovered?

CRUZ: From Mr. Barnett's right jacket pocket I recovered a paper bag, inside of which was a double glassine bag containing white powder. And from his right pants pocket I recovered five hundred dollars.

The white powder again field-tested positive for opiates and was delivered to the chemist. The serial numbers of the bills were compared to a photocopy of those supplied earlier that day to Agent St. James. Each of the serial numbers matched.

At that point Miki Shaughnessey produced four sealed evidence envelopes. One by one, she handed them to the witness and had him identify them from serial numbers and initials on the outside. Then she handed him scissors so he could cut the seals and open the envelopes. The first contained the small glass vial from buy number one; the second, the glassine envelope from buy number two; the third, the paper bag and double glassine envelope recovered from the defendant's right jacket pocket during buy number three; and the fourth, the five hundred dollars recovered from Barnett's right pants pocket.

Just as time intervals were always twenty minutes, so were pockets all right-side ones. And had there been testimony about which hand Barnett had used to give Agent St. James a package and which hand St. James had received it with, those would have both been right hands, too. Amazing how that happened.

But while Jaywalker waxed cynical, the jurors appeared to be mesmerized by the physical evidence. And while looking at four ounces of white powder may not sound like much, hearing from a federal agent that those four ounces are high-quality heroin worth five thousand dollars—or forty-five hundred, if you wanted to deduct the defendant's cut—is bound to have an impact upon a dozen people who've probably never seen hard drugs in their lives. Build up to it with sealed evidence envelopes, serial numbers and initials, and then top it off by allowing the jurors to pass the items among themselves, though only under the watchful eyes of a pair of large uniformed court officers, and the overall impact is high drama. Miki Shaughnessey instinctively knew that and played it for all it was worth, but to her credit, she never overdid it. Then again, she didn't have to.

Jaywalker began his cross-examination after the midmorning recess. There wasn't all that much he needed from Agent Cruz, but there were a couple of points he wanted to make.

JAYWALKER: Agent Cruz, were you involved in the surveillance of Mr. Barnett during the time period before Agent St. James joined the investigation?

CRUZ: Yes, I was.

JAYWALKER: Do you know what prompted the investigation in the first place?

CRUZ: I was told it began with an anonymous phone call.

JAYWALKER: Did you ever speak with the anonymous caller?

CRUZ: No, I didn't. Not personally.

JAYWALKER: And in the period before Agent St. James got involved, did you see Mr. Barnett make any sales?

It would have been a dangerous question, but Jaywalker already knew the answer from the reports. "No," said Agent Cruz, and in response to Jaywalker's next question, he admitted that neither he nor any other member of the team had seen anything that even remotely resembled a sale.

JAYWALKER: I see. Now, during the first buy that Agent St. James made, you say you stayed in your vehicle, while your partner got out and followed Mr. Barnett on foot. Is that correct?

CRUZ: You got it.

JAYWALKER: Whose decision was that?

CRUZ: I'm not sure what you mean by that.

JAYWALKER: Well, who decided who'd stay in the car and who'd get out?

CRUZ: I did.

JAYWALKER: Based upon what?

CRUZ: I was in the driver's seat.

JAYWALKER: That was it?

CRUZ: That was it, Counselor. Plus the fact that I had seniority.

A couple of the jurors laughed at the obviousness of the answer. But to Jaywalker the decision had been not only wrong but suspiciously wrong, and therefore probably dishonest. So at this point he was willing to put up with a little laughter.

JAYWALKER: Who was your partner that day?

CRUZ: Investigator Lance Bucknell.

JAYWALKER: Of the New York State Police?

CRUZ: That's right.

JAYWALKER: From Plattsburgh, New York?

CRUZ: I have no idea at all where he's from. Somewhere in upstate New York, I'd guess.

JAYWALKER: But you do have an idea what he looks like, don't you?

CRUZ: Yes.

For the first time since they'd begun, Agent Cruz had limited his answer to a single word. It's what sometimes happens when a slightly cocky witness begins to realize the cross-examiner is taking him somewhere that he doesn't particularly want to go.

Not that Jaywalker knew Investigator Bucknell. He didn't. But as usual, he'd done his homework and was willing to bet that Bucknell was the guy he'd seen earlier that morning out in the hallway talking with Cruz. Rehearsing. And from his clean-cut appearance, he certainly *should* have had a name like Lance Bucknell. So Jaywalker decided it was worth a shot.

JAYWALKER: Fair to say he's blond, blue-eyed, young and about six feet four?

CRUZ: Yes.

JAYWALKER: And has "cop" written all over him?

SHAUGHNESSEY: Objection.

THE COURT: Overruled. I assume you understand the question, Agent Cruz?

CRUZ: I think I do.

THE COURT: Does he look like a cop?

CRUZ: *[Shrugs]*

JAYWALKER: Did it ever occur to you, Agent Cruz, that you, being a somewhat dark-complexioned Hispanic about five feet six and what—forty years old?—might have blended into the Harlem neighborhood that day just a bit better than Lance Bucknell from upstate New York?

CRUZ: *[No response]*

JAYWALKER: After all, you figured Mr. Barnett was going to go and get the drugs Agent St. James had ordered. Right?

CRUZ: Right.

JAYWALKER: And you knew that Agent St. James, sitting in his Cadillac, was in no position to see where Mr. Barnett was going. Right?

CRUZ: Right.

JAYWALKER: So it was left to the backup team to try to discover Mr. Barnett's source. Right?

CRUZ: If we could.

JAYWALKER: Which, of course, is one of the major goals of any buy operation, to identify the source, the higher-up, and make a prosecutable case against him, as well. Agreed?

CRUZ: Yes.

JAYWALKER: So you decided to stay in the car and send Lance Bucknell to do the job instead. Yet you *did* want to identify the source of the drugs, didn't you?

CRUZ: If at all possible.

JAYWALKER: Investigator Bucknell does know how to
    drive a car, doesn't he? I mean, he *is* a state trooper.

CRUZ: Yes.

JAYWALKER: And who followed Mr. Barnett on foot
    during the second and third transactions?

CRUZ: Investigator Bucknell.

Jaywalker had gone over the reports so many times
that he could recite much of them verbatim. He knew
the answer before he'd asked the question. But even if
he hadn't, he would have guessed anyway. Once again,
he knew from experience that the team members would
have gone to great lengths to simplify things, just as they
had with the twenty-minute intervals and the right-side
pockets, and just as they would have with the right-handed
exchanges. That way, when it came time to testify, they
would know how to answer if they couldn't actually remember, without running the risk of contradicting each
other.

JAYWALKER: We already know from Agent St. James
    that he was never able to identify Mr. Barnett's source.
    How about the backup team? Did you succeed in iden-
    tifying him?

CRUZ: No, we didn't.

JAYWALKER: But you did succeed in arresting "Stump,"
    didn't you?

CRUZ: We did.

JAYWALKER: How did that happen?

CRUZ: By accident, actually. We'd just arrested Mr. Barnett and patted him down. One of the team members was about to handcuff him and read him his rights when out of nowhere, Stump walks up. So I patted him down, too.

JAYWALKER: And lo and behold, I suppose you detected something in his right pants pocket that felt like drugs. Right?

CRUZ: That's right.

Of course it was right. It had been in the reports.

JAYWALKER: And when it turned out to be heroin, you arrested him, too?

CRUZ: Not me personally. One of the NYPD guys took that collar.

JAYWALKER: And you learned that Stump's true name was Clarence Hightower, and that he'd done time with Mr. Barnett?

CRUZ: We learned that later.

JAYWALKER: And naturally you charged Mr. Hightower with acting in concert with Mr. Barnett, since he'd been the one who'd brought Agent St. James to Mr. Barnett in the first place, for the express purpose of buying drugs. Correct?

CRUZ: No, that's not correct. Mr. Hightower was charged only with possession.

JAYWALKER: Felony possession? Or just misdemeanor possession?

CRUZ: Misdemeanor possession. It was a small amount of heroin, which he told us he'd bought across town and was for his own use.

JAYWALKER: And you believed him?

CRUZ: *[Shrugs]*

JAYWALKER: I'm sorry, I didn't hear you.

CRUZ: Lieutenant Pascarella said we didn't have enough on Mr. Hightower to charge him with sale. And he was in charge of things.

JAYWALKER: Mr. Hightower was in charge of things?

CRUZ: No, Lieutenant Pascarella was.

JAYWALKER: So you never did learn who Mr. Barnett got the drugs from. And the guy who set everything up in the first place, you never charged him in connection with any of the three sales. Right?

CRUZ: That's right.

JAYWALKER: Who arrested Mr. Barnett?

CRUZ: I did.

JAYWALKER: Who processed him? Searched him, took his pedigree, vouchered his belongings?

CRUZ: I did.

JAYWALKER: Did you ever ask him who he got the drugs from?

This time it was nothing but a shot in the dark. Barnett had told Jaywalker that he'd never been asked about his source, which made no sense. But even if that was true, Agent Cruz could hardly admit it. Chances were he'd say that Barnett had refused to discuss the subject, asked to speak with a lawyer or gotten belligerent. But Cruz surprised Jaywalker.

"To tell you the truth, Counselor, I honestly don't remember if I asked him or not."

Which might have won him points with the jurors for honesty and politeness, but it really true broke a cardinal rule of drug enforcement. Still, Jaywalker decided to leave the answer alone. Not that it wouldn't continue to nag at him, though.

"No further questions," he said.

They broke for lunch.

"The People call Investigator Lance Bucknell," Miki Shaughnessey announced when the trial resumed that afternoon. And the moment Bucknell entered the courtroom, the jurors nodded in recognition. Apparently they had taken to heart Jaywalker's point that Investigator Bucknell's all-American looks hardly equipped him to blend in with the brothers in Harlem.

Because of that, Jaywalker was curious as to exactly why Shaughnessey had decided to call Bucknell. The best guess he could come up with was that she'd thought the investigator's good looks would help win over the women on the jury. Or perhaps it was a desire on her part to bring in a representative from the third and final agency that had made up the joint task force, the New York State Police. Ten minutes into Investigator Bucknell's testimony, it occurred to Jaywalker that Shaughnessey might be playing defense with her witness, using him to preempt any further attack by Jaywalker on the failure of the backup team to identify Alonzo Barnett's source of supply. But if that was her goal, she'd picked a strange witness to do it with.

SHAUGHNESSEY: Did there come a time during the course of that first buy, Investigator Bucknell, when you got out of your surveillance vehicle and followed the defendant on foot?

BUCKNELL: Yes, ma'am.

SHAUGHNESSEY: And were you able to see where he went?

BUCKNELL: Yes, ma'am, I was. He walked to number 345 West 127th Street, a large apartment building on the uptown side of the street.

SHAUGHNESSEY: What did he do when he got there?

BUCKNELL: He walked through the outer set of doors into a vestibule area. There he appeared to press a button on a large board of names. A moment later he appeared to be speaking over an intercom system. Then he stepped to the inner set of doors and, after a second or two, pushed one of those open, entered the lobby and disappeared from my view.

SHAUGHNESSEY: Did you attempt to follow him into the building?

BUCKNELL: No, ma'am. Not on this occasion.

SHAUGHNESSEY: How about on the second buy? Did you also follow him on foot during that event?

BUCKNELL: Yes, ma'am. On the second buy I followed him to the same building. And after I saw him get buzzed in, I entered the vestibule. But I found the inner doors locked, and I was unable to proceed farther. Eventually someone came out of the building and I was able to gain entry as she exited, but by that time the defendant was nowhere in sight.

SHAUGHNESSEY: And on the third buy?

BUCKNELL: On the third buy, anticipating that the defendant would go to the same building, I wore a disguise and stationed myself inside the lobby even before his arrival.

SHAUGHNESSEY: How did you get inside the lobby?

BUCKNELL: I slipped the lock with a credit card.

SHAUGHNESSEY: And did there come a time when you saw Mr. Barnett?

BUCKNELL: Yes, ma'am. About twenty minutes later he entered the vestibule area from outside the building, pressed a button on the board and was buzzed in.

SHAUGHNESSEY: Were you able to see which button
   he pressed?

BUCKNELL: No, ma'am.

SHAUGHNESSEY: What happened next?

BUCKNELL: The defendant walked to one of the el-
   evators, pushed the button and got on when the door
   opened. I…I got on behind him. I waited for him to
   push a floor button so I could push a higher one and
   see where he got off. But he pushed twelve, which was
   the top floor. I pushed ten, so it wouldn't look like I
   was following him. When the elevator door opened
   on ten, I figured I better get off. I looked around for
   the stairs, but it took me a moment to find them, and
   by the time I did and ran up to the twelfth floor, the
   defendant was out of sight.

Even as Jaywalker struggled to jot all that down in
his own cryptic version of shorthand, he could feel his
client nudging his elbow to get his attention. Jaywalker
put him off for a moment, afraid he might miss something. Other lawyers solved the problem by instructing
their clients to pass them notes whenever necessary. Jaywalker discouraged the practice, fearful that a note-taking
defendant might be perceived by the jurors as a jailhouse
lawyer, a smart-ass who thought he knew better than his
lawyer. So only when he'd finished his note-taking did
Jaywalker lean his head toward his client and ask him
what he wanted.

   "He's lying," Barnett whispered. "I went to the eighth
floor. And I've never seen this guy in my life. Believe
me, I'd remember."

   Interesting.

SHAUGHNESSEY: Did you stay there on the twelfth floor, Investigator Bucknell, in order to see which apartment Mr. Barnett came out of?

BUCKNELL: No, ma'am. I was afraid it would look too suspicious for me to still be there. Also, I could see the apartment doors had peepholes, and I was afraid I'd be visible standing there. So I left and went back downstairs and out of the building.

Shaughnessey left it there, concluding her questioning of the witness. She evidently figured that the jurors would understand that the obstacles Investigator Bucknell had run into would have stymied any member of the backup team.

As Jaywalker rose to cross-examine Bucknell, he knew better.

He knew better because on at least half a dozen occasions in his DEA days he'd encountered the same problem, or a pretty close cousin of it. Once he and another agent had gotten hold of a couple of elevator repairman uniforms and a bunch of cast-iron test weights, just so they could see what floor a dealer was heading to. On the next buy they'd hidden in a utility closet on that floor, cracking the door ajar just enough to see which apartment the guy entered. During another investigation, knowing it would be only a matter of time until they zeroed in on a particular apartment in a ten-floor building, Jaywalker had been confident enough to set up an office pool, copying the names from the tenant board onto slips of paper, putting them in a hat and charging five bucks a pick against a chance to win $250. *Stymied?* Stymied was nothing but a state of mind, a seeing-the-glass-half-empty sense of defeatism.

JAYWALKER: Have you ever made any undercover buys, Investigator Bucknell?

BUCKNELL: Yes, sir. I have.

JAYWALKER: Where was that?

BUCKNELL: It was at a NASCAR event in Watkins Glen.

JAYWALKER: Where's Watkins Glen?

BUCKNELL: It's in Schuyler County, New York. That's over in the Finger Lakes region.

JAYWALKER: And what kind of drugs did you buy there?

BUCKNELL: It wasn't drugs, sir. I bought a beer from a vendor when I was still a probationary trooper and not yet twenty-one years old. So it was illegal for him to sell alcohol to me.

JAYWALKER: I see. Anything else?

BUCKNELL: No, sir.

JAYWALKER: Any idea why not?

BUCKNELL: Why not what?

JAYWALKER: Why you haven't been given more undercover assignments?

BUCKNELL: They keep telling me I'm too clean-cut looking for undercover work. I'm working on it, though.

[Laughter]

JAYWALKER: And the disguise you mentioned earlier. Was that part of your working on it?

BUCKNELL: Yes, sir. Exactly.

JAYWALKER: May I ask what you disguised yourself as?

He expected to hear "a black man" or "a kid stoned on crack," or something like that. Maybe even a meter reader from Con Ed, or a cable TV installer, both of which Jaywalker had impersonated in his DEA days.

BUCKNELL: An encyclopedia salesman.

JAYWALKER: Excuse me? You went in there carrying a set of encyclopedias?

BUCKNELL: Not exactly. I did carry a briefcase, though. And it was definitely big enough to hold several volumes.

JAYWALKER: Sell any of them?

It was a dumb question, and Jaywalker was sorry he'd asked it as soon as it came out of his mouth. The last thing he wanted was to make fun of the witness and get

the jurors feeling sorry for him. So when Miki Shaughnessey stood up, Jaywalker hastily apologized and with-
drew the question even before the judge could sustain the
objection.

Still, it was frustrating. There'd been a time early on in
his involvement in the case when Jaywalker had hoped to
learn that Clarence Hightower had been acting as a government informer when he'd prevailed upon Alonzo Barnett to bring him to somebody who was dealing weight.
Had that been the case, Jaywalker would have had a viable
entrapment defense for Barnett. But those hopes had been
dashed by the disclosure about the anonymous caller and
the form Daniel Pulaski had shown him indicating that
no CI had been used in the case. Even so, it continued to
look as though the task force had gone to great lengths
to keep Hightower out of the case, rather than tie him to
it, as might have been expected.

Now the same thing was happening at the other end.
Both the undercover agent and the backup team should
have been doing everything they possibly could have not
only to find out who Barnett had gotten the drugs from
but to make a case against that guy, as well. Surely they
had black officers who could have gone into the building without arousing suspicion. Even Angel Cruz could
have done the job. So what had they done? They'd gone
and picked a guy whose white-bread WASPy looks all
but guaranteed that he'd fail. And that "disguise" business of his? That had been nothing but a joke, a joke so
lame that Jaywalker had succumbed to sarcasm.

But it got even worse. If Alonzo Barnett was telling
the truth—and Jaywalker had no reason to believe he
wasn't—then Investigator Bucknell had never even made

it upstairs after he'd followed Barnett inside the building. He was making up the whole twelfth-floor business in order to give himself an excuse for not having been able to see which floor Barnett had ridden the elevator to and which apartment he'd entered.

But how did you prove that? How did you show the jury that this innocent-looking, fresh-faced kid from upstate was deliberately lying through his teeth?

JAYWALKER: Tell me, Investigator Bucknell. Did you attend the team meeting prior to the third and final transaction?

BUCKNELL: Yes, sir.

JAYWALKER: And was it made clear at that meeting that Mr. Barnett was to be taken down—I'm sorry, arrested—once he was seen emerging from the building and walking back toward Agent St. James's Cadillac?

BUCKNELL: Yes, sir. That was made clear.

JAYWALKER: So you knew this was going to be your very last opportunity to see which apartment in the building he was going to in order to get the drugs?

BUCKNELL: I suppose so.

JAYWALKER: Well, was there any question about that in your mind?

BUCKNELL: I guess not.

JAYWALKER: It was now or never, wasn't it?

BUCKNELL: I guess.

JAYWALKER: Time to take a chance.

BUCKNELL: *[No response]*

JAYWALKER: And yet you chose to play it safe, didn't you?

BUCKNELL: I'm not sure what you mean.

JAYWALKER: I mean the team already had two solid buys against Mr. Barnett at that point, two hand-to-hand sales of heroin. So what if the third buy didn't go down exactly according to plan? You were primarily interested in the *connection* at that point, the *source of supply*. Weren't you?

BUCKNELL: I was only doing what I'd been told to do, sir.

JAYWALKER: And what was that? What had you been told, and by whom?

BUCKNELL: Lieutenant…Lieutenant—

JAYWALKER: Pascarella?

BUCKNELL: Right. He told me to be very careful, that Mr. Barnett was a high-value target. And he didn't want me to blow it by being too aggressive inside the building.

JAYWALKER: And you took that to mean "Don't try

too hard to identify which apartment he's going to."
Right?

BUCKNELL: In a way. I suppose so.

JAYWALKER: Well, that's exactly what it sounded like.
Didn't it?

Miki Shaughnessey's objection was sustained, but not
before the witness had already nodded his head and begun
to agree.

The problem was, where did you go from there? Did
you attack Lance Bucknell, accuse him of making up the
business about having been up on the twelfth floor? In
television and movie portrayals, witnesses were always
breaking down and admitting they'd been lying. In real
life, Jaywalker knew, that almost never happened. No
matter how hard he went after Bucknell, the guy wasn't
going to fold. He couldn't very well suddenly reverse
course and say, "Oh, yeah, I lied about that." To do so
would cost him not only his job but several years of prison
time for perjury. Besides, Jaywalker had nothing to go
after him *with*. It wasn't like he had a videotape of what
had gone on inside the building. He'd already checked,
and while there was a security camera, it was nothing
but a dummy. All he had was his own client's whisper in
his ear that almost two years ago he'd gone to the eighth
floor and not the twelfth. And while Jaywalker believed
the whisper, it simply wasn't enough to go on. Bucknell
would duck and parry whatever Jaywalker could throw
at him, and in the end, the jury would believe him and
feel sorry for him, not to mention regard Jaywalker as a
bully and take it out on his client.

So he thanked Investigator Bucknell and sat down.

* * *

It was only four-thirty, but up at the bench Miki Shaughnessey explained that she had only one remaining witness, the chemist, who was testifying in federal court and wouldn't be available until the following morning. "I have another member of the backup team here," she said, "but I've decided against calling him. I think his testimony would be nothing but cumulative."

"Who is he?" Jaywalker asked. *Cumulative* was a funny word, he knew. It was supposed to mean that the witness wouldn't really add anything new to the testimony. What it really meant, Jaywalker had learned over the years, was that the prosecutor didn't want to call the witness because he might remember things differently from the way previous witnesses had remembered them.

"Detective Lopata," said Shaughnessey.

"Give me a minute?" Jaywalker asked the judge. When she nodded, he went back to the defense table and found a file he had for Lopata. He pretty much knew the contents by heart but wanted to double-check, just in case he wanted the detective kept on call as a possible defense witness. But from scanning the reports, Jaywalker could see that Lopata's testimony would indeed add nothing new. He'd counted out and photocopied the official advance funds, weighed the drugs and performed a few other administrative tasks. But in terms of surveillance, he'd stayed back in one of the cars during each buy and had seen nothing of interest.

So it didn't look like Shaughnessey was trying to hide anything by deciding not to call him. If anything, it showed she was confident that her case was solid without him. And even Jaywalker would have had to agree. Three witnesses down and one to go, and he'd barely made a dent so far. And with the remaining witness being the chemist, what hope did he have? That he was going to be able to somehow show that it hadn't been heroin at all that his client had sold, but baby powder?

Back up at the bench, Jaywalker told Shaughnessey that she could let Lopata go. Without a good reason for doing so, he wasn't about to put some detective on the stand without ever having spoken to the guy. The upside was negligible, while the potential for getting clobbered was virtually unlimited.

But having only one prosecution witness remaining created something of a logistical problem for Jaywalker. As ready as he was to put Alonzo Barnett on the stand, he didn't want to begin with him on a Friday afternoon, only to have his testimony broken up by the weekend. Worse yet, doing so would give Miki Shaughnessey two full days to refine her cross-examination.

"I'm afraid I won't be prepared to go forward with the defense case until Monday morning," he said.

The judge shot him a look. In all the years she'd dealt with Jaywalker, he'd never once been unprepared to do anything. Overprepared? Yes. Absurdly overprepared? To a fault. Like the time he'd convinced her he was fluent in Swahili because he'd corrected an interpreter's translation of a witness's answer. All he'd done, of course, had been to memorize what the witness had said at an earlier hearing in response to the identical question. But the word had quickly gotten around the courthouse that Jaywalker wasn't to be fooled, not in English, Spanish, French, Italian, German, Hebrew, Yiddish, Creole, Patois, Hindi, Farsi, Mandarin, or any of a dozen other languages and dialects. While it was as far from the truth as it could have been, Jaywalker wasn't about to deny the rumor.

"Monday it shall be," said the judge, evidently knowing

that, were she to push Jaywalker to begin earlier, he'd no doubt come down with a migraine, set off a fire alarm or pull some other stunt to get what he wanted. So she turned to the jurors and told them they'd be working only a half day on Friday.

From their reactions, you would have thought they'd been given a reprieve from a death sentence.

That night, long after his wife had kissed him good-night and headed to bed, Jaywalker pored over his file on the chemist. Very few defense lawyers insisted that the chemist be brought in to testify. The vast majority were more than willing to concede that the drugs were heroin or cocaine or angel dust, or whatever the lab report said they were. Indeed, Jaywalker himself often stipulated to the same thing, especially in cases where he had a viable defense of some sort to focus on. But in this case he had no defense, viable or otherwise. So whether out of mounting frustration or mere stubbornness, he'd told Miki Shaughnessey some time ago that he wanted the chemist brought in to testify.

"Why?" she'd asked, the surprise evident in her raised eyebrows.

"Because," was all the answer he'd been able to give her.

Now, as he reviewed and re-reviewed lab reports he'd already reviewed a dozen times before, he tried his hardest to find a legitimate reason that, at least in hindsight, might justify his refusal to stipulate as something other than mere childish petulance.

It took him until nearly three o'clock in the morning to find one, but he did. The problem was that by that time he was so exhausted that he had no way of knowing whether it was a meaningful point or not. He finally fell asleep, but not before wondering if all those other defense lawyers didn't have the right idea. Instead of driving themselves relentlessly over every little thing, they conserved their energy so they'd be ready to recognize a real opportunity if one came along, then pounce on it. Jaywalker was too tired to recognize anything anymore, let alone pounce on it.

11

Chemistry lessons

Miki Shaughnessey's direct examination of the chemist was as basic as it could be. The previous afternoon she'd asked Jaywalker what he hoped to accomplish with the witness, and Jaywalker had answered that he honestly had no idea. It had been a truthful response at the time he'd made it. Shaughnessey had then volunteered that she'd checked and found that most of her colleagues had never once had to call a chemist at trial, having relied each time upon the defense lawyer's willingness to stipulate as to what the chemist would have said if put on the witness stand.

"Don't worry about it," Jaywalker had told her. "I'm just frustrated with your cops and agents. I want the jurors to hear what a truthful witness sounds like."

"You don't believe the cops have been truthful?"

"About the basics, sure. But," he'd added, "not about some of the little things. Though I'm honestly not sure why."

"What kind of little things?" she'd wanted to know.

Either she'd been genuinely curious about why her witnesses might have done a bit of fudging here or there, or she'd been looking to gain a tactical advantage from whatever Jaywalker might tell her. But she was young and cute, and Jaywalker, though happily married, had always been a sucker for the combination. So he'd decided to give her the benefit of the doubt.

"Oh, the business about the anonymous caller," he'd started with. "That just doesn't ring true. My client wasn't dealing out in the open on his stoop. In fact, he wasn't dealing at all until Clarence Hightower came along and twisted his arm. Next, the fact that Hightower was never charged with sale, even though he introduced St. James to Barnett for the express purpose of buying drugs. Finally, the fact that no real attempt was ever made to get to Barnett's connection. That should have been the ultimate goal of the operation. Instead they send some overgrown Boy Scout to do the job, and then tie his hands to make sure he doesn't find out anything."

"So what does all that have to do with the chemist?" Shaughnessey had asked.

"Nothing," Jaywalker had admitted. "Like I said, I'm frustrated, and I don't know what else to do."

That had been then.

Now it was Friday morning, and Miki Shaughnessey rose to announce that the People were prepared to call their fourth and final witness, Olga Kasmirov.

Just as not all doctors are lucky enough to be on staff at the Mayo Clinic or the National Institutes of Health, so too are there chemists in this world who don't pull down fat six-figure salaries at DuPont or Eli Lily. Scan down the rolls of the psychiatrists who perform the half hour court-ordered evaluations for the criminal justice system, or the technicians who spend their days peering through old-fashioned microscopes at drugs bought or seized on the streets of the city, and in no time you'll think you've stumbled upon a veritable roster of United Nations delegates. Except that the pay isn't nearly as good.

So the name Olga Kasmirov barely registered on Jaywalker's radar, any more than did her explanation two minutes into her testimony that while she'd once been a leading expert in polymer conductivity in the former Soviet Union, these days she made her living analyzing samples of white powder or green vegetation at the New York City office of the United States Chemist.

Shaughnessey's direct examination was just that—direct and to the point. She spent a few minutes asking the witness about her education and experience, but she needn't have bothered; Jaywalker quickly rose and offered to stipulate that the witness qualified as an expert in the analysis of controlled substances. Thanking Jaywalker for the concession, Shaughnessey moved on to the drugs bought and seized from Alonzo Barnett.

SHAUGHNESSEY: With respect to the substance from the first buy, what did you do?

KASMIROV: I emptied the powder onto a scale and determined its net weight to be 1.01 grams. We use the metric system. That comes out to about one twenty-eighth of an ounce. Then I conducted several tests for the presence of heroin hydrochloride, and the results were consistently and conclusively positive.

SHAUGHNESSEY: How about with respect to the second buy?

KASMIROV: For the second buy, I found the weight to be 26.02 grams. That's a little less than one ounce. As before, tests for the presence of heroin hydrochloride proved positive.

SHAUGHNESSEY: And the package seized from the defendant at the time of his arrest?

KASMIROV: I found the weight to be 124.8 grams. That's just under an eighth of a kilogram, or about 4.4 ounces. Once again, I tested for the presence of heroin hydrochloride and the results were positive.

SHAUGHNESSEY: Now, these lab reports you prepared. Were they prepared in the ordinary course of business at the lab?

Jaywalker knew the ritual, the legalese required to admit business records as an exception to the hearsay rule. The next question would be, "And was it the ordinary course of business at the lab to prepare such reports?" He rose to his feet and magnanimously stated that he had no objection to the reports being received in evidence.

The fact was, he actually wanted them in.

He *needed* them in.

"Received in evidence," said the judge.

Miki Shaughnessey thanked her witness and sat down. Her entire direct examination had taken less than fourteen minutes.

Jaywalker's cross would take considerably longer.

JAYWALKER: Good morning. Is it Ms. Kasmirov, or Dr. Kasmirov?

KASMIROV: In the Soviet Union I was Dr. Kasmirov. Here I'm not sure how it works.

JAYWALKER: But you won't object if I call you Doctor?

KASMIROV: I won't object.

JAYWALKER: Good. Dr. Kasmirov, in response to Ms. Shaughnessey's questions, you essentially described performing both a quantitative analysis of the drugs you examined in connection with this case and a qualitative analysis. Correct?

KASMIROV: That is correct.

JAYWALKER: In other words, how much the substances weighed and what they contained.

KASMIROV: Correct.

JAYWALKER: Let's talk about the weights first, okay?

KASMIROV: Okay.

JAYWALKER: Starting with the first buy. You found that its net weight was 1.01 grams. Can you tell us how close that was to weighing exactly one gram?

KASMIROV: It was off by only one one-hundredth of a gram. In other words, if it was supposed to be a gram, it was off by about one percentage point.

JAYWALKER: And skipping to the third quantity of drugs you analyzed. That you found to weigh 124.8 grams. If that was supposed to be an eighth of a kilogram, how close was it?

KASMIROV: Well, a kilogram is a thousand grams. An eighth of that would be 125 grams. So 124.8 would be off by only two-tenths of a gram. I would need a calculator or paper and pencil to compute the margin of error.

JAYWALKER: Here. *[Hands calculator to witness]*

KASMIROV: It comes out to .00016, or sixteen-thousandths. That's a small fraction of one percentage point.

JAYWALKER: In other words, very, very close.

KASMIROV: Yes.

JAYWALKER: So close as to suggest that whoever had measured it out used a very sophisticated scale. Would you agree?

KASMIROV: I would agree, yes.

JAYWALKER: Now let's go back to the one we skipped, the second buy. There you found the net weight to be 25.8 grams. Correct?

KASMIROV: Correct.

JAYWALKER: Assume for a moment that that buy was supposed to have been one ounce. Can you tell us how close it actually was?

KASMIROV: Well, an ounce contains 28.35 grams, rounded off to two decimal points. The difference would have been 2.55 grams.

JAYWALKER: In other words it was *more than two and a half grams short?*

KASMIROV: Yes.

JAYWALKER: And the margin of error?

KASMIROV: May I use the calculator?

JAYWALKER: Of course.

KASMIROV: More than nine percent off, almost ten.

JAYWALKER: Where did it all go?

KASMIROV: Some might have been lost during field-testing.

JAYWALKER: But only a tiny bit, right?

KASMIROV: I should think so.

JAYWALKER: And if the first and third batches were field-tested, as well, they appear to have lost almost nothing in the process. Agreed?

KASMIROV: I agree.

JAYWALKER: So where did those two and half grams— almost ten percent of an ounce—go?

KASMIROV: I can't tell you.

Jaywalker walked back to the defense table and dug out a file. Although *dug out* was only what it looked like.

OFFICIAL OPINION POLL

Dear Reader,

Since you are a book enthusiast, we would like to know what you think.

Inside you will find a short Opinion Poll. Please participate in our poll by sharing your opinion on 3 subjects that are very important to all of us.

To thank you for your participation, we would like to send you **2 FREE BOOKS** and **2 FREE GIFTS!**

Please enjoy them with our compliments.

Sincerely,

Pam Powers

YOUR OPINION POLL
THANK-YOU FREE GIFTS INCLUDE:

▶ **2 SUSPENSE BOOKS**

▶ **2 LOVELY SURPRISE GIFTS**

▶ **DETACH AND MAIL CARD TODAY!** ▶

OFFICIAL OPINION POLL

YOUR OPINION COUNTS!
Please check TRUE or FALSE below to express your opinion about the following statements:

Q1 Do you believe in "true love"?

"TRUE LOVE HAPPENS ONLY ONCE IN A LIFETIME."
○ TRUE
○ FALSE

Q2 Do you think marriage has any value in today's world?

"YOU CAN BE TOTALLY COMMITTED TO SOMEONE WITHOUT BEING MARRIED."
○ TRUE
○ FALSE

Q3 What kind of books do you enjoy?

"A GREAT NOVEL MUST HAVE A SATISFYING ENDING."
○ TRUE
○ FALSE

YES! I have placed my sticker in the space provided below. Please send me the **2 FREE books** and **2 FREE gifts** for which I qualify. I understand that I am under no obligation to purchase anything further, as explained on the back of this card.

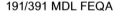

191/391 MDL FEQA

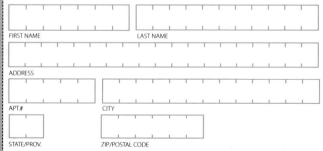

FIRST NAME

LAST NAME

ADDRESS

APT.#

CITY

STATE/PROV.

ZIP/POSTAL CODE

TF-SUS-11
Printed in the U.S.A.
© 2011 HARLEQUIN ENTERPRISES LIMITED.

The Reader Service—Here's How It Works:

Accepting your 2 free books and 2 free gifts (gifts valued at approximately $10.00) places you under no obligation to buy anything. You may keep the books and gifts and return the shipping statement marked "cancel." If you do not cancel, about a month later we'll send you 4 additional books and bill you just $5.99 each in the U.S. or $6.49 each in Canada. That is a savings of at least 25% off the cover price. It's quite a bargain! Shipping and handling is just 50¢ per book in the U.S. and 75¢ per book in Canada.* You may cancel at any time, but if you choose to continue, every month we'll send you 4 more books, which you may either purchase at the discount price or return to us and cancel your subscription.

*Terms and prices subject to change without notice. Prices do not include applicable taxes. Sales tax applicable in N.Y. Canadian residents will be charged applicable taxes. Offer not valid in Quebec. Books received may not be as shown. All orders subject to credit approval. Credit or debit balances in a customer's account(s) may be offset by any other outstanding balance owed by or to the customer. Please allow 4 to 6 weeks for delivery. Offer available while quantities last.

If offer card is missing write to: The Reader Service, P.O. Box 1867, Buffalo NY 14240-1867 or visit: www.ReaderService.com

BUSINESS REPLY MAIL
FIRST-CLASS MAIL   PERMIT NO. 717   BUFFALO, NY

POSTAGE WILL BE PAID BY ADDRESSEE

THE READER SERVICE
PO BOX 1341
BUFFALO NY 14240-8571

NO POSTAGE
NECESSARY
IF MAILED
IN THE
UNITED STATES

The truth was, he'd had the file right where he could find it since three o'clock that morning. Now he drew two sheets of paper from it. One he handed to Miki Shaughnessey. The other, the original, he gave to the court reporter, asking that it be marked Defendant's Exhibit A for identification.

JAYWALKER: Dr. Kasmirov, I hand you this item and ask you to take a look at it.

KASMIROV: *[Complies]*

JAYWALKER: Have you seen it before?

KASMIROV: No, I don't believe so.

JAYWALKER: Are you able to tell us what it is?

KASMIROV: Yes. It's a lab report prepared by someone at the police department's lab. It describes an analysis of drugs recovered from a man named Clarence Hightower, also known as "Stump," at the time of his arrest.

JAYWALKER: I offer it in evidence.

Now by rights Miki Shaughnessey could have objected. For one thing, it was hearsay, since Jaywalker hadn't subpoenaed anyone from the lab to authenticate it as a business record. There simply hadn't been time for him to do it the right way. Beyond that, its relevance was far from clear.

But one of the things that happens when the defense allows the prosecution to do things without objection is that the prosecutor—particularly a young and inexperienced prosecutor—feels compelled to match that display of goodwill. Jaywalker was betting that the last thing Shaughnessey wanted to do was seem threatened by a piece of paper. She had a winner of a case, an open-and-shut conviction. Would she dare jeopardize that by being perceived as fighting to keep evidence out of the trial?

SHAUGHNESSEY: No objection.

THE COURT: Received as Defendant's A.

JAYWALKER: Thank you. What does this lab report tell you, Dr. Kasmirov?

KASMIROV: It tells me that what was recovered from Mr. Hightower had a net weight of one-eleventh of an ounce plus 4.6 grains. They use avoirdupois weight over there.

JAYWALKER: And the metric equivalent?

KASMIROV: *[Using calculator]* Let me see. It comes out to just about two and a half grams. *Aha!*

If any of the jurors had missed the significance, there was Olga Kasmirov's spontaneous *"Aha!"* to highlight it for them. Was it just a coincidence that Clarence Hightower had ended up with the exact amount of heroin in his pocket that had mysteriously disappeared from the ounce Agent St. James had received from Alonzo Barnett on the second buy?

But Jaywalker was only halfway there.

JAYWALKER: Now, the lab report tells you still more, doesn't it, Dr. Kasmirov?

KASMIROV: Like what?

JAYWALKER: Like what else was in those two and a half grams besides heroin. Right?

KASMIROV: *[Examining report]* Right.

JAYWALKER: What else was in there?

KASMIROV: *[Reading]* Lactose, dextrose and quinine. Although it doesn't say how much of each.

JAYWALKER: Yes, too bad about that.

SHAUGHNESSEY: Objection.

THE COURT: Sustained. Strike the comment.

JAYWALKER: What is lactose?

KASMIROV: Lactose is milk sugar.

JAYWALKER: And what is dextrose?

KASMIROV: Dextrose is sugar from fruits or vegetables. In this case it's most likely from corn syrup.

JAYWALKER: What are they doing in heroin?

SHAUGHNESSEY: Objection. How can she say?

JAYWALKER: She's an expert. I'm asking her to give us her opinion.

THE COURT: Yes, overruled. You may answer the question if you can.

KASMIROV: A seller will add either lactose or dextrose to heroin as a diluent, to bulk up the heroin and make more of it. At the same time, it reduces the strength of the heroin, brings it down to a level where it can be safely injected or snorted by the user. Though it's a bit unusual to see both lactose and dextrose present in a single sample. It's redundant. They do exactly the same thing.

JAYWALKER: And quinine. What's that?

KASMIROV: Quinine is a salt made from an alkaloid from the bark of a tree. It used to be used to treat malaria. Although I forget the name of the tree right now.

JAYWALKER: How about the cinchona?

KASMIROV: That's it.

JAYWALKER: And what's quinine doing in there?

KASMIROV: Lactose and dextrose are sugars. Add enough of either one and the sweetness becomes detectable. The buyer will know the percentage of heroin isn't what it should be. Quinine, on the other hand, is bitter. It cuts the sweetness, like lemon would cut the sweetness in sugared tea. By adding a little quinine to counteract the sugar, it's possible to fool someone who tastes the drug into believing it contains more heroin than it really does.

JAYWALKER: I see. Now, with respect to your own analyses, Dr. Kasmirov, the three that you made. Did you find substances other than heroin?

KASMIROV: Yes, I did.

JAYWALKER: And unlike the police chemist, did you quantify the various substances you found in each analysis?

KASMIROV: Yes.

JAYWALKER: Please tell us what you found.

Even as the witness began reading from her lab reports, Jaywalker produced a huge piece of white-oak tag he'd brought along with him that morning and a thick black marking pen. By the time Dr. Kasmirov was finished answering and he was finished writing, he had diagrammed her testimony for all to see. What it showed was that there was no discernible difference in the 2.55 grams of heroin seized from Hightower and the 2.55 grams of heroin that were unaccounted for in the second buy made from Alonzo Barnett. Not in terms of weight, strength or additives. Right down to the redundant lactose and dextrose.

On redirect, Miki Shaughnessey got Dr. Kasmirov to agree that, absent a breakdown of the percentages of heroin, lactose, dextrose and quinine in the drugs seized from Clarence Hightower, it was nothing more than speculation that they'd come from the second Barnett sale. After all, weren't those three additives very common ones? Yes, they were, Kasmirov agreed. "And," Shaughnessey asked her, "regardless of whatever Hightower possessed or didn't possess, is there any question in your mind that what Alonzo Barnett sold twice and was caught with on a third occasion contained heroin?"

"No," Dr. Kasmirov replied. "About that there's absolutely no question at all."

That night, as Jaywalker lay in the darkness on his side of the bed, too tired to keep his eyes open but too wired to sleep, his wife asked him about the chart he'd brought home with him.

"What does it show?" she wanted to know.

"It shows that this guy Hightower ended up with some of the identical heroin that Barnett sold to the undercover."

"I understand that," she said. "But what does *that* show? What does it *mean?* What's the jury supposed to make of it?"

"It could mean Barnett gave him some of it," said Jaywalker. "But Barnett swears he didn't."

"And of course you believe him."

It was one of their private little jokes, that Jaywalker invariably believed whatever his murderers, rapists, thieves and drug dealers told him. Not always, he'd tell her. But once they'd gotten to know him and trust him? Once they understood that he was really on their side and would fight for them even if he knew the full truth? Yeah, then they'd tell him the truth.

Almost always.

"Suppose Hightower had simply bought some of the

same stuff?" she asked him. "Directly from the same guy Barnett was buying from?"

"Didn't happen," he assured her. "Barnett insists his source wouldn't sell to anyone but him. Refused to even meet with Hightower, or with his so-called friend from Philadelphia. It's the only reason Barnett's in the hot seat now."

"So what, then?"

"I don't know," Jaywalker confessed. "Maybe the agents thought Hightower was a pain in the ass, coming up on them like he did while they were trying to arrest Barnett. Those can be scary situations. Buncha white guys surrounding a brother in the middle of Harlem. Who knows? Maybe they got pissed off and flaked him."

"Flaked him?"

"Took some of the drugs they'd skimmed off from the second buy and planted it on Hightower."

"They *do* things like that?" she asked.

"Occasionally."

"Did *you?*"

"*Moi?* No. But I know that kind of thing used to happen back then, and I'm sure it still happens today."

"Great system you work in," she said. And even in the dark, he could feel her turning away from him.

"So what am I supposed to do? Pretend I don't know stuff like that goes on? Not argue that cops lie? Roll over and give up?"

"No," she said, her voice softening. "What you're supposed to do is roll over and try to get some sleep."

Which turned out to be easy for her to say. For another hour Jaywalker continued to lie in the darkness, listening to the rise and fall of his wife's breathing. He'd been able to go only so far with Olga Kasmirov and her lab reports, he knew. Even as he'd been busy with his chart-making,

he'd noticed blank stares coming his way from the jury
box. Sure, he'd had them there for a moment when the
numbers had matched perfectly, Hightower's drugs with
what was missing from Barnett's. But his wife was right,
as she almost always was. What inference were the jurors
supposed to draw from that match that could possibly
steer them in the direction of acquitting Alonzo Barnett?
Especially when Jaywalker himself couldn't come up with
an answer to that question.

He lay awake for another forty-five minutes. At one
point he reached down to the floor by his side of the bed
and groped around until he found the pen and pad of
paper he always kept there. Blindly, he scribbled down
two words. It was the last thing he remembered before
finally falling asleep.

12

Hightower

Helping his wife make their bed that Saturday morning, Jaywalker stepped on something with his bare foot. When he bent down to see what it was, he found a crumpled piece of paper with scribbling on one side of it. It took him a moment to recognize his own handwriting and another moment to decipher it.

Call Miki

was all it said. With no pockets in his pajama top—and no pajama top, either, for that matter—he held on to it and didn't put it down until he got to the kitchen. There he poured himself a glass of iced tea and grabbed a handful of Cheez-It crackers. Breakfast, Jaywalker style.

"So who's this Miki?" his wife wanted to know.

"The D.A. I'm up against," he said between mouthfuls.

"You're going to call her on a weekend?"

"Yeah," said Jaywalker. "I got an idea."

His wife rolled her eyes but said nothing more. She was familiar with Jaywalker and his ideas. It was when he was most creative that he was also most dangerous. Like the time he'd decided their living room needed a fireplace. For two full years they'd lived with a blue plastic tarpaulin draped over an entire wall. But eventually they'd ended up with a pretty cool fireplace. So she'd learned to get out of the way and give her husband room while she feared for the worst and hoped for the best.

It took him a while to get hold of Miki Shaughnessey's home phone number, because, like those of all A.D.A.'s, it was unlisted. But with a little lying and cajoling, he got it.

"How'd you get my number?" was the first thing she wanted to know.

They spent a few minutes on that, before moving on to the purpose of Jaywalker's call. "I want you to have Clarence Hightower's drugs tested by Dr. Kasmirov, so we can hear the percentages of the various additives. That way we'll know for sure if there's a match."

"What difference could it possibly make?"

His wife couldn't have said it better.

He spent the next five minutes trying to convince Shaughnessey that it *did* make a difference. He even went so far as to try out his flake theory on her. But if her re-action was any indication of what the jury's might be, it left Jaywalker with second thoughts about whether his argument would fly.

Finally she relented, but he strongly suspected it was just to get him off the phone. And even then, all she said was that she'd run it by her supervisor.

"Promise?" he asked, reduced to begging.

"Promise."

"Cross your heart and hope to die?"

"Stick a needle in my eye."

First thing Sunday morning, Jaywalker got a call from his former client Kenny Smith. Naturally Smith had his home number. All his clients and former clients did. It was what you did when you refused to own a cell phone but still wanted to be accessible to important people. Like your clients on Rikers Island, say.

"What's going on?" Jaywalker asked Smith.

"Can we talk?" Kenny asked.

Ever since his voice had been identified on a wiretap ten or twelve years back, Smith had been totally paranoid about saying more than hello and goodbye on the phone. And while Jaywalker considered it unlikely that anyone might be listening in on either of their phones, he wasn't willing to bet on it, having made an enemy or two in law enforcement over the years. Besides, he had absolutely no idea what Kenny was about to tell him. The last thing he wanted to do was assure him it was okay to talk, only to hear a murder confession and then have it played back in court six months from now.

"Have you had breakfast?" he asked Kenny.

"No. You wanna meet somewhere?"

"Nah," Jaywalker told him. "Come on over here."

And the thing was, he didn't even need to give Kenny the address. "Do me a favor," he told his wife. "Make some more of whatever you're making?" It was a drill she'd become familiar with over time. It came down to a choice of having strange people drop over from time to time, or having her husband go out even more than he did to meet them in what she considered scary neighborhoods. So she reached into the refrigerator for a couple more eggs.

"It's Kenny," he told her.

Make that four more eggs.

It was only while he was putting a third plate on the kitchen table that Jaywalker realized why Kenny had called him. A week or two ago he'd asked Smith to look around and see if he could locate one Clarence Hightower, more commonly known as Stump. No doubt Kenny was coming to report on his progress—or lack of it. That was certainly something they could have discussed on the phone, wiretap or no wiretap. But no big deal. It was only four eggs, five pieces of toast and a quart of coffee, after all. He'd once gone so far as to suggest to his wife that she learn how to make grits, but she'd drawn the line at that.

Kenny showed up an hour later. "So you want the good news?" he asked Jaywalker. "Or the bad?"

"Both."

"The good news," said Smith, "is I found your man Hightower. The bad news is he ran away before I could lay the suspeena on him."

Kenny had a problem pronouncing certain words. Not that it would have disqualified him from becoming President or anything like that.

"Ran away?"

"Bet."

Back in 1986, *bet* passed for Yes. As in *you bet*.

"And check this out," said Kenny between mouthfuls. "'Cordin to people who knows him, dude was gettin' some sorta *allowance* from someone. Ev'ry Friday, he'd come around with, like, a hundred bucks in his pocket— cash money."

"Welfare?" Jaywalker asked. "SSI?"

"You ain't lissenin', Jay. I said *ev'ry* week, not ev'ry two weeks or ev'ry month."

"So what was it?"

"I dunno what it was," Kenny admitted. "I only know what he *tol'* people it was."

"And what was that?"

"Tol' people it was from workin' for his uncle."

"So?" asked Jaywalker.

"So I axed around," said Kenny. "And far as anyone knows, the guy never worked a day in his life. And he don't even *have* no uncle."

Jaywalker rubbed his temples, trying to will his headache to go away. So Clarence Hightower was a liar. Great. What else was new?

It was noon Sunday by the time Miki Shaughnessey called Jaywalker back as she'd promised to do. But two words into the conversation, he could tell from the tone in her voice that she was going to disappoint him.

"My supervisor says there's no way. To begin with, Hightower's case is officially sealed, so it would take a court order to do anything. And since none of the NYPD lab's stuff is computerized, it would take them weeks just to find out if those drugs still exist or have already been destroyed. So he says we can forget about it."

"Terrific," was all Jaywalker could think to say. Well, that and one other thing. "Who *is* your supervisor, anyway?"

"You know him. Dan Pulaski."

Long after he'd hung up the phone, Jaywalker continued to seethe. Pulaski's point about Hightower's case being sealed, while technically true, was an obstacle only if you wanted to let it be one. The computer story was a bit more plausible. These days, everything's on computers, no more than a click away. But back in 1986 computers were only just beginning to show up in the system. And they were doing it with all the speed that feet had once begun to show up on fish.

Still, Jaywalker's distrust of Daniel Pulaski was so deep that he couldn't help wondering if he might not be onto something. The only problem was, he had absolutely no idea what that something might be.

13

Offer of proof

"The defendant calls Kenny Smith."

With those five words, Jaywalker began his defense of Alonzo Barnett. And got no further. Miki Shaughnessey was on her toes, both figuratively and literally, asking to approach the bench. There she told Judge Levine that she wanted an offer of proof.

An offer of proof is pretty much what you might guess it is. It's a brief oral statement from the lawyer who's putting a witness on the stand, and it's intended to show what he or she intends to prove through the witness. That way the opposing lawyer can argue to the judge, out of the hearing of the jury, that the witness shouldn't be permitted to testify because whatever he has to say is irrelevant, immaterial, hearsay, privileged or otherwise objectionable.

The offer of proof was also one of Jaywalker's pet peeves, and he lost no time in sharing that sentiment with Levine and Shaughnessey. "How come it's only when the defense calls a witness that there's got to be a preview? Why should we assume that I know the rules of evidence any less than the prosecution does?"

"We don't assume that at all," the judge assured him.

"But we do know how *creative* you can sometimes be. So I'm going to grant Ms. Shaughnessey's request and ask you to let us know what Mr. Smith's going to tell us."

"Then you'd better excuse the jury," Jaywalker suggested, "because I have a feeling this is going to take a while."

The judge agreed and ordered the jurors led out of the courtroom. One or two of them could be heard grumbling over the fact that they were being banished before they'd heard a single word. Once the last of them had left, the judge signaled the court reporter that the colloquy they were about to have would be on the record. That way, were she to prohibit the witness from testifying, the offer of proof would be preserved for an appellate court to consider. Finally she turned to Jaywalker.

"Now," she said, "who is Kenny Smith, and why are you calling him?"

Jaywalker stood, though he needn't have. The jury was gone, and Shirley Levine wasn't into formality. But Jaywalker worked better on his feet, especially when it was an uphill climb. "Kenny Smith is a private citizen," he began. "A private citizen and convicted felon who happens to be a former client of mine."

"Don't tell me you lost a case."

"It was a long time ago."

"And what is Mr. Smith going to tell us?"

"He's going to tell us things that, if believed by the jury, will lead them to conclude that Clarence Hightower is and continues to be a paid informer of law enforcement."

Okay, it was a stretch. But at some point Sunday night it had occurred to Jaywalker that the uncle Hightower was getting weekly payments from might just be named Sam. As in Uncle Sam.

"What sort of *things* is Mr. Smith going to tell us?" the judge wanted to know.

"Among others, that Mr. Hightower was, at least until recently, receiving regular weekly cash payments from an undisclosed source. That he was given favorable treatment consistent with his being an informer on at least three separate occasions, first at the time of his arrest, later in court, and finally with the state parole authorities. And that when Mr. Smith attempted to serve a subpoena on him, Hightower responded by running away."

"Suppose for a moment that you're right about Mr. Hightower's being an informer," said the judge. "How is that relevant to this trial?"

"I can think of two reasons right off the bat," said Jaywalker. "First, it means that the jury's been deliberately lied to. Second, it means that Hightower is under the control of the prosecution. I want him brought here so I can call him as a defense witness. If the prosecution won't do that, I want them sanctioned. I want a missing witness charge. And third, if Mr. Hightower was indeed an informer, my client has a legitimate entrapment defense."

Jaywalker sat down. It was more than he'd wanted to say, but he was beginning to get angry—angry and frustrated. Those who knew him knew it could be a dangerous combination.

"Ms. Shaughnessey?" said the judge.

Miki Shaughnessey rose. "The issue isn't whether or not Mr. Hightower has ever been an informer, or even if he is one now. So far as I know, he never has been and he isn't now. But none of that matters. The issue is whether he was acting as an informer back in September of 1984, when he introduced Agent St. James to the defendant for the purpose of buying drugs. And the answer to that question is an unequivocal no. I even have a document,

an official New York Police Department document that
Mr. Jaywalker has seen with his own eyes, that makes
that crystal clear."

"Is that true, Mr. Jaywalker?"

"It's true that I have seen such a document, and that
the document says that no informer was utilized in this
case."

"So why," asked the judge, "isn't that the end of it? If
he wasn't an informer in this case, there can be no entrapment as a matter of law. Wouldn't you have to agree,
Mr. Jaywalker?"

"Yes," Jaywalker was forced to concede.

"And Ms. Shaughnessey would therefore be right in
wanting Mr. Smith's testimony precluded. Right?"

"Right again."

"So why isn't that the end of the inquiry?"

"Ahhh," said Jaywalker, back up on his feet. Here,
finally, was the best part. The part that had kept him up
most of the previous night, long after Kenny Smith had
finished eating breakfast and left, long after Miki Shaughnessey had called back with word that Daniel Pulaski had
refused to authorize the retesting of Hightower's drugs. It
was the part that had finally dawned on Jaywalker not too
long before dawn itself had. The part that had prompted
him to pick up the phone, call Kenny Smith and tell him
to be in court at nine-thirty sharp that morning.

Lawyers are advocates, paid to argue positions. Those
positions can be as lofty as a client's factual innocence
or as mundane as whether a particular witness should
be addressed as Miss or Ms. Sometimes the position is
supported by the facts, the law and the equities of the
issue, and when those three considerations align, arguing
is easy. But there are other times, times when a lawyer
must—*must*—argue just as vigorously while standing on

ground so shaky that it feels as though it's going to give
way any second. So fearful had Jaywalker been that his
position on Clarence Hightower bordered on the frivolous
that at one point Sunday night he'd thought about showing up in court Monday morning wearing hip boots and
carrying a shovel.

And then the perfect, irrefutable argument had come
to him. Perfect because it was absolutely bombproof. And
irrefutable because it was dictated by nothing less than
the United States Constitution.

"It's not the end of the inquiry," he now told the judge,
"for the simple reason that for the life of me, I can't remember my client ever requesting a trial in front of either
the police commissioner or the district attorney. Nor, most
respectfully, did he request a bench trial in front of Your
Honor, though we did actually give that serious consideration. What my client requested was a trial by jury.
And whether or not a particular individual was acting as
an informer in a particular case becomes a question of
fact. Nothing more, nothing less. As a result, the NYPD
doesn't get to decide that fact, not even by writing something on a piece of paper. Mr. Pulaski and Ms. Shaughnessey don't get to decide that fact. Nor do I. Not even
you get to decide that fact, Your Honor. The only ones
who get to decide the facts in this case are those twelve
people we just sent out of the room and down to the principal's office."

And the thing was, he was right. He knew it, Miki
Shaughnessey knew it, and—most importantly—the
judge knew it.

Not that Shaughnessey didn't continue to contest the
point. First she argued that the court had the discretion
to preclude testimony that promised to be so vague as to
be nothing short of speculative. Then she complained that

permitting the testimony would force her to recall witnesses on rebuttal and perhaps even call additional ones, causing the trial to go on endlessly. Next she pointed out that she was being put in the impossible position of being forced to prove a negative. Finally she asked the judge to force Mr. Smith to testify first in the jury's absence, to see if anything he had to say deserved to be heard by the jury.

"You're suggesting an *audition?*" was Jaywalker's comment.

In the end, Shaughnessey's objections were overruled one by one. The Constitution has a pretty neat way of ensuring that.

JAYWALKER: What do you do for a living, Mr. Smith?

SMITH: I press clothes in a dry cleaner's, and I work for Mr. Jaywalker.

JAYWALKER: Have you ever been convicted of a crime?

SMITH: Oh, yeah, about fifteen of them. But none since I last got out of prison. So far it's been eight years, two months and seven days. And it's going to stay that way.

JAYWALKER: How long have you worked for me, Mr. Smith?

SMITH: Eight years, two months and seven days.

THE COURT: Listen carefully to the questions, Mr. Smith. He asked you a different one this time.

SMITH: I know, ma'am, but the answer is the same. The same day I got of prison, I goes to see Mr. Jaywalker. It was the first thing I did, before I even went home. He'd promised me when I went in that he'd have a job waiting for me if I came to see him, and he did as he said.

THE COURT: And did he have a job for you?

SMITH: He sure did. He made me his Official Unofficial Investigator. The unofficial part is on account of I've got a criminal record, so I can't get a license or carry a gun or get paid by the state.

THE COURT: And do you still work for him?

SMITH: From time to time I do, whenever he asks me. And as long as it don't conflicate with my other job.

THE COURT: I see. Thank you, Mr. Smith. Sorry for the interruption, Mr. Jaywalker.

Any other lawyer would have been beaming at the inadvertent endorsement of his largesse. Jaywalker, who was unlike any other lawyer, had no need of endorsements and didn't normally appreciate being interrupted during his examination of a witness. But even he had to suppress a grin at how nicely things had just worked out.

Pretty much as he'd planned.

JAYWALKER: And did there come a time, Mr. Smith, when I asked you to do something in connection with this case?

SMITH: Yes, there did.

JAYWALKER: When and what was that?

SMITH: About two weeks ago. You asked me to try to find a man named Clarence Hightower.

JAYWALKER: And did you try to find him?

SMITH: Yes.

JAYWALKER: And?

Smith described the places he'd gone and the things he'd done over a two-week period of searching for Hightower. Jaywalker had given him a crash course in the rules of evidence that morning, and Kenny was a pretty quick study. Understanding that whatever he'd heard on the street would be hearsay, he omitted the business about the weekly cash allowance Hightower was rumored to be getting. And having been warned that he couldn't speculate or offer his opinion about anything, Smith refrained from suggesting that the money was supposedly coming from an uncle who didn't exist. Still, Kenny was permitted to describe the one-and-only meeting he'd had with Hightower. That was neither hearsay nor opinion.

JAYWALKER: When did that occur?

SMITH: Two nights ago. Just after midnight Saturday. So I guess that was more like very early Sunday morning.

JAYWALKER: Where was that?

SMITH: I finally tracked him down in a bar on 125th Street called the Red Rose Tavern. I cornered him and told him I needed to talk to him for five minutes.

JAYWALKER: What did he say?

SMITH: First he said he wasn't Clarence Hightower. But I told him I knew who he was. Then he agreed to talk with me, but said he had to use the men's room. Although that's not exactly how he put it. He'd been drinking beers, he said, and a lot of them. And I guess all them beers ran right through—

THE COURT: Yes, I think we get the picture, Mr. Smith. What happened next?

SMITH: I said okay, but I waited, like, right outside the door for him. After about five minutes, when he hadn't come out, I went in. The men's room was completely empty, and the window was wide-open. Seems he'd ducked out before I could give him the suspeena.

SHAUGHNESSEY: Objection. Move to strike the last part.

SMITH: Suspayna.

THE COURT: Sustained. Stricken.

SMITH: Suspen—

THE COURT: It's not your pronunciation, Mr. Smith. It's that you're not allowed to give us your conclusion. You told us the men's room was empty and the window was open. That's all you know for a fact.

SMITH: Oh, no, ma'am. I checked the stalls. I know for a fact he had to have gone out that—

The rest of his answer was drowned out by Miki Shaughnessey's objections and Shirley Levine's gavel. But it hardly mattered. Just as Kenny Smith had managed to put two and two together, so could the jurors.

Not that Shaughnessey didn't do her best to undermine Smith's testimony on cross-examination. First she spent a full half hour going over the details of his prior criminal record. If the jurors ended up convinced that for many years Smith had been a career criminal, they also learned that his assertion that he'd been arrest-free for the past eight and a half years was true. And by candidly owning up to his past crimes without trying to minimize them, Kenny was able to offset much of the damage. Then Shaughnessey brought out that Smith had never had—or even *seen,* for that matter—a photograph of Hightower. Next, that Smith's imposing size could very easily have frightened Hightower—if indeed it had been Hightower—into fleeing out of a natural fear that he was about to be harmed.

SHAUGHNESSEY: Anyway, why didn't you give him the subpoena as soon as you saw him?

It was something Jaywalker himself had wondered about. But he hadn't wanted to risk offending Kenny, who, after all, had been doing him a favor.

SMITH: I didn't want to freak him out or nothing.

SHAUGHNESSEY: So instead you're telling us he disappeared before you could serve him.

SMITH: I'm not *telling* you—it's what happened. See, if
I was gonna lie about it, I'd say I served him and *then*
he ran away, wouldn't I?

He actually had a pretty good point there.

Kenny Smith hadn't been the best witness in the history of the world, but he hadn't been the worst, either.
Still, Jaywalker was acutely aware that even if the jurors
were to believe every word of Smith's testimony—that it
had taken him a full two weeks to find Clarence Hightower, and that when he finally had, the guy had pulled
a disappearing act—that by no means established that
Hightower had been working as an informer. That gap in
the testimony was still there, and as long as it remained,
Jaywalker was going to have a hard time arguing entrapment. As things stood, he was going to be forced to ask
the jurors to make a huge leap of faith with him, to conclude that despite the denials of law enforcement and the
absence of any real proof, the only way the case made
sense was if Stump had been working for the Man.

Because the fact was, Jaywalker was now down to his
final witness. And that witness, no matter how persuasive
he might turn out to be, wasn't going to be able to shed
any light on the issue. Then again, he was the witness the
jurors had been waiting to hear from for a week now, ever
since Jaywalker had promised them during jury selection
that they would. The name of the witness, of course, was
Alonzo Barnett, and the time had finally come for him to
rise from his seat at the defense table and make his way
to the witness stand.

But not quite yet.

The argument over whether Kenny Smith should be
permitted to testify in the first place, followed by his

actual direct and cross-examinations, had taken most of the morning. Rather than begin with a new and no doubt lengthy witness, only to have to stop fifteen minutes into testimony, Judge Levine broke for lunch.

"But please be back here promptly at two o'clock," she told the jurors, and waited until she heard a chorus of yesses. Then, turning to the tables where the lawyers sat, she added, "That means you, too."

"Yes, ma'am," said Alonzo Barnett. They were the first two words the jurors had heard from him, and they reacted with good-natured laughter. Under the rules, they really weren't supposed to know he was a guest of the city. But of course they did. Jurors always do.

May the rest of what he has to say go over half as well as his first two words, prayed Jaywalker the atheist.

14

Somebody showed up

"The defense calls Alonzo Barnett."

And with those five words, the man who for a week now had done pretty much nothing but sit quietly at a table rose and made his way slowly but purposefully to the witness box. Slowly, because he'd been warned by the court officers to refrain from making any sudden movements. Purposefully, because the fact was, he'd been waiting for this moment for nearly two years.

As Jaywalker watched Alonzo Barnett mount the single step that led to the witness chair before turning to face the court clerk, he had little doubt that Barnett would make a good witness, perhaps even a compelling one. By this time the two of them had spent something like fifty hours going over the facts, plumbing for the tiny details that would attest to Barnett's truthfulness, and searching for the visual images and precise wording that would stay with the jurors into their deliberations. Together they'd run through half a dozen mock direct examinations and twice as many crosses. If those numbers sound excessive, they are, and there are lawyers who would scoff at them as either absurdly inflated or totally unnecessary. But even back then, Jaywalker knew only one way to try a case.

And that way compelled him to overprepare as though his very life depended on the outcome. He might not have been able to win all of his cases, but on the increasingly rare occasion when he lost one, no one was ever going to accuse him of giving it less than a thousand percent.

Not that he wouldn't blame himself anyway.

Now, as he watched Alonzo Barnett raise his right hand as instructed and place his left upon a book that had no place in his particular religion, Jaywalker sensed the enormity of the task in front of both of them. Until this moment, the trial had pretty much followed the familiar script of all sale cases. A midlevel law enforcement official—in this instance Lieutenant Dino Pascarella—had set the table for the jurors, describing the receipt of an anonymous phone tip about a man dealing drugs. Surveillance of the man had proved of limited value. A veteran undercover officer had been brought in from out of state. That undercover officer, Agent Trevor St. James, had described his success in gaining the unwitting confidence of an associate of the suspect, a man known to him only as "Stump." Following an introduction to the suspect, Agent St. James had ordered heroin from the target three times, each time in dramatically escalating amounts. Twice the deals had been completed. On the third occasion the target had been arrested just prior to making delivery. On his person had been not only the drugs, but some of the prerecorded money St. James had given him earlier.

Three additional witnesses had been called by the prosecution. Two members of the backup team, Agent Angel Cruz and Investigator Lance Bucknell, had described their roles in the surveillance and arrest of the defendant. And a chemist, Olga Kasmirov, had certified that on each of the three occasions, the drugs sold or seized had contained heroin.

So it was all there, neatly laid out, wrapped up and tied with a bow. An *absolute lock,* in the jargon of prosecutors. A *dead-bang loser,* any defense lawyer would have called it. And were you to take those two polar opposites and try to reconcile them, you'd end up with a third phrase. A *guilty plea,* it was called, and it was how such differences were invariably settled.

Only not in this case.

In the matter of *The People of the State of New York versus Alonzo Barnett,* the rule had been broken, the script tossed aside. There'd been no guilty plea. Instead there'd been a trial, a trial that had finally come down to its last witness.

Now, as Jaywalker sat and listened as his client swore to tell the truth, the whole truth and nothing but the truth, he knew how powerless he was to change the story the prosecution witnesses had recounted. This wasn't one of those cases, after all, where there were two competing versions of the facts. Just about everything Pascarella and St. James and Cruz and Bucknell and Kasmirov had testified to was true. Alonzo Barnett had indeed sold heroin twice and been caught in the act of doing it a third time. Now he was about to confirm that, waiving his constitutional right to silence so that he could admit it under oath in open court. He was going to tell the jurors, in other words, that he was guilty, exactly as charged.

Why?

It was a question Jaywalker had been asking for several months now, first of Barnett and eventually of himself. A question that had occurred to him even before the two of them had met, way back when Lorraine Wilson had called him with the assignment, and he'd read the charges and examined the court file. A question that had nagged at him when he'd realized early on that only two things were likely to result from a trial. First, Barnett would end up serving substantially more time than if he had taken a plea. Second, Jaywalker would lose. Now, a week into the trial, those two things seemed as inevitable as they ever had.

Yet a few things *had* changed.

For starters, the way the investigation had been conducted had raised more questions for Jaywalker than it answered. Had there really been an anonymous phone call, or was that a fabrication? Had the case truly been made without the use of a confidential informer? Why had Stump, now known to be Clarence Hightower, been treated with such unusual deference? And why hadn't more of an effort been made to identify, arrest and prosecute Barnett's source of supply?

But it wasn't just the answers to these questions that eluded and intrigued Jaywalker. It was the way each question interlocked with the next one. Was it merely coincidental that they had all arisen in the same case? Or was there a pattern to them, a pattern that Jaywalker was for some reason unable to discern? Was he onto something that lay just out of sight? Or was his searching for it just the latest example of his penchant for tilting at windmills? A comment came back to him, something uttered by a client of his long ago, as he'd sat on a secure psychiatric ward in Bellevue Hospital. The guy's name had been Simberg, William Simberg, and he'd been locked up— again—this time for accusing the police commissioner of watching his every move or the mayor of monitoring his thought waves. Something along those lines.

"Just because I happen to be a diagnosed paranoid

schizophrenic," Simberg had whispered to Jaywalker, "doesn't mean I'm not being followed."

So maybe Jaywalker was just being his usual obsessive self, asking questions for which there were no answers, searching for patterns where there were none to be found. But then again...

Something else had changed, too.

Over the weeks since Jaywalker had accepted the assignment and agreed to represent a defendant who'd already been through several other lawyers, he'd gotten to know the man behind the name. The charges and the court papers and the rap sheet had promised a hard case, a career criminal who'd spent half his life in prison without ever learning a thing from it. And when Alonzo Barnett had predictably insisted on a trial in spite of his admitted and demonstrable guilt, Jaywalker had resigned himself to a menu of extremely limited choices. Talk him out of it or go down with him.

But the Alonzo Barnett who'd gradually emerged from the file had surprised him. Here was a man who'd come from absolutely nothing, been through terrible adversity, and finally managed to turn things around completely. And then, just when he'd been firmly on the road to redemption, a tragic flaw had tripped him up, a misguided sense that he still owed a debt he'd incurred long ago. Yet even when things had imploded and he'd landed back in jail, he hadn't rued repaying that debt, railed against the fates or whined over his predicament. He'd simply asked for a chance to tell his story, to speak and to be heard.

And Jaywalker?

Jaywalker had been drawn to this defendant as he'd been drawn to few others in his career. There was a nobility to Alonzo Barnett, a calm, quiet grace that Jaywalker had never quite encountered before in a client, whether through the bars of a jailhouse or across the desk in his office. In spite of Barnett's long and serious criminal record, in spite of the horribly self-destructive life choices he'd made, in spite of his ultimate willingness to trade heroin for money, Jaywalker had come to feel a unique connection to this particular man. By the time he rose from his seat and stepped to the podium to ask his first question on direct examination, he'd gotten to know and like Alonzo Barnett in a way he would have had great difficulty describing to a stranger. Hell, he'd had great difficulty describing it to his *wife,* who'd accused him of getting soft and mushy in his old age, and over an admitted heroin dealer, of all people.

So the question people would be forever asking Jaywalker would turn out to be the wrong one after all. It shouldn't be "How can you possibly represent someone you know is guilty?" The answer to that one was easy. It was because it was his job, so he did it the same way he would have done any other job, the best way he knew how. The far more interesting question, at least in this particular case, had become "How do you go about representing a defendant who admits his guilt, but whose conviction would bring about an infinitely greater injustice than his acquittal would?"

And the only answer Jaywalker had to that question was the same as he had to the first one. He would do his damnedest. He would spend the next day and a half trying to get twelve strangers to know Alonzo Barnett as well as he himself had gotten to know him. He would show them the man behind the criminal record, the man who'd somehow broken free of the revolving door of justice and finally made something of his life, only to be tripped up because, in a moment of blindness, he'd decided that no matter what the possible cost, honoring a debt was the right thing to do.

And while Jaywalker was busy trying to show all those things and more through the strange choreography of questions coupled with answers, maybe—just maybe— some clue would shake loose from the story, some pattern would emerge from the shadows, and he'd figure out how to win what until this moment looked like an absolutely unwinnable case.

JAYWALKER: How old are you, Mr. Barnett?

BARNETT: I'm fifty-one.

JAYWALKER: Where were you born?

BARNETT: I was born on a farm outside Forked Creek, Alabama.

JAYWALKER: How far did you go in school?

BARNETT: Not very far. About the middle of fourth grade, I guess. I was nine when they put me to work tending hogs.

It had always been Jaywalker's belief that life stories count almost as much as facts do. Sure, he'd won acquittals for defendants whose backgrounds and demeanor combined to make them less than likable, but those acquittals had come hard, after long uphill battles. In Alonzo Barnett, he had a lot of raw material to work with. Here was a man who was good to look at, for starters. Even as he'd sat silently at the defense table, he'd projected an inner calmness, a quiet dignity. Once he'd begun speaking in a resonant baritone that hinted ever so slightly at a distant West Indian heritage, those qualities had been not only confirmed but reinforced. Add to all that a backstory about an impoverished, exploited child-hood on a Southern farm and you had the whole package: a defendant fully capable of winning the jurors' hearts.

Which was good, Jaywalker knew, but could get you only so far. Empathy was a great place to start, but it wasn't enough to get you across the finish line. On the way, there were the facts to trip you up. Including the nastiest of them all, that Alonzo Barnett had indeed sold heroin to an undercover agent not once, not twice, but three times. So winning the jurors' hearts wasn't going to be good enough. If Jaywalker wanted to win their votes, as well, he was first going to have to draw them a road map showing them how to get there. And here he was, three questions into direct examination, and he still had no idea how to do that.

Then again, he couldn't let a little thing like that stop him from trying, could he?

JAYWALKER: Had you learned how to read and write by the time you left Alabama?

BARNETT: No, I hadn't.

JAYWALKER: Did you ever?

BARNETT: Yes, in my forties. In prison.

JAYWALKER: How old were you when you came to New York?

BARNETT: I was fourteen.

JAYWALKER: Who did you come with?

BARNETT: Myself. I came alone.

JAYWALKER: Who took care of you?

BARNETT: I took care of myself.

JAYWALKER: Where did you live?

BARNETT: Days, I lived on the street. Nights, I slept in a shooting gallery.

JAYWALKER: What's a shooting gallery?

BARNETT: It's where drug addicts congregate to shoot up heroin or smoke crack, and then sleep it off.

JAYWALKER: How did you support yourself?

BARNETT: Any way I could. When you're fourteen, they don't let you work legally, on the books. So you hustle, you do anything you can for a meal or a buck. Some kids, they steal or sell their bodies. Me, I swept the place up, cleaned the toilets, washed up the vomit, ran errands, whatever I could.

JAYWALKER: And did any of those errands you ran get you into trouble?

BARNETT: Yes, they did.

Jaywalker ran him through his rap sheet, beginning with his first arrest ten days after his fifteenth birthday and culminating in the charges he was on trial for. The jurors had known about Barnett's record ever since jury selection, when Jaywalker had made a point of warning them about it. Still, he went into greater detail now, for a couple of reasons. The first was preemptive. He knew if he didn't do it, Miki Shaughnessey would. The second was a little more counterintuitive. By having Barnett go into the particulars of his criminal past, Jaywalker hoped to demonstrate his client's honesty through his willingness to let them know the bad stuff. A guy who's going to level with you about having repeatedly broken the law is a guy you're going to be likely to trust to tell you the truth—about everything. Finally, Barnett's record, as long as it was, was the record of a drug seller. Almost all his arrests and convictions were for sale or possession. There were a few property crimes mixed in, but they were minor things. Nothing a Manhattan juror couldn't take in stride.

Except, that was, for the two charges that jumped off the page, just as they had on Barnett's arrival at Green Haven Prison a dozen years earlier. "Forcible Rape of a 15-year-old Female" and "Sale of a Controlled Substance on School Grounds," they'd read. Jaywalker needed to defuse them by having Barnett explain the rather innocuous facts that lay behind the damning labels. At the same time, he needed the jurors to understand how those labels had instantly made Barnett a target, a man literally marked for death.

JAYWALKER: Who was the fifteen-year-old female?

BARNETT: Her name was Jasmine Meadows, and she was the mother of my son. She later became my wife, and we had two more children together, two daughters.

JAYWALKER: Are you still married?

BARNETT: No, I'm not. My wife died four years ago. She was killed by a hit-and-run driver while she was crossing Edgecombe Avenue.

JAYWALKER: What became of your son?

BARNETT: My son was killed in Vietnam.

JAYWALKER: And your daughters?

BARNETT: My daughters are eleven and nine. They're in foster care right now. I see them on regular visits to my home. At least, I did until my arrest. And it's my hope to be reunited with them, if things work out.

If things work out.
They'd settled on that phrase together, Barnett and Jaywalker had. They'd rejected "if I'm lucky," "God willing," "if the jury sees fit," "if it's written," "if it's meant to be," "if it's Allah's will" and a dozen others.
They'd spent an hour deciding.
Add up enough of those hours and you begin to understand what it's like to be a Jaywalker. But you're also going to understand what it takes to win.

JAYWALKER: And the school grounds case. Were you in fact selling drugs on school grounds?

BARNETT: Yes, according to the law. But I honestly had no idea at the time. And I certainly wasn't standing in a school yard or selling drugs to children, or anything like that. It turned out that the law on the books at that time said school grounds were anything within half a mile of any school.

JAYWALKER: Would you be surprised to learn that under that definition, you're on school grounds right now?

Actually, Jaywalker had no idea if that was true or not. But he wasn't about to let that stop him from asking the question.

SHAUGHNESSEY: Objection.

THE COURT: Overruled. You may answer.

BARNETT: No, it wouldn't surprise me at all.

JAYWALKER: Yet those two charges remained on your rap sheet, which was in your file when you arrived at Green Haven. Is that correct?

BARNETT: That's correct.

JAYWALKER: Would you explain to the jurors, as best as you can, the problem that that created for you?

It was an open-ended question, the kind that Jaywalker might have hesitated to ask an ordinary witness. But Alonzo Barnett was no ordinary witness. And if there was any chance whatsoever of winning an acquittal in this case, Barnett was going to have to do his share of the heavy lifting. No "Yes, sir" or "No, sir" answers were going to do the trick. He was going to have to sell himself to the twelve men and women sitting in the jury box, and he was going to have to do it in his own words. Or at least in words that he and Jaywalker had arrived at together.

BARNETT: From the day I walked into Green Haven, I was a marked man. You have to understand this about prison—there are no secrets. Inmates work in the library, the record room, the administration room, the infirmary. Everywhere but at the front gate. So everything in your jacket—the file that follows you to prison—becomes common knowledge within hours of your arrival. I want to know your wife's home address or the name of the school your kid attends, I can get it. It may cost me a pack of smokes, but I can get it. My jacket had the rape case and the school-yard thing. They might just as well have painted a target on my back. I wasn't there three days before I had a contract on me.

JAYWALKER: A contract?

BARNETT: A price tag. To be collected by anyone lucky enough to kill me.

JAYWALKER: What did you do?

BARNETT: Nothing. There was nothing I could do but wait for it to happen, and hope that when it did it would be quick and relatively painless. And then somebody intervened. The inmate who ran the prison barbershop saw what was going on. And he felt sorry for me, I guess. He offered me a job in the barbershop, and by doing that he vouched for me. In other words, he made it clear that I was down with him and I was okay, and that no one was to mess with me.

The other thing I did was to join a group. Prison is all about which group you're down with. For the Hispanics there were the Bloods and the Crips and the Latin Kings. For the whites there were the Aryan Brotherhood guys. And for black people like me there were the Muslims. So I joined up. I got me a Koran and I studied Islam. I embraced Allah and became a Muslim.

JAYWALKER: Are you a Muslim to this day?

Part of being a Jaywalker is reminiscent of Bill Murray's fate in the movie *Groundhog Day*. You're doomed to try cases over and over in your head years after they've ended. *Decades* after they've ended. Not just the ones you've lost, hoping that by changing a word here or a phrase there you might somehow be able to make them turn out differently in the replay.

Jaywalker retries even the cases he *won*.

Yet when he looks back today to the trial of Alonzo Barnett, he shudders. Back then, being a Muslim was no big deal. Sure, you had Malcolm X, never a favorite among the synagogue crowd. You had Cassius Clay changing his name to Mohammed Ali and refusing to fight for his country, and Lew Alcindor becoming Kareem Abdul-Jabbar. And you had the Ten Percenters, the extremist fringe who'd run out of patience with Dr. King and his preaching about the virtues of nonviolence. But at least you didn't have to contend with September 11 and its repercussions.

Try playing a game of word association these days with the average American. Toss out the word *Muslim* and see what you hear in return. Nine out of ten responders aren't even going to blink before answering *Terrorist*. So if Jaywalker had some concerns about how the whole

Islam business was going to sit with the jurors, at least they were minor ones. At least Muslims weren't flying airplanes into buildings yet. At least Alonzo Barnett could say he was one of them without fear of being immediately demonized.

BARNETT: Yes, I still embrace Islam and consider myself a Muslim. I don't call myself by my Muslim name, and I don't go to a mosque as often as I might. But when I pray, I pray to Allah, and I thank Him for my salvation. And with His help I was able to give up drinking alcohol and smoking cigarettes and cursing. And after shooting heroin into my veins for over thirty years, I was able to give that up, too. So the way I look at it, Islam and me may have started out with a shotgun wedding, but we turned things into a marriage that lasted. And as I sit here today, it's no exaggeration to say I wouldn't be alive without my faith, any more than I would be if it hadn't been for that man who gave me the job in the barbershop.

JAYWALKER: And that man, the one who gave you the job in the barbershop. Do you happen to recall his name, by any chance?

BARNETT: Yes, I do. His name was Clarence Hightower.

If you watch enough trials, you learn that every once in a while there's a moment when things start to come together for the jury. Those who make it their business to follow Jaywalker's trials—and even back in 1986, there was a small but growing number of colleagues, opponents, reporters and retirees who did—had even coined a term for the phenomenon. Right now, with that simple question and the even simpler answer to it, anyone who happened to be lucky enough to be sitting in Part 91 of Manhattan Supreme Court knew they had just been treated to a Jaywalker Moment.

Shirley Levine seemed to know it, too. She declared a midafternoon recess and excused the jury for fifteen minutes.

Jaywalker couldn't have scripted things better if he'd tried. He loved sending the jurors out of the room on a good note, whether it was for the weekend, the evening, the lunch hour or even just a coffee break. Before each recess, New York law requires the judge to admonish the jurors to refrain from visiting the crime scene, from forming opinions until all the evidence is in and from discussing the case with each other. And although Levine dutifully did all that now for what must have been the twentieth time, Jaywalker knew that jurors were only human, after all. Of course they discussed the case— every chance they got. Maybe not as a group, but certainly in twos and threes. And right now, as they filed out of the courtroom, what they were going to discuss, in one way or another, was Clarence Hightower and the strange coincidence that he had once saved Alonzo Barnett's life.

All because Shirley Levine had decided to call a recess at a particular moment. Well, that and the fact that Jaywalker had paced his direct examination so that it would be just about time for her to do so, and had then paused for just a moment, as though he were about to go on to a different subject.

Still, he could have hugged her.

"So," he asked Alonzo Barnett once the trial had reconvened, "who got out of Green Haven first, you or Clarence Hightower?"

"I did," said Barnett. "I was doing a four-and-a-half-to-nine for a sale I'd pleaded guilty to. I got out in 1981. Mr. Hightower was still there when I left, doing ten to twenty for aggravated assault. He still had another three years to go."

Jaywalker spent a few minutes getting Barnett to recite the things he'd managed to accomplish in those three years. An okay job, followed by a better one. An apartment of his own. No heroin, no alcohol, no drugs of any sort. No criminal activity whatsoever. Not that he couldn't see that stuff going on everywhere in the neighborhood. It was the early 1980s, after all, and it was Harlem. Crack was in every doorway, crime on every street corner.

Just not for Alonzo Barnett.

JAYWALKER: Besides working and taking care of your apartment, what else did you do with your time?

BARNETT: I reported to my parole officer. I never missed a single appointment, not one. I took fifteen regular urine tests and eight unannounced ones to check on whether there were drugs in my system. I passed all twenty-three of them. I volunteered at a big brother program. I asked to be paired up with the worst of the worst of the kids they had. Kids with no parents, kids who couldn't read or write, kids in real danger. I like to think I helped one or two of them a little bit. And, most important—

And right there, Barnett's voice cracked, and he had to wait just a second before repeating the words *most important* and continuing. Had you been sitting in the back row of the courtroom, you might have missed it. It was over and done that quickly.

The jurors weren't sitting in the back row.

As much as Jaywalker would have liked to take credit for the moment, he couldn't. Sometimes you planned little things like that, choreographed them down to the tiniest detail. But other times, stuff just happened. And when it did, there was no mistaking how real it was. This was one of those times.

BARNETT: —I went to Family Court and won permission to have visits with my daughters.

JAYWALKER: How did that go?

BARNETT: It was hard at first, very hard. My daughters were angry at me, and rightfully so. I'd gone to prison. I'd abandoned them. At first the visits had to be supervised and conducted at BCW, the Bureau of Child Welfare. But after a while, once they were going smoothly and we'd dealt with the anger, the visits became unsupervised and freer. I was allowed to bring my daughters to my apartment, though not overnight. I was working on that, too, when…when…

This time his voice didn't crack; it just tailed off into silence. Jaywalker waited a few seconds before asking if something had happened.

"Yes," said Barnett.

"What happened?" Jaywalker asked.

"Somebody showed up."

Again Jaywalker paused a beat before asking his next question. This was the quiet part of his direct examination, the part conducted in barely a whisper. This was the sad part.

"Who showed up?" he asked.

But he needn't have. Even before Alonzo Barnett had a chance to answer, the jurors answered for him. They answered in their nods and their grimaces, some of them going so far as to mouth the name silently to themselves, or not so silently to those on either side of them.

"Clarence Hightower."

For the next forty minutes Jaywalker engaged Barnett in a re-creation of the tug-of-war that had taken place between the two men nearly two years ago. They broke it down into seven separate visits in which Hightower played Iago to Barnett's Othello. Six times Hightower begged Barnett to cut him into his former heroin connection, pleading in turn sickness, poverty, profit, old times' sake and whatever else he could think of. Six times Barnett refused him. Finally, on the seventh visit, Hightower pulled out his trump card and played it.

"Listen up," he said. "You owe me. I saved your life. Now it's your turn to save mine."

JAYWALKER: What happened when he said that?

BARNETT: For a long time I didn't say anything. I just thought about what he'd said, as hard as I could. And then, when I was done thinking, I nodded and I said okay.

JAYWALKER: Why did you do that?

BARNETT: Because he was right. He *had* saved my life. I couldn't argue with that. I *did* owe him. At least that's the way I figured it.

JAYWALKER: Do you still figure it that way?

BARNETT: Yes and no. I wish I hadn't succumbed to the pressure he put on me. But I'm an adult, and nobody put a gun to my head. My decision ended up costing me everything I'd accomplished. It cost me my freedom, my job, my home, my self-respect. Most of all, it cost me my daughters. So on the one hand, it's obvious that I figured very wrong.

JAYWALKER: And on the other hand?

BARNETT: I don't know. Prison is a tough place, ten times tougher than your worst imagination of it. I was a dead man…I really was. When no one else would reach out and help me, one man did. He saved my life. So did I owe him a debt? Yes. Did that mean I had to repay it when he called on me to? I'm not sure. I held out as long as I could, and then I said yes.

JAYWALKER: And if you had to do it all over again, would you still say yes?

BARNETT: I honestly can't say. A debt is a debt, after all. So I might. I hope not, but I might.

By asking his questions softly, almost gently, Jaywalker had elicited responses from his client that were just as soft, just as gentle. *Thoughtful,* he hoped, thoughtful and honest. Anyone can say, "No way. I've learned my lesson. I'd never do that again." It takes some real soul-searching to admit that, in spite of the horrendous price you've paid for doing something, you're not sure how you'd react if asked to do it all over again.

For better or for worse, the quiet portion of Alonzo Barnett's testimony was over. Jaywalker stepped back a few paces and, in a matter-of-fact tone, asked his client if after saying yes, he'd agreed to meet Hightower's man and bring him to someone he knew for the purpose of buying heroin. Yes, said Barnett, he'd done that. Only the guy had refused to meet either Hightower or his man. He said he'd deal only through Barnett, who he'd known for years. So three times Barnett had taken money from the man he now knew to be Agent Trevor St. James. Three times he'd exchanged it for heroin, each time in increasing amounts. And three times it had been his intention to deliver the heroin to St. James. Twice he'd succeeded; on the third occasion he'd been arrested before he'd made it back to the agent's car.

Just like they'd said.

JAYWALKER: Did you know it was heroin each time?

BARNETT: Yes, I did.

JAYWALKER: Did you know it was against the law to possess heroin?

BARNETT: Yes, I did.

JAYWALKER: Did you know it was against the law to sell heroin?

BARNETT: Yes, I did.

JAYWALKER: But you did those things nonetheless?

BARNETT: Yes, I did. I'm ashamed to say so. But yes, I did.

Jaywalker looked up at the clock, saw it was nearly five. He had a few minor questions left on his notepad, but Alonzo Barnett's last answer had been a good one, and it seemed an okay place to leave things. Miki Shaughnessey would have the whole night to work on her cross-examination, of course, but there was nothing Jaywalker could do about that.

"Thank you," he said, and sat down.

15

One-Eyed Jack

The typical defense lawyer will allow himself the luxury of relaxing just a bit following a lengthy direct examination of his final witness. Next up is the prosecutor, after all, who conducts cross-examination while the defense lawyer gets to sit and relax. But relaxing simply wasn't part of Jaywalker's vocabulary when he was on trial.

On trial.

A friend, a banking lawyer, had once accused Jaywalker of misusing the phrase. "It's the *defendant* who's on trial," she'd said. "Not *you*."

She'd obviously never tried a case. Certainly not a criminal case.

So Jaywalker didn't even think about taking the evening off. Time off was something he treated himself to *after* a trial, not during it, and even then, only if he'd won. Until the moment he heard the verdict delivered, there was simply too much to do. And if he lost, there would be still more. It was one of the reasons he fought so hard to win, so it would be over. He could still feel the sting of learning he'd flunked the bar exam the first time he'd taken it. Not because he felt stupid or because his pride was hurt. Jaywalker and pride had barely been on speaking terms for as long as he could remember. No, it was the realization that he'd have to go through it all over again, that it wasn't *over*.

Which was why he spent what was left of Monday, as well as the first hour or two of Tuesday, preparing his redirect examination of Alonzo Barnett. Even though he hadn't yet heard a word of Miki Shaughnessey's cross, Jaywalker knew what she'd ask. Despite the fact that Jaywalker had preemptively gone into Barnett's criminal record three times now—during jury selection, in his opening statement and now on direct examination—no young, inexperienced prosecutor was going to be able to avoid the temptation of covering the same ground on cross. After that, she'd try to challenge Barnett's notion that owing a debt to another man constituted a moral justification to sell heroin, or a legal defense to having done so. She'd pin him down on the amounts involved, which had gradually grown from small to significant to substantial. She'd bring out that as a former addict himself, Barnett had to have been aware of the consequences of his actions. And she'd use that same "former addict" label to accuse him of being that worst of all combinations: a seller without the excuse of being a user needing to support his own habit. She'd pointedly ask him about the money he'd made or hoped to make from the sales. She'd want to know why he hadn't considered his debt to Hightower paid off after the first sale, or at least the second. She'd suggest through her questions that, had Barnett not been arrested when he was, there might have been a fourth sale, then a fifth, and that the sales might still be going on to this day. Then, mostly because Jaywalker hadn't—in fact *especially* because Jaywalker hadn't—she would go into the details of how the three transactions had gone down, in order to show how accurate and honest her own witnesses had been in describing them. Finally, she'd try to put Barnett on the hot seat by asking him about his source, the person he'd gotten the drugs from on each occasion. It was a question no dealer ever wanted to answer, whether out of fear, loyalty or a combination of both. And it was a subject Jaywalker had purposefully avoided going into on direct.

In other words, by asking certain questions on direct and refraining from asking certain others, Jaywalker was able to not only predict what his adversary would ask on cross but to consciously and purposefully *dictate* her questions. So even as he was able to prepare his wit-ness—in this case his client—to answer her questions, he could also prepare himself for his own next round of questions on his redirect examination.

But doing that was by no means all that Jaywalker did that Monday night into Tuesday morning. He consid-ered it a distinct possibility that once they'd finished with Barnett's testimony and the defense had rested, Shaugh-nessey would begin calling rebuttal witnesses. That, too, was something that inexperienced prosecutors tended to do. She'd recall agents and detectives—or call new ones—in an attempt to assure the jurors that Hightower hadn't been working as an informer, and that the dangers involved in following Barnett too closely had been real ones. So Jaywalker prepared for those rebuttal witnesses, too, even though at this point they existed only in his imagination.

And when he'd finished working on his redirect ex-amination of Barnett and his cross-examination of the imaginary rebuttal witnesses, he worked on his summa-tion. Though the truth is, he'd begun working on it the day he'd met Alonzo Barnett and had been working on it ever since.

It certainly wasn't easy, being Jaywalker. But it was the price he paid for being an obsessive-compulsive whose obsession forced him to do everything he possibly could in each case he tried, and whose compulsion drove him to avoid losing at any cost.

He finally climbed into bed around two in the morning, kissing his wife's neck gently, so as not to wake her. Then he rolled over in the dark and blindly ran his hand along the floor by his side of the bed, until he felt the pen and notepad that were there, as they always were.

Just in case.

Miki Shaughnessey didn't disappoint Jaywalker. She cross-examined on each of the areas he'd expected her to, though not in the order he would have bet on. Okay, so maybe he wasn't quite Nostradamus yet. But by anticipating what she'd do, Jaywalker had been able to take a smart defendant with a nice manner of speaking and prepare him for just about every question that would come his way. Now, as he sat and listened to things play out, Jaywalker wondered if the combination of his preparation and his client's receptiveness would be enough to offset what he was up against: the fact that no matter how well Barnett came off as a witness, he was going to be forced to admit that he'd knowingly and repeatedly sold large amounts of heroin for profit when he, of all people, should have known better.

It didn't take too long to find out.

SHAUGHNESSEY: If I understand what you said yesterday, Mr. Barnett, you sold heroin to Agent St. James only because you felt you owed some kind of a debt to Clarence Hightower. Is that correct?

BARNETT: Yes, except that I wouldn't call it "some kind
of a debt." It was a very specific debt. The man saved
my life.

SHAUGHNESSEY: And you sold heroin to repay him.

BARNETT: That's what it came to. I'd hoped to get off
the hook by simply introducing Mr. Hightower to
someone he could buy from. But it didn't work out that
way. So yes, it ended up with me getting the heroin for
his friend, who turned out to be a federal agent.

SHAUGHNESSEY: Did you make any money in the process of repaying this debt?

BARNETT: Yes, I did.

SHAUGHNESSEY: How much?

BARNETT: I'd have to break it down for you.

SHAUGHNESSEY: Please do.

BARNETT: The first time I was given one hundred dollars and spent eighty of it.

SHAUGHNESSEY: So you made twenty dollars?

BARNETT: No, I gave the twenty dollars to Mr. Hightower.

SHAUGHNESSEY: All of it?

BARNETT: All of it. I wanted no part of it.

SHAUGHNESSEY: And the second time?

BARNETT: The second time I was given fifteen hundred dollars and spent twelve hundred. Of the three hundred left over, I gave Mr. Hightower two hundred, and kept one hundred.

SHAUGHNESSEY: Suddenly you *did* want part of it?

BARNETT: I'm human. I was behind in my rent, and I figured I'd earned it. It was wrong of me to keep it, but I did. I'm not going to lie about it.

SHAUGHNESSEY: And the third time?

BARNETT: The third time I was given five thousand dollars and spent four thousand five hundred.

SHAUGHNESSEY: So you would have made five hundred on that occasion alone, had you not been arrested. Correct?

BARNETT: No, that's not correct.

SHAUGHNESSEY: No?

BARNETT: No. It wasn't just a coincidence that Mr. Hightower showed up right after I was arrested. He was there to hit me up for some of the five hundred dollars.

SHAUGHNESSEY: Was your rent paid up by that time?

BARNETT: Yes, it was.

SHAUGHNESSEY: So you would have given him the whole five hundred. Right?

BARNETT: No, ma'am. I'd be lying to you if I said that. I was going to keep one hundred of it again, maybe even two hundred. I hadn't decided which. I was going to keep it to buy something nice for my daughters. They were in foster care at the time, and were on a pretty tight budget. No new clothes, no new books or school supplies. Nothing but bare essentials. So the way I figured it, it was better spent on them than going into Mr. Hightower's veins.

Bravo, thought Jaywalker. He and Barnett had worked hard trying to come up with zingers like that, hoping there'd be opportunities to use them. Score one for the bad guys.

SHAUGHNESSEY: You knew Mr. Hightower was using?

BARNETT: He told me he was. It was one of the things he told me, trying to convince me to help him.

SHAUGHNESSEY: So you helped him get money to feed his drug habit. You *enabled* him.

BARNETT: Actually, I was still refusing to help him at that point. It was only when he reminded me about the debt that I agreed to help him.

SHAUGHNESSEY: I see. You yourself weren't using drugs at that point, were you?

Here it comes, thought Jaywalker. *You're a seller, not a user.*

BARNETT: No, ma'am, I wasn't.

SHAUGHNESSEY: You had no habit of your own to support, did you?

BARNETT: No, ma'am.

SHAUGHNESSEY: Yet you thought it was okay to sell heroin so others could use it?

BARNETT: I never thought it was okay, not even back when I used to sell to support my own habit. I always knew it was wrong.

SHAUGHNESSEY: And being a member of the Muslim religion, you knew it was wrong to use alcohol or illegal drugs. Did it ever occur to you that it might also be wrong to *sell* illegal drugs?

Good question, thought Jaywalker, and one he hadn't seen coming. He bit down on the inside of his mouth, hoping that Barnett wouldn't try to split hairs and insist that while using was prohibited by the Koran, selling wasn't covered.

BARNETT: Please forgive me, ma'am, but the religion is called Islam. One who practices it is a Muslim. And yes, it was wrong of me, as a practicing Muslim, to do what I did, and I knew that. I am by no means perfect, and I have never claimed to be. I've made more than my share of mistakes in my life, and this was certainly one of them. For a lot of reasons, not just religious.

Not bad for an ad lib.

Looking to regroup, Shaughnessey sought a safe place and apparently figured a good bet could be found in Alonzo Barnett's criminal record. But she hadn't counted on the weeks of drilling Jaywalker and his client had put in on just that subject. For the next half hour, she tried to catch Barnett denying his guilt of some twenty-year-old arrest or hedging about some conviction from a decade ago. But she got nowhere. Alonzo Barnett was that rare defendant who truly understood, actually *got* it, that his record was his record, and as bad as it was, he could only make it worse by attempting to minimize it.

He was, in other words, a Jaywalker defendant.

Finally Shaughnessey turned her attention to the one area Jaywalker expected his client to have real difficulty with. She asked him who'd sold him the drugs.

Not that Jaywalker hadn't anticipated the question; he had. Still, asking a man to name and identify his drug connection is pretty much the same as asking him to become a snitch. And the problem is only heightened when the man being asked has done time and spent years living under a code that reduces snitches to the lowest of the low. In prison you have your general population, comprised of inmates who are free to mingle with each other. *Free to mingle* is something of a misnomer in this case, of course, and is generally limited to mealtimes and yard time, with an extra hour thrown in now and then.

Then you have younger inmates, those below twenty-one or maybe nineteen, who are almost always separately housed for a variety of reasons, including preventing them from expanding their knowledge as apprentices of hardened criminals. After them come homosexuals—prison administrators will no doubt get around to adopting the word *gay* eventually, but seem in no particular rush to do so—psychiatric cases, the very old, the very weak, sex offenders, and anyone else who might be considered a likely target of violence. A corrupt cop or public official, say, or a transgendered individual. And finally, way down at the bottom of the barrel where the scum settles, the snitches.

Alonzo Barnett had no interest in being labeled a snitch, certainly not while he was in jail, and not now, when the overwhelming odds were that he'd soon be shipped back to prison. He'd told Jaywalker that, and Jaywalker hadn't needed to ask him why. His suggestion to Barnett had been to make up a name and an apartment number on the twelfth floor of 345 West 127th Street, where Investigator Lance Bucknell claimed he'd gone during the third transaction. After all, according to Barnett, Bucknell had been lying; the apartment Barnett had actually gone to was on the eighth floor. In either event, almost two years had passed, and even were Barnett to now pinpoint a particular apartment, no judge in his right mind was going to sign a search warrant on information that stale. Which narrowed it down to the handful of judges who would.

Barnett had initially balked at the suggestion. He didn't like the idea of supplying a name and identifying an apartment, even if the name was fictitious and the apartment wasn't the one he'd gone to. But over the weeks they'd talked about it, he'd been forced to agree that if asked, he had to come up with something; he couldn't refuse to answer the question. There was the doctor-patient privilege, the priest-penitent privilege, the husband-wife privilege, and lately the president-advisor privilege. But no one had gone so far as to argue the existence of a dealer-supplier privilege. Not even Jaywalker.

But even as Alonzo Barnett had acknowledged that he'd have to answer the question if it were put to him, he never had told Jaywalker what his answer might be. Eventually Jaywalker had stopped pressing him, figuring that if and when the time came, Barnett would deal with it as best as he could. Though to Jaywalker's way of thinking, it had always been a matter of *when,* rather than *if.*

And now they were there.

SHAUGHNESSEY: Did you indeed go to 345 West 127th Street on each of the three occasions?

BARNETT: Yes, I did.

SHAUGHNESSEY: Exactly as Investigator Bucknell testified?

BARNETT: Yes, ma'am.

SHAUGHNESSEY: And did you go to that building to obtain heroin from your connection?

BARNETT: I went there to obtain heroin. I have a bit of problem with your use of the term *connection.* I went to the person who I'd agreed to introduce Mr. Hightower and his friend to. When he refused to meet with either of them, I agreed to take the money and get the drugs for them. But if you want to call him my connection, I'm willing to use your term.

SHAUGHNESSEY: Thank you. And did you in fact go to the twelfth floor, as Investigator Bucknell testified you did?

BARNETT: No, ma'am, I did not.

SHAUGHNESSEY: You did hear Bucknell say that?

BARNETT: Yes, I did. Absolutely.

SHAUGHNESSEY: Are you telling us he lied when he said that?

BARNETT: I honestly don't know why he said that. He may have been lying. He may have been mistaken. He may have made it up to cover for the fact that he wasn't able to see where I went. All I can tell you is the truth. And the truth is, I didn't go to the twelfth floor.

SHAUGHNESSEY: Ever?

BARNETT: Ever.

SHAUGHNESSEY: So when Investigator Bucknell testified that he rode in the elevator with you and saw you press the button for the twelfth floor, that never happened?

BARNETT: That's right. That never happened. If that man had gotten onto the elevator with me, I would have immediately stepped off and walked out of the building. He has *cop* written all over him.

SHAUGHNESSEY: So where *did* you go?

BARNETT: To the eighth floor.

SHAUGHNESSEY: What apartment?

BARNETT: Eight-oh-five.

SHAUGHNESSEY: Whose apartment was that?

BARNETT: A man they use to call "One-Eyed Jack." Got the nickname because he'd lost an eye in a shoot-out. I never did know his real name. But not too long after my arrest, the word got around that he was a snitch, an informer for the police. So he left town in a hurry.

SHAUGHNESSEY: And just how do you happen to know all that?

BARNETT: I've been on Rikers Island going on two years now. Guys don't have much to do out there except talk about other guys. And One-Eyed Jack was one of the guys they talked about.

SHAUGHNESSEY: And you expect me to believe that?

BARNETT: Most respectfully, ma'am, I don't care too much what you believe. What I care is what these folks sitting over here believe. *[Points to jury]* And I suspect they can recognize the truth when they hear it.

To her credit, Miki Shaughnessey plunged on without taking time out to wipe the egg off her face. She got Barnett to admit that with the exception of the twelfth-floor/eighth-floor business, just about everything else her witnesses had testified to was true.

"So why should they lie about that?" she asked him.

"I have no idea," said Barnett. "Maybe you should ask them."

His response marked the only time in a lengthy cross-examination when he verged on testiness. But with that single exception, Alonzo Barnett had been that rarest of witnesses who somehow managed to exceed even Jaywalker's expectations. Without once raising his voice or losing his composure, he'd taken just about everything a talented cross-examiner had thrown at him and turned it to his advantage. When Miki Shaughnessey finally gave up a few minutes later, Jaywalker resisted the temptation to conduct a redirect examination aimed at rehabilitating his witness.

There was simply nothing to rehabilitate.

"The defense rests," he announced.

"And the People?" asked Judge Levine.

"The People intend to call rebuttal witnesses," said Shaughnessey.

Just as Jaywalker had expected her to.

That night Jaywalker replayed the day's events in his mind, as he always did when he was on trial. They'd ended with an early recess, with Shirley Levine granting Miki Shaughnessey's request to go over to Wednesday to give her a chance to assemble her rebuttal witnesses. But Shaughnessey's long cross-examination of Alonzo Barnett had clearly been a high-water mark for the defense.

If only Barnett hadn't taken the bait and stepped out of character at the very end, thought Jaywalker. Until then, he'd done everything right. Not content with simply stating that he had no idea why the prosecution's witnesses would choose to lie about something so minor and tangential as which floor in a building he'd gone to, he'd let himself slip and add "Maybe you should ask them" to his answer.

And now she was going to do just that, with her rebuttal witnesses.

"Idiot."

"Who, me?"

For a moment he mistook the voice for his client's and imagined they were talking together in the pen adjoining the courtroom. Though he couldn't explain the surrounding darkness. Then he realized that he was lying in bed and the voice had been his wife's, thick with sleep.

"Who's an idiot?" she asked again.

"My client." And he proceeded to describe Alonzo Barnett's exchange with the prosecutor.

Jaywalker had fully expected his wife to agree with him; she usually did. But she surprised him this time. Instead of sharing his annoyance over the impertinence of Barnett's comment, she seemed far more interested in what had led to it.

"So why *did* they lie about that?" she wanted to know.

"You're missing the point," Jaywalker told her.

Or was she?

The thought would keep him awake another hour. In his annoyance at his client for botching the extra-credit question and ending up with a score of only 100 instead of 105, was it possible that Jaywalker himself had missed the point? Was the reason Investigator Bucknell had lied about the twelfth floor business more complicated than Jaywalker had figured?

He'd learned a lifetime ago that cops lied. Hell, he'd been one of them, only on the federal payroll, so he knew it firsthand. But they didn't lie indiscriminately. They lied selectively, to cover their own asses or those of their partners or team, to make an arrest stand up here or a search pass muster there. In other words, they lied only when there was something to be gained by lying—or something to be hidden.

So what could they possibly be gaining by specifying that Alonzo Barnett had ridden the elevator to the twelfth floor, when he swore he hadn't and they had no knowledge of where he'd actually gone? And what could they possibly be hiding by denying that he'd gone to the eighth floor instead, as he insisted he had?

16

All Cretans are liars

"The People call Thomas Egan," Miki Shaughnessey announced once the trial resumed Wednesday morning.

For once, Jaywalker—whose organizational skills fell somewhere between extremely compulsive and certifiably insane—found himself at a total loss. He had no subfile for a Thomas Egan, no entry in his master index, no report of any sort. He'd never even *heard* of Thomas Egan.

"May we approach?" he asked Judge Levine.

Up at the bench, he took a page straight out of the Prosecutor's Primer and asked for an offer of proof. Only he did it slightly less formally than Shaughnessey had with Kenny Smith.

"Who the f— is this guy?" he asked. Actually said it that way, the *F* standing on its own, just in case Shirley Levine might have been in a rare testy mood.

Shaughnessey was more than happy to comply. "Captain Egan happens to be the commanding officer of the Manhattan Narcotics Division," she explained. "Just as he was in the fall of 1984, when this case was made. As such, he not only oversees all field operations but is the police department's official custodian of all records pertaining to confidential drug informers. Mr. Jaywalker has suggested through his questioning that Clarence High-tower may have been acting as an informer."

"*May* have been?" Jaywalker interjected, before Levine silenced him with a withering stare.

"He's also insinuated," Shaughnessey continued, "that the task force was remiss in failing to make a serious effort to identify the defendant's source of supply. Captain Egan's testimony will put both of those notions to rest once and for all."

"Mr. Jaywalker?" said the judge.

Jaywalker could do nothing but stand there and shrug helplessly. The truth was, he'd never held out much hope that the whole twelfth-floor/eighth-floor business would fly with the jury, or that Hightower had truly been acting as an informer. But with nothing else to talk about, he'd been reduced to probing those possibilities. After all, the way the burden of proof operated, it wasn't up to him to convince the jurors about anything on these points; it was up to the prosecution to dispel any lingering doubts as to the defendant's guilt. Now Miki Shaughnessey was about to do just that, apparently, and in very impressive fashion.

It didn't hurt that Captain Egan was an extremely good-looking man with a thick mane of silver hair and a pair of piercing Paul Newman blue eyes. Or that he was well-spoken, with an economy to his words, no trace of an outer-borough accent, and none of the usual cop-speak that infected the testimony of so many of his fellow officers.

Shaughnessey began her direct examination with a run-through of Captain Egan's background and responsibilities within the police department. It was hard to tell which was more impressive. At one time Egan had aspired to be a priest, but the violent murder of a younger brother had steered him toward law enforcement. There he'd risen steadily through the ranks to his present position, accumulating a long list of medals, awards and commendations along the way.

Only when he sensed that Shaughnessey was done with the preliminaries and about to get down to business did Jaywalker pick up his pen and get ready to do some serious note-taking. By sitting back during the résumé portion and trying to look mildly bemused, it had been his hope to suggest to any jurors looking his way that this was nothing but window dressing that had no real relevance to the case. The problem was that no jurors had been looking his way. All eyes were glued to Thomas Egan's silver hair and blue eyes, just as all ears were attuned to his rich baritone voice.

Then, just when Jaywalker was prepared for the worst, Miki Shaughnessey surprised him again. "At this point," she told the judge, "I think it might be best if we were to approach the bench."

"Come up," said Levine.

Once both lawyers and the court reporter had formed a semicircle in front of the judge, Shaughnessey explained that she had an application to make. "Captain Egan is about to name and discuss a highly valued confidential informer of the NYPD. In order to protect that informer from public exposure and possible retaliation, the People ask that the courtroom be cleared and the door locked for the balance of the witness's testimony."

Jaywalker was about to oppose the application, but Levine silenced him with a raised hand. Then she stood back and addressed the jury.

"I'm sorry," she told them, saying the words as though she truly meant them. "But something has come up that requires me to confer with the lawyers at some length. I know it's still early, but I'm going to have to excuse you for twenty minutes or so. Go have a cup of coffee, or take a walk around the block. Don't discuss the case. Don't speculate as to what we're talking about. Just be back by eleven o'clock. Okay?"

She was answered with a chorus of sixteen "Okays" from the twelve regular jurors and the four alternates. Jaywalker forced back a smile. If all judges treated people the way Shirley Levine did, *jury duty* might cease to be thought of as a pair of four-letter words.

As he pivoted to walk back to his seat, Jaywalker got another surprise. During the colloquy at the bench, someone had quietly slid into Miki Shaughnessey's chair at the prosecution table. It took Jaywalker a second to recognize him, but recognize him he did. Staring back at him was Daniel Pulaski, the assistant district attorney who'd had the case originally, before handing it off to Shaughnessey. Jaywalker, never a fan, gave Pulaski a perfunctory nod. As far as he was concerned, the man was a lowlife, a rarity in an office pretty much filled with decent people. Not only that, but he was nowhere near as good to look at as Miki Shaughnessey was.

But look at him was apparently something Jaywalker was going to have to do. As soon as the jurors had filed out of the courtroom, it was Pulaski, and not Shaughnessey, who rose to address the judge and make the case for sealing the courtroom.

PULASKI: If it please the court, Captain Egan is here because I subpoenaed him. I did that out of an awareness of the People's continuing obligation under *Brady versus Maryland*.

Under normal circumstances, this would have sounded like nothing but good news to Jaywalker. Under *Brady,* the prosecution is supposed to promptly turn over anything that might reasonably be regarded as exculpatory—in other words, helpful to the defense.

But these weren't normal circumstances. First of all, this was the prosecution's rebuttal case, and Miki Shaughnessey had already said that Captain Egan was there to put to rest any notion that the task force hadn't tried hard enough to identify Alonzo Barnett's source of supply, as well as any suggestion that Clarence Hightower was an informer. Beyond that, there was quite another reason for Jaywalker to be suspicious.

Daniel Pulaski.

So Jaywalker listened carefully as Pulaski spoke, hoping for the best, but fully expecting the worst.

PULASKI: It has recently come to my attention that a witness called by the People earlier in this trial may have given answers that were less than a hundred percent complete. That witness, I have no doubt, was testifying in good faith and, to his credit, was doing his best to protect the identity of a confidential informer. But as a result of his testimony, the record as it now stands contains what I would characterize as a few minor inaccuracies. I subpoenaed Captain Egan so that we could correct those inaccuracies and set the record straight. However, in order to do that, it will be necessary for Captain Egan to name and reveal the cooperation of a highly valued confidential informer who continues to work with the police department in that capacity. For that reason, the People request that all persons not immediately involved in the trial be excluded from the courtroom during the balance of his testimony.

Jaywalker couldn't believe his ears. He would have loved to believe that the prosecution was about to admit not a *few minor inaccuracies* but a lie that was so huge as to be absolutely verdict-changing. That in spite of all their denials and assurances, in spite of that official-looking form Pulaski had shown him weeks ago, Clarence Hightower actually *had* been acting as an informer when he'd approached Alonzo Barnett. And if that was so, then it *had* been entrapment, and the case had just gone from a dead-bang loser to a toss-up.

Which meant, of course, that it couldn't possibly be true.

Pulaski was up to something. He had to be.

For confirmation, Jaywalker looked over at Miki Shaughnessey, suddenly reduced to the status of a spectator seated at the prosecution table. As soon as she caught his glance, she averted her eyes and devoted her full attention to playing with a paper clip.

She was being shoved to the sidelines.

And whatever witness had introduced the *minor inaccuracies* during the course of his testimony was being hung out to dry.

"Mr. Jaywalker?"

He looked back to the judge, who was evidently awaiting his response to Pulaski's application.

"The defense objects," he told her. Then he followed up with a pretty good three-minute, off-the-cuff argument against closing the courtroom.

Not too many years back, excluding the public for substantial portions of a trial was something done on a fairly regular basis. An undercover officer, an informer, a child or the victim of a sex crime was about to testify? Seal the courtroom. Standard operating practice. Then the Supreme Court, the real one, down in Washington, reminded everyone that under the Constitution a defendant was entitled not only to a trial but a *public* trial. Ever since, judges have been compelled to devise briefer and less restrictive alternatives than simply tossing everyone out and bolting the doors.

Which was the point Jaywalker made, with some degree of success. He made it succinctly, without being overly pedantic about it, and then he sat down. Shirley Levine didn't need him to teach her the law. She continued writing for a minute before looking up and speaking.

"After full consideration," she said, "I've decided that we'll keep the courtroom open right up to the point where the witness is about to identify the informer. Then—" She looked from Pulaski to Shaughnessey and back again. "Which one of you is going to do the direct examination?" she asked.

"I am," they answered in tandem.

"I am," Pulaski repeated.

Jaywalker watched Shaughnessey as she silently bent the paper clip back and forth. He could imagine the metal growing hot to the touch. Finally it broke. "Mr. Pulaski is," she said.

"Please let me know when we're right at that point," said the judge, "and we'll ask the spectators to step out."

Ask, not *tell.*

They don't make judges like that anymore.

Once the jurors were back in their places, the trial resumed. The judge introduced Daniel Pulaski to them and explained that he'd be conducting the balance of Captain Egan's testimony for reasons they shouldn't speculate about. Miki Shaughnessey fumed silently. But Jaywalker, as sorry as he felt for her unexpected benching, couldn't dwell on it. He was about to hear Clarence Hightower branded an informer.

Wasn't he?

PULASKI: Captain Egan, did there come a time when you learned that some slightly misleading testimony may have been given in this trial?

EGAN: Yes, there did.

PULASKI: And did you learn that from me?

EGAN: Yes. Apparently an officer who testified earlier in the trial had some concerns and reported them to A.D.A. Shaughnessey. As I understand it, she in turn took them to you. And you called me.

This was all improper testimony, as far as Jaywalker was concerned. Not only were the questions leading, but they called for hearsay. The right way to do it would have been to recall the offending witness and give him an opportunity to correct his misstatements. Still, there was a decision for Jaywalker to make, and make quickly. A good lawyer is someone who knows when to object. A *really good* lawyer is someone who knows when *not* to. And right now something in Jaywalker told him to keep quiet, that the ultimate payoff was going to be worth the *see-what-good-guys-we-are* preliminaries. So he let it go.

PULASKI: Who was that officer, and what about his testimony may have been misleading?

EGAN: The officer was Investigator Lance Bucknell, from the New York State Police. And the testimony in question was with regard to his following the defendant into a building located at 345 West 127th Street.

Shit, thought Jaywalker, angrily enough that for a moment he worried he might have said it out loud. This wasn't going to be about Clarence Hightower at all. This was going to be about something totally different. Something that would benefit the prosecution and end up doing absolutely nothing for the defense.

Why should he have expected anything else from Daniel Pulaski?

PULASKI: Exactly what portion of Investigator Bucknell's testimony may have been misleading?

EGAN: As I understand it, Investigator Bucknell testified that he got onto the same elevator as the defendant and saw the defendant press the button for the twelfth floor. That wasn't entirely accurate.

PULASKI: What actually happened?

Again, this was all going to be hearsay, and Jaywalker could have kept it out had he wanted to. But not only was Egan going to tell the jurors that Bucknell had lied—or given *slightly misleading testimony,* to use his euphemism—he was going to tell them what had actually happened. What would the upshot be? Jaywalker had no way of knowing. All he could do at this point was tighten his seat belt and hang on for the ride.

EGAN: What actually happened was that Investigator Bucknell made it into the building, just as he said. But by the time he did, the elevator door had already closed and the defendant was riding up in it. Bucknell watched the lights on the panel above the door and saw that the elevator stopped on the eighth floor. He left the building and reported that observation to his supervisor on the task force, Lieutenant Dino Pascarella.

PULASKI: And what did Pascarella do?

EGAN: Pascarella got in touch with me. He said he was concerned because it just so happened that he knew of a confidential informer who lived on the eighth floor of that particular building.

PULASKI: And what did you do?

EGAN: I have a master cross-index of all confidential informers involved in narcotics investigations with the NYPD. That means it can be accessed by name, nickname, address or telephone. I went to the list and conducted a search referencing 345 West 127th Street. And I got a hit. On the eighth floor was the apartment of an extremely high-value informer, someone who'd been providing the department with critical intelligence in major undercover operations for a number of years.

The way he said it conjured up images of special ops capers in Vietnam or Cambodia. Which was no accident, Jaywalker knew.

PULASKI: What did you do when you made that discovery?

EGAN: I convened a meeting with Lieutenant Pascarella, Deputy Chief Finn Murphy—that's my boss—and a detective named Jeremiah Yarborough. Yarborough was running the CI in question.

THE COURT: Would you mind giving us that in English, Captain?

EGAN: Sorry. Detective Yarborough was the department's contact with the informer.

THE COURT: Thank you.

PULASKI: What was the result of that meeting?

EGAN: It was decided that the identity of the informer had to be protected at all costs. He was that important. So Lieutenant Pascarella was directed to speak with Investigator Bucknell and have him sanitize his reports in such a way as to keep the eighth floor destination out of them. At the same time, he was instructed to do so without adversely prejudicing the rights of the target of the investigation, Alonzo Barnett, in any way.

PULASKI: And did Bucknell do that?

EGAN: He did.

PULASKI: And that accounts for the fact that he told us in court that Mr. Barnett rode to the twelfth floor instead of the eighth floor?

EGAN: That's correct.

　　Years later, Jaywalker would read in astonishment each time the Supreme Court upheld the State Secrets Act, not just permitting, but *requiring,* lower courts to throw out lawsuits whenever the federal government claimed that letting such suits proceed would compromise national security. Not that he'd be the only citizen to recoil at the notion. But thanks to what he was listening to right now, he'd be one of a precious few to experience a déjà vu moment. He would truly be able to say he'd been there, heard that.

But if anything, this was even worse. Egan wasn't merely suggesting that the authorities could avoid litigating an issue by making the naked assertion that it was too sensitive to talk about, he was advancing the proposition that committing perjury in open court during a criminal trial was acceptable. That it all came down to a balancing test of sorts, in which the end could justify the means.

And the defendant?

Tough shit.

After all, the defendant was nothing but a two-bit dope dealer with a criminal record as long as his arm. How could he possibly stack up against *an extremely high-value informer who'd been providing critical intelligence in major undercover operations for a number of years?* And this nonsense about doing things in such a way as to not prejudice the defendant's rights? While that must have sounded good to the jury, since when had it been left up to the police department to be the judge of that?

Unfuckingbelieveable.

Yet for the moment, all Jaywalker could do was shake his head in bewilderment and listen as Daniel Pulaski turned to the judge and said, "This might be a good point for us to take up my application again."

Once the jurors were out of the courtroom, Pulaski stated the obvious, that he was about to ask his witness to reveal the name of the informer. Judge Levine responded by saying that unless Jaywalker had something to add to his previous objection, she was prepared to close the courtroom.

"You bet I have something to add," said Jaywalker. "Based upon Captain Egan's admission that there's not only been perjury committed by a previous prosecution witness, but that the perjury was the result of a deliberate, concerted effort to mislead the court, the defense and the jury, I move to dismiss all charges against my client."

The judge turned to the prosecution table. "Tell me," she said. "Did either of you know about this? Did you know, either in advance or at the time Investigator Bucknell testified, that he was telling anything other than the truth?"

"Absolutely not," said Miki Shaughnessey.

"No," said Daniel Pulaski.

Jaywalker was inclined to give Shaughnessey the benefit of the doubt. Pulaski was a different story. Still, there was no way he could show that either of them wasn't telling the truth.

"If I may use a sports metaphor," said Pulaski, "this is really a case of no harm, no foul. In no way has the defense been prejudiced by—"

"Sit down," Levine told him. "I'm frankly not interested in your sports metaphors. Mr. Jaywalker is right in characterizing this as a deliberate, concerted effort to mislead the jury. And if I thought for a moment that you or any member of your office was involved in the deception, I would grant the motion. That said, I'm not sure Investigator Bucknell's lie rises to the level of perjury. Perjury requires that the lie be about some material fact. Can you convince me, Mr. Jaywalker, that changing where the defendant went, from the eighth floor to the twelfth floor, was a material misstatement?"

Jaywalker spent the next five minutes on his feet, giving it his best shot. But the strongest argument he could come up with was that Bucknell's lie may have led the jurors to disbelieve Alonzo Barnett's testimony that it had been to the eighth floor, specifically to Apartment 805, that he'd gone. And if they disbelieved him on that point, they could well conclude that he'd lied about other things, as well. But as the judge was quick to point out, Egan's testimony now supported Barnett's version. And if that remained unclear to the jurors, Jaywalker was free to emphasize it on cross-examination and argue it on summation.

"So," Levine continued, "while I think some sanction against the People is warranted, I don't find that the situation requires dismissal. Any suggestions short of that, Mr. Jaywalker? Such as an instruction that the balance of Bucknell's testimony be regarded with skepticism?"

"No," said Jaywalker. For one thing, he couldn't think of a lesser remedy. For another, he was afraid that anything less than outright dismissal might satisfy an appellate court without really accomplishing anything for the defense.

"I'm willing to tell the jury that Investigator Bucknell may face departmental charges as a result of what he did."

"Absolutely not," said Jaywalker. As he saw it, Bucknell was a patsy taking the fall for others. He'd done his job by originally reporting to Pascarella that he'd seen the elevator stop at eight. Then he was told to sanitize his testimony. *Sanitize.* Now he was being outed as a liar. The last thing Jaywalker wanted was for the jurors to

feel sorry for him and return a conviction in an attempt
to protect him from being disciplined.

So in the end the judge did nothing.

But Jaywalker had been around the block often enough
to know that didn't mean the incident had had no effect.
The fact was, Shirley Levine was now pissed off at the
prosecution, and rightfully so. Jaywalker knew that, and
while there might be nothing he could do with it at the
moment, sooner or later he was going to find an opportunity to turn it to his advantage—and Alonzo Barnett's.
That opportunity might come during cross-examination,
summation, or even deliberations, should the jurors, for
instance, have a question about what they should make
of Egan's testimony.

But for now, all Jaywalker could do was fret.

When they resumed, the spectator section was cleared.
There was some complaining, but a run-of-the-mill drug
case doesn't exactly bring out the scalpers. Had there been
reporters present, one of them might have put in a call to
his or her legal department. But there were no reporters
present. Nothing about Alonzo Barnett's case had been
newsworthy up to this point, and nothing was about to
be. The people who were most upset at having to leave
were the four of five Jaywalker groupies, retired guys
who magically materialized whenever he was involved
in a trial.

PULASKI: Captain Egan, would you tell us the name
    of the informer who at that time resided on the eighth
    floor of 345 West 127th Street?

EGAN: Only if I'm directed to do so.

Another cute stunt, this one no doubt choreographed
by Daniel Pulaski.

THE COURT: Consider yourself directed.

EGAN: The informer's name was Jackson Davis.

PULASKI: Thank you.

And with that, Pulaski sat down.

As Jaywalker rose to cross-examine, he half suspected a trap. Why hadn't Pulaski had Egan pinpoint the apartment Davis lived in? Was it something other than 805, as Alonzo Barnett had testified? But Jaywalker knew he couldn't afford to be cautious at this point. Sometimes you tested the waters, gingerly dipping in a toe. Other times you sucked in a deep breath and dived in. For better or for worse, this was going to be one of those other times.

JAYWALKER: Tell me, Captain Egan, does this master cross-index of yours include apartment numbers?

EGAN: Yes, it does.

JAYWALKER: So what apartment number did Jackson Davis reside in at 345 West 127th Street?

EGAN: Apartment 805.

JAYWALKER: Which just happens to be precisely where Alonzo Barnett said he went. Correct?

PULASKI: Objection. Captain Egan wasn't present during Barnett's testimony.

THE COURT: Yes, but I was, and the jury was. And Mr. Barnett did indeed say he went to Apartment Number 805. Next question, Mr. Jaywalker.

JAYWALKER: You also said that your cross-index can be accessed by nickname. Correct?

EGAN: Yes, as long as the nickname is unusual enough. Something like "Lefty" or "Shorty" might pose a problem, for example.

JAYWALKER: How about something like "One-Eyed Jack?" Do you think that might pose a problem? Or would that be unusual enough?

EGAN: No, I'd have to agree that's pretty unusual.

JAYWALKER: So did Jackson Davis have a nickname, by any chance?

EGAN: Yes.

JAYWALKER: What was his nickname?

EGAN: One-Eyed Jack.

JAYWALKER: Do you happen to know how he got that nickname?

EGAN: I have no idea.

JAYWALKER: Was Mr. Davis working off a case of his own in order to stay out of prison? Cooperating out of the goodness of his heart? Or was he being paid for his services?

PULASKI: Objection. That's privileged information.

THE COURT: Overruled. Now if you'd said "That's three questions in one," Mr. Pulaski, or "It's irrelevant," I might have sustained your objection. But as far as privilege goes, there is none. And if there ever was, it's been waived by Captain Egan's taking the stand and testifying about the subject on direct examination.

PULASKI: Objection. That's three questions in one, and it's irrelevant.

THE COURT: Sorry, too late. Was Mr. Davis paid, Captain Egan? Yes or no?

EGAN: Yes, Your Honor, he was.

THE COURT: Next subject, Mr. Jaywalker.

And by using the word *subject* rather than *question,* Judge Levine was making it clear to Jaywalker that he was to move on, that there weren't to be any follow-up questions like *Who was paying him, how much,* and *on what basis?* Because the judge was right. It was irrelevant. Jackson Davis hadn't testified, so his credibility wasn't at issue. Technically speaking, the details of his payment had no bearing upon Alonzo Barnett's guilt or lack thereof.

Needless to say, *technically speaking* wasn't exactly Jaywalker's native tongue. Still, he had to admit that Shirley Levine had given him a couple of favorable rulings to get even with the prosecution. But there were limits to her generosity. So he'd have to try some other way of helping the jurors get acquainted with Jackson Davis.

JAYWALKER: Do you by any chance have a photo of
    Mr. Davis?

Egan thumbed through his papers and eventually
pulled out a photograph, a three-by-five color glossy,
and handed it to Jaywalker. It was a mug shot, a pair
of side-by-side images of a middle-aged black man, one
full face, the other in profile. On the left image, the one
where the subject had been directly facing the camera, a
placard held against his chest displayed in movie-marquis
style the initials NYPD, the department's blue-and-white
shield, the name DAVIS, Jackson, and the date, 01-09-79.
You didn't have to look too closely to see that one of
the subject's eyes was real and focused, while the other
was glass, or whatever they made fake eyes out of back
then.
    Jaywalker had the photo marked into evidence as
Defendant's Exhibit A and passed among the jurors. He
wanted to make sure they saw the bad eye for themselves.
At the same time, he wanted them to get a good look at
the guy their tax dollars were subsidizing because the
poor fellow couldn't make enough of a living selling
heroin under the police department's protection.

JAYWALKER: How about Clarence Hightower? Is he
    in your index, too?

EGAN: No, he isn't.

JAYWALKER: You've checked?

EGAN: I have.

JAYWALKER: By name, address and nickname?

EGAN: All three.

JAYWALKER: No entry for him?

EGAN: None at all.

JAYWALKER: Did you check under "Stump"?

EGAN: Yes, I did. Negative.

JAYWALKER: So I assume you have no photograph of him?

EGAN: Actually, I do. But only because I took the trouble of hunting one down. Miss Shaughnessey over there *[Gestures]* told me you'd probably be asking me about him.

Even as Jaywalker looked at "Miss Shaughnessey over there" and the two of them fought off grins, Egan busied himself digging out the photograph and handing it over. It, too, was in color, but it contained only a single exposure and bore no placard with lettering. Jaywalker recognized it as an old-fashioned Polaroid print, the kind you used to snap and wait a minute for it to develop before sticking it onto a piece of gummed cardboard. He'd thought those things had gone the way of hot-water bottles and seltzer dispensers. Leave it to the NYPD to still be using them. Jaywalker flipped the photo over. Early in his career, he'd once made the mistake of not checking the back of an exhibit, resulting in the jury learning that his client was nicknamed "Jimmy the Strangler." So he'd been burned by his carelessness. But only once. This time Jaywalker saw nothing but the word "asp" inked on the back of the cardboard. Another nickname, perhaps? If so, how fitting.

Jaywalker turned the photo back over. He'd never seen Clarence Hightower in person, but he'd seen another photo of him back when he'd checked his court file, not too long after being appointed to represent Alonzo Barnett. His reaction now was pretty much the same as it had been then. Clarence Hightower was one ugly dude. Not menacing or deformed or anything like that. Just ugly. Still, the photo certainly wasn't important enough to circulate among the jurors, as the one of Jackson Davis had been, showing as it did the bad eye and hence the nickname. But come summation time, Jaywalker might nonetheless want to hold up Hightower's photo for the jury to see, as a way of putting a face—and an ugly one at that—on the guy who'd gotten Barnett into all this trouble. Would it have an impact on the verdict? Probably not. But then again, who was to say? Jaywalker had won cases before on things as unlikely as ugliness. So he offered the photo into evidence as Defendant's B. And with Daniel Pulaski shrugging his shoulders and raising no objection, it was received.

Up to this point, as surprising as Thomas Egan's testimony had been—one cop admitting that another cop had lied under oath—nothing he'd said had really helped Alonzo Barnett. Sure, it showed Barnett had been telling the truth when he said he'd gone to Apartment 805 and gotten the heroin from One-Eyed Jack. And that Lance Bucknell had made up the business about the twelfth floor. And maybe it made the task force witnesses look bad for protecting an informer at the expense of the truth. Beyond that, however, any advantage gained by the defense was minimal. Now, if Captain Egan had said Clarence Hightower had been acting as an informer instead of Jackson Davis, that would have been a different story. It would have meant something in terms of an entrapment defense. But now Egan had all but slammed the door on that possibility.

JAYWALKER: Does the nickname "Asp" by any chance mean anything to you?

EGAN: "Asp"? No.

JAYWALKER: Would you check your cross-index?

EGAN: *[Complies]*

EGAN: Sorry. Nothing for "Asp."

Still, Jaywalker decided to give it one last shot. After all, wasn't that what you were supposed to do when you were down to a single bullet? Did any gunslinger ever dream of being buried with a live round still left in his six-shooter?

JAYWALKER: Tell me, Captain Egan. Did you yourself ever work narcotics?

EGAN: Yes, I did. For about eleven years, actually.

JAYWALKER: Made a number of drug arrests?

EGAN: More than I can count.

JAYWALKER: What does it mean to "flip" someone, or "turn" someone?

EGAN: Those terms refer to convincing someone to cooperate, in the hope that he'll be treated more leniently.

JAYWALKER: You've done that?

EGAN: Many times.

JAYWALKER: When in the course of a case would you try to do that?

EGAN: Any time after the arrest.

JAYWALKER: Sometimes right away?

EGAN: Sometimes.

JAYWALKER: Would there be any advantage to doing it right away?

EGAN: Sure, I suppose so.

JAYWALKER: What sort of advantage?

EGAN: I'm not sure what you're driving at, Counselor.

Jaywalker loved it whenever a witness said something like that on cross-examination. He took it as a golden opportunity to testify, no oath required.

JAYWALKER: Here's what I'm driving at. You make an arrest. Right there on the spot, you flip the guy, convince him to cooperate in order to stay out of prison. Then, before the word gets out that the guy's been arrested, you have him introduce an undercover to his supplier to make a buy. The supplier doesn't suspect anything because he doesn't even know the guy got busted. Anything like that ever happen in your experience?

EGAN: Yes, I suppose so.

JAYWALKER: You suppose so, or you know so?

EGAN: It's happened.

JAYWALKER: More than once?

EGAN: Probably.

So far, so good. But that had been the easy part, baiting the hook. Getting the fish to bite was another thing altogether.

JAYWALKER: And isn't that in fact precisely what happened between Detective Pascarella and Clarence Hightower? Sometime in early September, say, Pascarella arrested Hightower, a man with an extremely long record who happened to be on parole. They both knew what that meant for Hightower. Pascarella offered him a deal, right on the spot. "Help us out by introducing an undercover to your man, and we'll help you out." Hightower, knowing full well that the alternative meant going back upstate, very possibly for the rest of his life, agreed. In other words, Pascarella flipped him right then and there. And Hightower delivered. It took him a lot of time and a lot of arm-twisting, but he delivered. He delivered Alonzo Barnett, didn't he?

PULASKI: Objection.

THE COURT: On what basis?

PULASKI: This is all purely speculative.

THE COURT: Overruled. You may answer if you know, Captain.

EGAN: No, that didn't happen.

JAYWALKER: How do you know?

EGAN: Several reasons. First of all, Hightower would have had to be registered as an informer. He never was. He's not in the index. Second of all, I've spoken with Detective Pascarella, and he told me for a fact that it never happened.

JAYWALKER: So you suspected it, too.

EGAN: Now you're putting words in my mouth, Counselor. What I mean is, we discussed the case in full. Detective Pascarella told me it began with an anonymous phone tip, that there was no informer involved. And I believe Detective Pascarella.

JAYWALKER: Is that the same Detective Pascarella who directed Investigator Bucknell to leave out the business about the eighth floor and change it to the twelfth floor?

EGAN: *[No response]*

JAYWALKER: The same Detective Pascarella who orchestrated a witness lying under oath in this trial in order to protect an informer who lived on the eighth floor?

EGAN: *[No response]*

JAYWALKER: Tell us, Captain Egan. Do you think Detective Pascarella would lie, or have someone else lie, in order to shield the identity of an informer?

EGAN: Yes. No. Maybe. I don't know.

JAYWALKER: Well, isn't that exactly what he did with respect to Jackson Davis and the eighth floor business?

EGAN: Only if you choose to look at it that way.

JAYWALKER: And how do you choose to look at it?

EGAN: Jackson Davis was and continues to be an extremely valuable confidential informer. Certain necessary steps were taken to protect him. Steps that in no way jeopardized your client's right to a fair trial.

JAYWALKER: Suppose Clarence Hightower was an extremely valuable confidential informer. Might it not be equally reasonable to believe that Detective Pascarella would have taken certain necessary steps to protect him, too?

EGAN: Hightower was never an informer.

JAYWALKER: How can we possibly know that, if Pascarella lies to protect his informers?

EGAN: I don't know how to answer that question, Counselor.

JAYWALKER: Well, maybe the jury will.

It was, as Judge Levine was quick to point out, a comment that was totally uncalled for, and she instructed the jurors to disregard it. But Jaywalker hadn't been able to help himself. If Hightower, like Davis, had indeed been working with the task force while trying to get Alonzo Barnett back into the drug business, then Jaywalker had a beauty of an entrapment defense. But with Egan adamant that there was no truth to the suggestion, what was left for Jaywalker to do but rant? The whole thing reminded him of a paradox he'd heard as a young boy, back before he had any idea what a paradox was.

All Cretans are liars.
I am a Cretan.
Am I really?

Daniel Pulaski spent ten minutes on redirect, during which he elicited from Captain Egan his assurances that there was a big difference between protecting a highly valued informer like Jackson Davis and an absolute nobody like Clarence Hightower. Besides, Egan insisted, Pascarella never would have made up the stuff about the anonymous caller to shield Hightower. Why not? Because there'd been no reason to. *And* it would have been wrong. "Also," Egan added, "that's the kind of thing you can get into real trouble for."

"No further questions," said Pulaski.

"Any re-cross?" the judge asked.

"No," said Jaywalker. He'd given up trying to crack Captain Egan. He'd even considered the possibility that Egan was telling the truth, that as far as he knew, Hightower hadn't been an informer. Which narrowed things down to one remaining possibility.

As soon as Egan had left the courtroom, Pulaski stood and announced that the People were resting, having concluded their rebuttal case with a single witness.

"Mr. Jaywalker?"

Meaning, *does the defense rest, too?*

"No," said Jaywalker, rising to his feet. "The defense has a surrebuttal witness." He loved that word, *surrebuttal*. It sounded devious and underhanded, kind of like *surreptitious*. He half wondered if he'd decided to drag the case out further just so he could hear himself say it.

But the other half of him was dead serious. If he and Alonzo Barnett were going down, then they might as well go down in flames. There was no way Jaywalker was going to let Captain Egan's denial be the last word of the trial. No way he was going to wake up the morning after the conviction wondering what else he could have done. He lost cases from time to time, Jaywalker did, but never because he hadn't bothered doing something.

"Very well," said the judge. "Who's your witness?"

"Lieutenant Dino Pascarella."

17

The Asp

Jaywalker's announcement that he intended to recall Lieutenant Pascarella in rebuttal essentially ended Thursday's court session. Pascarella, as it turned out, had called in sick that morning with a stomach ailment and, when finally reached by phone at home, said he didn't think he'd be feeling well enough to come back to court until the next day. Which actually solved a problem Jaywalker had been worried about. Had the evidence been completed on Thursday, he would have been required to sum up on Friday, followed immediately by Shaughnessey or Pulaski. That would have put the defense at a huge disadvantage, inasmuch as it would have meant sending the jurors off for the weekend with the prosecution's summation still ringing in their ears. Now, with more testimony scheduled for Friday, Jaywalker knew he'd be able to convince Levine to defer summations until Monday morning, putting both sides on a more even footing.

But even as Pascarella's stomach had solved one problem for Jaywalker, it had created another. "Tomorrow happens to be a holy day in the Islamic calendar," he'd told the judge once the jury had left the courtroom. "Normally, my client would ask that he not be required to come to court at all. But under the circumstances he's perfectly willing to, so long as Your Honor can see to it that he's allowed ten minutes to pray in the morning, and another ten minutes in the afternoon."

Even as he'd heard Daniel Pulaski muttering "Who cares?" under his breath and Judge Levine saying that it should pose no problem, Jaywalker had felt Barnett tugging at his sleeve, reminding him not to forget his second request.

"One other thing," Jaywalker had added. "Mr. Barnett would like your permission to wear his prayer garb over his clothes. It consists of a robe and a— What do you call that thing again?"

"Just tell her it looks like a yarmulke," Barnett had whispered.

"And something that looks like a yarmulke."

"Excuse me?"

It was a new voice, belonging to the court reporter, a young woman with blue eyes and straight blond hair. "How am I supposed to spell that?"

Levine and Jaywalker had taken turns trying, without too much success. They'd been able to agree that there was supposed to be an *L* in there somewhere, but neither of them had known exactly where it belonged. Shaughnessey and Pulaski had been no help at all.

A few months later Jaywalker would get around to reading the official transcript of the entire trial. Win or lose, he made a habit of doing that, figuring he was bound to learn a thing or two in the process. This particular time it would turn out to be a new word to add to his vocabulary. Today he can still picture the dictionary entry in his mind, just as he did twenty-five years ago.

Yamika (yä'ma·keh), n. 1. a brand name of motorized
scooters. 2. a famous maker of concert pianos. 3. A small
skullcap favored by the Chinese.

God bless the gentiles.

It was only late that night, long after Jaywalker and
his wife had finished dinner and he'd kissed her good-
night and retreated to their spare bedroom/den/office/
laundry-sorting room, that he was forced to ask himself
exactly why he'd told Shirley Levine that he intended to
recall Dino Pascarella as a rebuttal witness. The simple
answer, once again, was that he'd been angry. Angry and
frustrated and unwilling to quit while he was behind. And
since Pascarella's name had happened to be the one on
his tongue at the moment, he'd spat it out without giving
it serious thought.

That was then.

Now he had to figure out what to do about it.

He spent an hour reviewing every shred of paper he
had with Pascarella's name on it. Documents, reports,
photocopies of the prosecution's exhibits, notes Jaywalker
had scribbled to himself during the testimony. Nothing
jumped out at him. Yet he wasn't ready to admit that
his instincts had been wrong. He kept coming back to
the nagging feeling that the guy was holding something
back.

He called Kenny Smith, who'd come so close to in-
terviewing Clarence Hightower, only to lose him out a
restroom window.

"Any luck?" Jaywalker asked him.

"No, man," said Smith. "The guy's disappeared, with
a capital *D*. Gone. Vanished off the face of the earth."

Jaywalker spent another hour flipping through the rest

of the reports. His head was throbbing, and he was beginning to see two of every word on the pages in front of him.

Still nothing.

He made himself a pot of strong coffee. Downed two cups black and sweet and hot enough to burn his tongue. The combination of caffeine and sugar made his heart race, but did nothing for his headache and double vision.

He pulled out his own exhibits. The way it worked was that each side was responsible for the custody of whatever items it had put into evidence. The drugs and lab reports and the money that had been seized from Alonzo Barnett all belonged to the prosecution, People's 1 through 7. All the defense had contributed were two measly photographs. Defendant's A was the double mug shot of Jackson Davis, showing his glass eye. Jaywalker had introduced it to show that Barnett had been telling the truth about having obtained the heroin from "One-Eyed Jack." Defendant's B was the single Polaroid photo of Hightower. About the only reason Jaywalker'd had for putting that in was to show the jury how ugly the guy was.

He looked at it again now, forcing his eyes to focus on the face. "Talk to me," he told it. "Say something. *Anything*. Give me a fucking clue, will you?"

But the face wasn't talking. Not the thick lips, not the broad nose, not the crooked teeth or the short gray hair. Not the double chin or the thick neck. Not the dirty gray sweatshirt or the navy T-shirt peeking out from underneath it at the collar.

Nothing.

He turned the photo over, just as he'd done in the courtroom after Captain Egan had dug it out and handed it to him. The word *asp* was still there, still a perfect

descriptive for the man who'd set this whole case in
motion some twenty months ago by insisting that another
man repay an old favor. But at such a terrible price. For
in a few days, for all practical purposes Alonzo Barnett's
life would be over. Already over fifty, he was pretty much
guaranteed to spend the next fifteen to twenty-five years
sitting in state prison. Damn near a death sentence, when
you thought about it.

And the guy who'd called in the favor, who'd set the
whole thing in motion? The asp? He was in the wind,
nowhere to be found.

Just as he had in the courtroom, Jaywalker turned the
photo back over and studied the image once more. There
had to be something more to the story. There *had* to be.
But he had absolutely no idea what it might be, what he
was missing.

"The defense calls Dino Pascarella in rebuttal," Jaywalker announced when the trial reconvened Friday
morning.

Although there had been no spectators in the audience
when they'd recessed on Thursday, there were a handful now. Asked by Judge Levine if his examination of
Pascarella would reveal the identity of any confidential
informers, Jaywalker had replied, "I sure hope so," and
she'd cleared the courtroom again.

Again Jaywalker found himself double-teamed by
Daniel Pulaski and Miki Shaughnessey. Though from
the sullen expression on her face, Jaywalker guessed that
Shaughnessey wasn't happy about reprising her new role
as a nonspeaking extra.

One more thing bears mentioning.

The average lawyer wouldn't even dream of putting a
witness on the stand without having spoken to him in advance. Jaywalker, of course, was about as far from average

as possible in just about everything he did. So he'd called witnesses "cold" several times in his career and would continue to do so whenever the situation warranted it. But almost invariably those witnesses were minor players. An interpreter to testify to some nuance in translation from Spanish to English, a court clerk to read from a file, a corrections officer to describe a defendant as a model prisoner. Never before had he called a central figure in the trial without so much as a run-through of the questions he'd be asking and the answers he'd be expecting.

Lawyers have been suspended or even disbarred for such omissions, convictions overturned for ineffective assistance of counsel. Not to mention that no lawyer in his right mind would risk getting clobbered by a hostile witness he hadn't taken the trouble to interview in advance.

Then again, no one had ever accused Jaywalker of being in his right mind. He paid attention to conventional wisdom about as much as he did to the daily horoscopes in the supermarket tabloids. His thinking on the subject tended to be simple and straightforward. If you're winning, play it safe. If you're not, what do you have to lose?

JAYWALKER: So who's the asp?

PASCARELLA: The asp?

JAYWALKER: Yeah, you know. Asp, *A-S-P*. Like snake?

PASCARELLA: I have no idea what you're talking about.

JAYWALKER: The word means nothing to you?

PASCARELLA: Nothing at all.

Jaywalker pulled a photo out of his pocket and handed it to the witness.

JAYWALKER: I show you Defendant's Exhibit B in evidence. Do you know who that is?

PASCARELLA: I'm not sure. It looks like Clarence Hightower.

JAYWALKER: Very good. Have you ever seen that photo before?

Jaywalker watched as Pascarella turned it over, just as he himself had. Only where he'd seen writing on the back of it, he knew Pascarella wouldn't. Jaywalker had seen to that.

PASCARELLA: No, not that I know of.

JAYWALKER: Yet you were able to recognize Mr. Hightower, weren't you?

PASCARELLA: Yes.

JAYWALKER: From where and when?

PASCARELLA: From arresting him the same day we arrested Mr. Barnett. And from processing him later that day at the precinct house.

JAYWALKER: Anything else?

PASCARELLA: Like what?

JAYWALKER: Well, was that the only day you saw him? The day of his arrest?

PASCARELLA: Yes.

Jaywalker pulled out another photo. This one he'd retrieved earlier that morning, with the help of the same friendly court clerk who'd helped him early on in his investigation of the case. He had it marked now as Defendant's C for identification and handed it to the witness.

JAYWALKER: How about this one? Recognize it?

PASCARELLA: I'm pretty sure that's Hightower, too.

JAYWALKER: I offer it in evidence.

THE COURT: Mr. Pulaski? Or is it Ms. Shaughnessey today?

PULASKI: No objection.

THE COURT: Received in evidence as Defendant's C.

JAYWALKER: What can you tell us about this photo, Detective?

PASCARELLA: Like I said, I'm pretty sure it's Clarence Hightower. It looks like it's his official arrest photo, taken at Central Booking, right downstairs in this building. You must have gotten it from his court file.

JAYWALKER: I'll stipulate that the witness is correct. I did.

THE COURT: Mr. Pulaski?

PULASKI: So stipulated.

JAYWALKER: Let's go back to Defendant's B, the other photo of Mr. Hightower. What can you tell us about that one?

Pascarella put down C and picked up B again. Once more he turned it over and checked the back, almost as if he'd expected writing to have magically appeared since he'd last looked at it. Much the same way the Polaroid image on the front of it must have gradually appeared twenty-some months earlier. But no writing had appeared. Jaywalker watched as the witness seemed to struggle to absorb that fact, as if he was wondering if he could rely upon the blank piece of cardboard in front of him.

JAYWALKER: I'm sorry. We couldn't hear your answer.

PASCARELLA: I'm afraid I can't help you, Counselor. Like I said, I can't remember ever seeing this photo here.

JAYWALKER: Ever?

PASCARELLA: Ever.

Well, thought Jaywalker, that was about as much as he was going to be able to pin Pascarella down on that point. Before moving on to his next area of questioning, he paused and drew a deep breath. This was going to be it, he knew, *his* last chance and Alonzo Barnett's last hope. Jaywalker had a hunch, an idea that had come to him about four o'clock that morning. If it turned out he was wrong about it, the Fat Lady would have sung, and the case would pretty much be over. So here went nothing.

JAYWALKER: Detective, do you by any chance have a middle name?

PULASKI: Objection. Totally irrelevant.

THE COURT: Mr. Jaywalker?

JAYWALKER: Give me a minute and I'll connect it.

THE COURT: You've got half a minute. We'll take it subject to connection. You may answer the question, Detective.

PASCARELLA: Yeah, I have a middle name.

JAYWALKER: What is it?

PASCARELLA: Salvatore.

Jaywalker exhaled a breath he didn't realize he'd been holding. He was two-thirds of the way there, but it was the easy two-thirds. The final third was going to be a serious leap.

JAYWALKER: And your first name?

PASCARELLA: Dino.

JAYWALKER: Isn't that short for something?

PULASKI: Objection.

THE COURT: Overruled.

PASCARELLA: Everyone calls me Dino. I've been Dino for as long as I can remember.

JAYWALKER: So it's not a nickname?

PASCARELLA: No.

JAYWALKER: It's the name that's on your birth certificate?

PASCARELLA: You mean officially like?

JAYWALKER: Yeah, officially like.

PASCARELLA: No, it's not on my birth certificate.

JAYWALKER: So what's the first name on your birth certificate?

PASCARELLA: On my birth certificate?

JAYWALKER: Yes, on your birth certificate.

And as he waited for an answer, Jaywalker held up a piece of paper for the witness to see. It may have been old and yellowed around the edges, but it was a genuine New York City Department of Health birth certificate, right down to its Old English type font, its official inked-in signature and its circular raised seal.

PASCARELLA: On my birth certificate it's Andino. My mother's family name. But like I'm telling you, everyone calls me Dino. Everyone.

JAYWALKER: Would you spell that for us, please?

PASCARELLA: Spell what?

JAYWALKER: Andino.

PASCARELLA: *A-N-D-I-N-O.*

THE COURT: Excuse me, Mr. Jaywalker. Would you like to offer the document into evidence?

JAYWALKER: The birth certificate?

THE COURT: Yes.

JAYWALKER: My own birth certificate?

THE COURT: Never mind. I should have known.

Jaywalker approached the witness and took the photo from him. Gently he peeled away the backing from it. Not the original Polaroid backing, but the second one, the one he'd added that morning using double-faced tape but being careful to steer clear of the part where the lettering was. Then he handed the photo back to the witness.

JAYWALKER: Would you please read what's written on the back of the photo?

PASCARELLA: It says "asp."

JAYWALKER: How is that spelled?

PASCARELLA: *A-S-P.*

JAYWALKER: Whose initials are ASP?

PASCARELLA: I guess they're my initials, if you want
to get really technical about it.

JAYWALKER: I want to get really technical about it.
Who put them there?

PASCARELLA: I guess I must have.

JAYWALKER: You guess?

PASCARELLA: I put them there. I forgot, was all. I...I
didn't notice them.

All of a sudden, he was a different witness. Gone were
the swagger, the cockiness, replaced by a meekness that
would have been almost comical if another man's freedom
hadn't been at stake. It was almost like watching all the
helium go out of one of those giant Thanksgiving Day
balloon characters.

JAYWALKER: Why did you put your initials there?

PASCARELLA: I honestly don't remember. It's what
we do.

JAYWALKER: When did you put them there?

PASCARELLA: It would have had to be on the day we
arrested Mr. Hightower, the same day the other photo
of him was taken.

JAYWALKER: Are you certain about that?

PASCARELLA: Yes.

JAYWALKER: Where did you take it?

PASCARELLA: In the squad room at the precinct house.

JAYWALKER: Is that where you kept the Polaroid camera?

PASCARELLA: Yeah.

JAYWALKER: It was no use to you on the street, was it?

PASCARELLA: No.

JAYWALKER: Too bulky, too cumbersome, too slow?

PASCARELLA: Right.

JAYWALKER: Now, you didn't take Mr. Hightower home with you at any point, did you?

PASCARELLA: Home? No, of course not.

JAYWALKER: So he could shave and shower, perhaps?

PASCARELLA: No way.

JAYWALKER: Or take him shopping for clothes?

PASCARELLA: Not a chance. The man was under arrest.

JAYWALKER: Then I don't suppose you can explain to the jurors the reason why Mr. Hightower seems to be wearing two different sets of clothes in the two photos.

Because there was no rise in the inflection of Jaywalker's voice as he reached the end of it, it came out sounding more like a statement of fact than a question. And the truth is, it hadn't really been a question at all. Questions have answers. This didn't.

JAYWALKER: Who took this photo, Detective? The one that's got your initials on the back of it, in your handwriting?

PASCARELLA: I guess I must have.

JAYWALKER: Now look carefully at the two photos, if you will. Not just at the clothing, but at the length of Mr. Hightower's hair and the stubble of his beard. Any doubt in your mind that they were taken on different days?

PASCARELLA: No, I guess not.

JAYWALKER: No doubt?

PASCARELLA: No doubt.

JAYWALKER: What happened to Mr. Hightower after he was arrested? Where was he taken?

PASCARELLA: Like I said, to the precinct house. Specifically, upstairs to the detective squad room.

JAYWALKER: And from there?

PASCARELLA: Central Booking.

JAYWALKER: And after that?

PASCARELLA: Court.

JAYWALKER: Did he make bail?

PASCARELLA: No.

JAYWALKER: Was that the last you ever saw of him?

It was one of those wonderful *shit-or-go-blind* questions Jaywalker loved so much. If Pascarella were to say no, that in fact he'd seen Hightower again—by going out to Rikers Island to visit him, for example—Jaywalker would use his answer as proof that the two of them had had a continuing relationship. From there it would be only a baby step to believe that Hightower had been Pascarella's informer.

So instead Pascarella said yes. Yes, the day of the arrests had been the last time he'd ever seen Hightower.

Jaywalker paused before asking his final two questions. And when he asked them, he did so quietly, gently, with no trace of anger, sarcasm or irony. He had no need for volume at this point, no desire to reach the back rows of the audience. The audience was out in the hallway, after all, locked out of the courtroom. So when the final questions were asked, they were asked with something that sounded very much like sadness, the way a morgue attendant might ask the next of kin to take a good look at the body of a loved one long missing and recently found.

JAYWALKER: In other words, Detective, you took this photo, the one that bears your initials in your handwriting on the back of it, days or even weeks earlier than the arrest photo. Am I correct?

PASCARELLA: *[No response]*

JAYWALKER: Back before the sales in this case ever took place. Am I correct again?

PASCARELLA: *[No response]*

As the old saying goes, silence can be deafening. And nowhere, *nowhere,* is that more true than the inside of a courtroom.

Jaywalker collected the photos from the witness, walked to the defense table and sat down. To his way of thinking, while he hadn't succeeded in getting Lieutenant Pascarella to admit that Clarence Hightower had in fact been working with him as an informer, he'd at least made it seem like a reasonable possibility. At this point, that was about the best he could do.

But Daniel Pulaski wasn't about to let things end there. Rising from the prosecution table, he walked to the lectern, then seemed to change his mind and kept walking another three or four steps before stopping. That put him squarely in front of Pascarella and only a body length away. Had Jaywalker taken up such a confrontational position, he would have been told to step back, that his closeness was intimidating to the witness. For a split second he considered objecting but then thought better of it. *Let's see where this goes,* he told himself.

It didn't take long to find out.

PULASKI: Is a detective permitted to use an informer without registering him? Or would that constitute a serious violation of police department rules?

PASCARELLA: That's not allowed. It would be a violation.

PULASKI: A violation serious enough that the detective could be disciplined, perhaps even discharged?

PASCARELLA: I would certainly think so.

PULASKI: How about giving false testimony at a trial? Is that an equally serious violation?

PASCARELLA: I'm sure it is.

PULASKI: And a felony, as well?

PASCARELLA: Yes, sir.

PULASKI: You testified last week that this case began with an anonymous phone call. Was that the absolute truth?

PASCARELLA: Yes, sir.

PULASKI: No doubt about it?

PASCARELLA: No, sir. No doubt at all.

PULASKI: Counsel seems to be suggesting—

Counsel.
When lawyers get angry at other lawyers, they stop

using their names and start referring to them as *counsel*.
Kind of the way an irate legislator calls a despised member
of the opposing party *my most esteemed colleague*.

PULASKI: —that these photographs of Clarence High-
    tower are some kind of proof that Mr. Hightower was
    working for you as a confidential informer. Was that
    the case?

PASCARELLA: No, sir. Absolutely not.

Pulaski took another two steps forward. By the time
he stopped to ask his next question, he was close enough
to Pascarella that he could have reached out and touched
him.

PULASKI: Was he ever your informer?

PASCARELLA: No, sir. Never.

PULASKI: Thank you. No further questions.

With that, he turned and headed back toward the prosecution table. Because Pulaski had been so close to the
witness box when he'd concluded his cross, Jaywalker
could now see the satisfied sneer spread across his face
that neither the judge, behind Pulaski, nor the jurors, off
to one side, could. But Jaywalker wasn't the only one in
a position to see it, and as Pulaski neared his table and
was about to take his seat, the morning's most remarkable event took place.

It wasn't Jaywalker's production of the second photo of
Hightower, or the revelation of the initials on the back of
it, or the dramatic lowering of his voice as he questioned

Pascarella about it. It wasn't Pascarella's pregnant silence when asked if he had taken the photo before the sales had even occurred. Nor was it Pulaski getting up in the witness's face and having him reiterate the business about the anonymous phone call and proclaim his flat-out denial that Hightower had ever been an informer.

No, the morning's most remarkable event wasn't engineered by Jaywalker or Pulaski or Pascarella or Judge Levine or, for that matter, any combination of the four of them. Instead it was the spontaneous act of one young woman.

Just as Pulaski pulled his chair away from the table and was about to resume his seat next to her, Miki Shaughnessey rose to her feet, nodded at the judge, silently excused herself, turned and walked out of the courtroom.

To this day, Shaughnessey will demur when asked if her departure amounted to a sign of protest, a wordless objection to the way in which an experienced senior colleague had intimidated a witness into delivering answers that might or might not have been truthful. She'll deflect the question and insist she retains little or no memory of the incident. She might not have felt well, she'll tell you, or perhaps she'd experienced a sudden need to use the ladies' room. And because she'd spoken not a single word at the time, who can possibly argue with her, especially now, after so many years have gone by?

Jaywalker can.

Because from his perfect vantage point, he'd needed no words. No sound track or subtitles could have made things any clearer to him. The expression on Miki Shaughnessey's face as Pulaski neared her said it all. It was almost as though a stranger had approached her from across the room, and only when he'd reached her had it hit her that he hadn't bothered to bathe, shower or brush his teeth in six months. It might not have been a literal stench emanating from Pulaski, but it was something very, very close. And whatever it was, Shaughnessey had suddenly reached her limit with him. Her expression told Jaywalker that she wanted nothing more to do with either Daniel Pulaski or the case he'd dropped into her lap a month earlier, then suddenly yanked back once the shit had begun to hit the fan. She was done with him and with the case, and though she'd show up to hear the summations, she'd listen to them from the audience section of the courtroom.

"Does the defense rest, Mr. Jaywalker?"

"No, Your Honor. I have one additional rebuttal witness. He's here, and his direct testimony should only take a few minutes."

"Are we going to be revealing the names of any informers?" she asked. "Or may we unbolt the doors and let the huddled masses in?"

"You may throw open the portals," Jaywalker told her.

A court officer walked to the front door of the courtroom, unlocked it and pushed it open. Five or six people trickled in and found seats.

"The defense," announced Jaywalker, "calls its final rebuttal witness, Alonzo Barnett."

Until the moment Alonzo Barnett stood, none of the jurors had taken much notice of his changed wardrobe that Friday morning. A kufi—see *yamika*—tends to be worn toward the back of the head and is therefore barely visible from the front, especially when it's a white kufi against gray-to-white hair. Even a long white robe looks a lot like a shirt when worn by a man sitting in an armchair pushed all the way up to the edge of a table for security reasons.

Now, as Barnett strode to the witness box—if indeed one can stride without hurrying—his appearance was suddenly riveting. *Majestic* wouldn't be too strong a word to describe it, with his loose, knee-length white tunic, trimmed in pale blue. *Regal* might be closer to it.

As he sat, he carefully gathered his tunic around him. The court clerk reminded him that he was still under oath, but he needn't have. Just to look at Barnett was enough to seriously doubt he was capable of telling anything but the absolute truth.

Or so Jaywalker hoped.

The judge spent a few minutes explaining the accommodations that had been made to the defendant out of respect for his day of observance. Then she nodded in Jaywalker's direction.

JAYWALKER: Mr. Barnett, did you on three occasions obtain heroin for Agent Trevor St. James?

BARNETT: I did.

JAYWALKER: Why did you do that?

BARNETT: In order to repay a debt I felt I owed Clarence Hightower for having saved my life.

JAYWALKER: Would it be fair to say that Mr. Hightower induced and encouraged you to do what you did?

BARNETT: It's more than fair to say. It's what happened, over and over again. Until he finally pressed the right button and I said yes.

JAYWALKER: Had Mr. Barnett not induced and encouraged you over and over again, would you have done what you did?

BARNETT: Never.

And that was it.

Even as Jaywalker sat down, Daniel Pulaski waved a hand dismissively, his way of signaling the jury that Barnett's assertions were so self-serving and meaningless that there was no need for Pulaski to cross-examine him.

THE COURT: Any further witnesses, Mr. Jaywalker?

JAYWALKER: No, Your Honor. The defense rests.

THE COURT: Mr. Pulaski?

PULASKI: The People rest, too.

And with that it was over, at least the evidence portion of the trial. The jurors were sent off for the weekend, some of them smiling at the prospect, others grumbling that their jury service would be going into its third week, more than they'd signed up for.

It was the grumblers who worried Jaywalker. They were the ones who were self-employed or considered themselves indispensable at work. They had small children, elderly parents or pets with bladder issues at home. Above all else, they wanted the case over with. Come deliberation time, their impatience could easily translate into a desire to arrive at a quick verdict, no matter which way it happened to go.

A quick verdict meant deciding whether the evidence proved beyond a reasonable doubt that the defendant had done what he was accused of doing. It left no room for nuance, no time to consider *why* he'd done it. Entrapment wasn't a simple concept, a black-or-white, either-or notion that lent itself to quick and easy analysis. And that could spell trouble for the defense.

Big trouble.

Even as the jurors were excused for the weekend, the lawyers had to come back that afternoon for the charge conference, a meeting between the judge and the lawyers about what the judge will be telling the jurors when, following the summations, she instructs them on the principles of law applicable to the trial. Somewhere along the line, those instructions have come to be called the judge's charge.

In most federal courts the lawyers are expected to submit detailed written requests to charge, often as early as the beginning of the trial. The practice in state court tends to be more relaxed, with oral requests being the norm. Nevertheless, Jaywalker took charge conferences seriously. What the judge told the jurors, and how she told it to them, was of critical importance. Juries don't always get cases right, but it's the rare jury that fails to take its job seriously. They listen to the judge and try to apply the principles of law to the facts, just as she tells them to.

A lot of any charge is boilerplate stuff. Presumption of innocence, burden of proof, credibility, reasonable doubt and unanimity of verdict don't change from trial to trial. But some things do. And Alonzo Barnett's case had several wrinkles that made it anything but ordinary.

So that afternoon, once Shirley Levine had run through

a list of standard things she intended to tell the jurors, she called upon first Pulaski and then Jaywalker to make additional requests, if they had any. The setting was far more relaxed than it had been when the jury had been present, and the lawyers were permitted to remain seated at their respective tables while they spoke. But the court reporter was present, taking down every word of the discussion. More cases get reversed by appellate courts because of things said during the charge—or things requested but omitted from the charge—than because of just about anything else.

Pulaski stated that he was satisfied with what the judge intended to tell the jurors, and that he had no objections or additional requests.

Then it was Jaywalker's turn.

"The defense requests that you charge the jury on both entrapment and agency," he said.

A half an hour later, they were still arguing about both requests. Pulaski took the position that there couldn't have been any entrapment as a matter of law. Since Clarence Hightower had been acting on his own when he approached Alonzo Barnett, it hadn't been law enforcement that was responsible for any pressure put on Barnett, if indeed there'd been any.

Jaywalker countered by arguing that whether Hightower had been acting on his own or in cooperation with the task force was a question of fact, and like all questions of fact it was up to the jury to decide. Even as Judge Levine agreed with Pulaski that most of the evidence supported his position, she expressed her concern that her refusal to at least present the issue to the jurors for their determination might be grounds for reversal. "It's not that I'm agreeing it was entrapment," she explained. "After all, we have a captain and a lieutenant denying that Mr.

Hightower ever worked with them. But Mr. Jaywalker does have a point. It's up to the jury to decide. So I'll read them the statutory language from section…section—"

"Forty point oh-five," said Jaywalker.

"Thank you."

Her reluctant acquiescence might not have sounded all that promising to anyone else. But it was good enough for Jaywalker. He was perfectly content to have Pulaski continue to think of entrapment as a nonstarter. All Jaywalker could ask for at this point was that the door be cracked open just enough for him to get a foot in. The rest, he knew, would be up to him.

He had an even harder time when it came to agency. As soon as he'd mentioned the word, he'd realized that neither Levine nor Pulaski had even considered it as a possible defense. The theory behind an agency defense is that although a sale occurred and the defendant took part in it, he was aligned not with the seller, but the buyer. If that was so, he could be convicted only of buying drugs, not selling them. And buying was no crime.

"Agency?" Pulaski repeated incredulously. "The defendant profited from these sales, by his own admission. He wasn't working for Agent St. James. He was *selling* to him. He was working for himself. The record couldn't be clearer. Give me a break, will you?"

Again the judge expressed skepticism that, given the facts, the defense should be available. But again she ended up siding with Jaywalker out of an abundance of caution and the fear of seeing a conviction reversed. "Personally," she said, "I don't think the jurors will spend five minutes on this one. But technically, Mr. Jaywalker's right again. It's up to them to rule it out, not me. So I'll include something on it. Though over your objection, Mr. Jaywalker, I'll instruct them that it's a defense only to sale, not possession. Anything else, gentlemen?"

"That's it for me," said Jaywalker.

"Nothing else," said Pulaski.

"Then I'll see you back here first thing Monday morning, nice and refreshed."

Right.

Over the three nights between now and then, Jaywalker would sleep for a combined total of less than ten hours, and fitfully at that.

So much for *nice and refreshed.*

18

How about sex?

Jaywalker had long been a card-carrying procrastinator, and he managed to put off working on his summation all of Friday evening and most of Saturday. But it wasn't as if doing so allowed him to enjoy himself. He and his wife even went for a walk Saturday afternoon, something they hadn't done together for months. But on the way back, after the third time Jaywalker had said "What?" to one of her questions, she finally told him he might as well get down to work, that until his summation was done he would be no good to her or anyone else.

"How about sex?" he suggested. "Maybe that would help."

"Right," she laughed. "And halfway through, you'd say, 'Wait a minute, an idea just came to me.' Thanks, but no thanks."

"Afterward?"

"Afterward," she agreed. But they both knew full well that there'd be no afterward until he'd actually given the damn thing. He'd work on it on and off until then, mostly on. He'd work on it that night, all day Sunday and long into Sunday night. He'd still be working on it Monday morning, right up until the moment the judge looked his

way and said, "Mr. Jaywalker?" And that was on top
of the fact that he'd been working on it for two months
now, ever since the first time he'd sat down with Alonzo
Barnett and learned about the favor Barnett had done for
Clarence Hightower.

He began with the Penal Law, as he often did.

§40.05 Entrapment

In any prosecution for an offense, it is an affirmative defense that the defendant engaged in the
proscribed conduct because he was induced or encouraged to do so by a public servant, or by a person
acting in cooperation with a public servant, seeking
to obtain evidence against him for the purpose of
criminal prosecution, and when the methods used
to obtain such evidence were such as to create a
substantial risk that the offense would be committed by a person not otherwise disposed to commit it. Inducement or encouragement to commit
an offense means active inducement or encouragement. Conduct merely affording a person an opportunity to commit an offense does not constitute
entrapment.

It was by no means the first time he'd read the section,
of course. He'd done so as recently as Thursday night,
which explained why he'd used the words *induced and
encouraged* during his rebuttal questioning of Alonzo
Barnett, and why a moment later he'd asked Barnett if he
would have obtained heroin for Trevor St. James but for
the pressure Hightower had exerted on him. No, Barnett
had said, never.

At the time, Daniel Pulaski had made a show of waving

off Barnett's answers as too self-serving to be worthy of cross-examination. Pulaski might have been better off had he spent a little less time practicing his gestures and paying more attention to reading section 40.05.

Now, as Jaywalker reread the language of the statute for the twentieth time, he was reminded that it contained plenty of *bad* news, too. For starters, it classified entrapment not as a "defense" but an "affirmative defense." That distinction might have seemed a minor one to some, a matter of mere semantics. But if you went back to section 25.00 the difference became clear, and its implications were nothing short of game-changing. In the case of a "defense"—such as insanity or justification—the prosecution bore not only the burden of disproving the claim, but of doing so beyond a reasonable doubt. But when it came to an "affirmative defense," the burden of proof became the defendant's. And although the standard of proof that had to be met was a lesser one, satisfied by a "preponderance of the evidence," that was still nothing to sneeze at.

Next came the requirement that the defendant committed the offense because he was induced or encouraged to do so. That, Jaywalker figured, was the easy part. If the jurors decided to credit Alonzo Barnett's testimony— and Jaywalker was pretty sure they would—then they shouldn't have too much trouble concluding that Clarence Hightower's conduct had risen to the level of inducement or encouragement. Hell, it had gone *miles* past that.

It was the next phrase that was going to be the tricky part, the requirement that the inducement or encouragement be done by a public servant or by someone cooperating with a public servant. That was where this case was going to be won or lost, Jaywalker knew. That was the threshold issue of the trial, the moat that he and his client had to cross before they could storm the castle and do battle. And on that issue, as well as all others pertaining to entrapment, the defense once again bore the burden of proof.

But exactly how was he supposed to go about meeting that burden? A high-ranking police captain, a senior lieutenant, an experienced federal agent and a supporting cast of characters had all testified, some implicitly but several quite explicitly, that Clarence Hightower hadn't been cooperating with them. Lying about that fact would have constituted not only a serious violation of departmental rules, one serious enough to justify firing the violator, but a felony punishable with prison time. Added to that was the fact that neither Hightower's name nor his nickname was to be found anywhere in the official cross-index of informers maintained by the NYPD.

And just in case Jaywalker was somehow able to bridge that gap, it would still be incumbent upon him to prove that the defendant wasn't "otherwise disposed to commit the offense." In other words, he'd have to convince the jurors that absent the inducement or encouragement, Barnett never would have made the sales. Finally, whoever had written the statute had gone to great lengths to add not just one but *two* additional caveats. First they'd inserted language requiring that the inducement or encouragement be "active." And just in case that wasn't enough of a hurdle, they'd added one last disqualifier, proclaiming that "conduct merely affording a person an opportunity to commit an offense does not constitute entrapment."

Talk about an uphill battle…

Still, Jaywalker felt that meeting those tests would be the easy part, *easy* being a relative term. The hard part, perhaps the impossible part, was going to be convincing the jurors that, despite all the denials and despite his absence from the cross-index, Clarence Hightower had nevertheless been working with the Man.

Which is why he'd spend the rest of the weekend working on his summation, not getting to bed until well after midnight Sunday. Why he'd awake bleary-eyed, why he'd cut himself while shaving, and why he'd end up wearing one black shoe to court and one brown one.

But he'd be ready to sum up.

19

The key to the case

Jaywalker was precisely one sentence into his summation Monday morning when it happened. As always, he'd dispensed with the silly formalities that all other trial lawyers seemed to feel obliged to start off with. There was no "Ladies and gentlemen of the jury" for Jaywalker, no "May it please the court." Not even a "My client and I are indebted to you for the close attention you've obviously paid throughout the trial."

He'd started out on the right foot ten years earlier, winning acquittals in the majority of his trials at the Legal Aid Society in an era when he would have gone to the head of the class simply by winning one out of three. Judges, prosecutors and colleagues quickly branded him a natural. But the truth was, it was his years as a DEA agent that had prepared him for the work. Even as he'd learned to talk like a defendant, he'd also figured out how to think like a cop. By the time he arrived at Legal Aid, Jaywalker could pick up a written complaint and, in the time it took him to read it, know not only what was true in it and what wasn't, but what had actually happened out there on the street.

Yet even though winning more often than losing gained

him respect and reputation, those things weren't nearly enough for Jaywalker. The acquittals were certainly sweet, both for him and his clients. But each conviction would plunge him into the depths of depression. So the very next time out, he'd change something in his approach. And if the change worked, he stuck with it. They could be big things, these changes, such as alerting the prospective jurors at the earliest possible opportunity that the defendant had a criminal record. Or they could be little tweaks, like dispensing with the niceties and jumping right into the narrative with the first words of his summation.

By the time of the Alonzo Barnett trial, Jaywalker had changed enough things in his repertoire that he was winning four out of every five cases he tried. Over time he'd manage to push that rate all the way up to nine out of ten, an absolutely unheard of statistic for a criminal defense lawyer.

By the time he stood that Monday morning to face Alonzo Barnett's jury, the Jaywalker Summation had already evolved from pretty good to absolutely riveting and was well on its way toward legendary. But the perfectionist in Jaywalker understood the hard reality that neither meeting nor exceeding any of those descriptives guaranteed success.

Convictions happened, as he knew only too well.

Earlier that very morning, in fact, he'd run into a friend, a fellow defense lawyer named Blackstone, while riding up to the fifteenth floor. Taking in Jaywalker's blue suit, white shirt and conservative tie—and evidently unable to notice the contrasting colors of his shoes in the crowded elevator—the guy had asked if he was summing up.

"Yup," Jaywalker had answered.

"What kind of case?"

"Sale."

Blackstone had grimaced almost reflexively. "Well,"
he'd said, "good fucking luck."

Translation? Because jurors invariably ended up believing cops, sale cases were all but unwinnable. Which
might have been a good enough excuse for Blackstone,
but not for Jaywalker. *All but unwinnable* was where they
separated the men from the boys. *All but unwinnable* was
Jaywalker's briar patch.

"It is a Monday, a Monday in September, perhaps
twenty months ago this very day," Jaywalker had begun,
taking the jurors back with him to that fateful day when
Clarence Hightower had first shown up on the stoop of
Alonzo Barnett's apartment building.

And that was as far as he got.

He never saw the court officer rise quietly from his
seat and walk to the wooden partition that separated the
well of the courtroom from the audience section. Nor did
he hear the officer whispering to the man standing on the
other side of the partition, ordering him to find a seat.
Because Jaywalker had been standing directly in front
of the jurors as he'd begun to address them, those things
had taken place behind him, out of his field of vision.

But he quickly became aware that as much as the jurors
were trying to give him their undivided attention, something was distracting them. First one pair of eyes, then
another, then five or six more, were looking past him and
focusing on someone or something else.

Almost reflexively, he turned to see what they were
watching. There at the partition, a uniformed court officer was pressing one index finger to his lips while using
the other to direct a tall black man toward an empty section of seats in the third row. But the man wasn't obey-
ing the officer's instructions. Instead he was gesturing

frantically in Jaywalker's direction, trying to make himself understood.

Which was right about when Jaywalker recognized the man. It was Kenny Smith, Jaywalker's official unofficial investigator, who'd testified earlier in the trial.

"Please excuse me," Jaywalker told the jurors, turning and stepping away from them. Then, even as Shirley Levine reached for her seldom-used gavel, he raised a hand and asked if he might be permitted to approach the man. Which he did, without bothering to wait for her response.

He quickly reached the partition and assured the court officer that he knew the man, and knew he wasn't a threat of any sort. Then he turned his attention to Smith.

"What are you *doing?*" he whispered.

"I've *got* him," Smith whispered back. "He's *here.*"

But there are whispers, and there are *not-quite-whispers.* And in Kenny Smith's inability to contain his excitement, his reply fell squarely into the latter category, the sort guaranteed to draw a sharp rebuke from any librarian within a hundred yards. But on this Monday morning in Part 91 there were no librarians in sight, only a gavel-banging judge, a bunch of jurors and a few rows of spectators.

"*Who's* here?" Jaywalker asked Smith.

"*Hightower.*"

"*Here* here?"

By way of an answer, Smith pivoted and pointed toward the front door of the courtroom, the one that led directly to the hallway just beyond it.

"Do you need a recess, Mr. Jaywalker?" Judge Levine was asking.

"No, Your Honor, no. What I need is to reopen the case

so that one more witness can testify. The defense calls
Clarence Hightower."

"Objection!" shouted Daniel Pulaski. "He can't do
that. He's already rested. It's too—"

"That's enough," barked the judge. "Everyone be
seated. Now. That includes both lawyers and the gentleman standing at the rail. All of you."

Kenny Smith mumbled "Sorry" and found a seat. So
did Pulaski and Jaywalker. But there was still an audible
buzz in the courtroom that refused to die down.

"Quiet," ordered the judge.

The buzz complied.

As she turned to face the jurors, Levine looked positively pained. "Please forgive us once again," she told
them. "But I'm afraid we're going to have to excuse you
while we sort this all out. I'm truly sorry."

In the twenty-minute argument that followed, Jaywalker formally asked permission to reopen his surrebuttal case in order to put Clarence Hightower on the
stand. "He hasn't been available until this very moment,"
he explained. "And he's the one person who's in a position to tell us whether he was actually cooperating or not.
The interests of justice demand that we hear what he has
to say."

Pulaski was equally fierce in his opposition. "Both
sides rested," he pointed out. "Then we had rebuttal, followed by surrebuttal. After that, both sides rested again.
At some point the evidence has to come to an end, Your
Honor. Enough has to be enough already."

Shirley Levine spent a lot of time listening to the arguments and trying to balance the equities. In the end,
the clincher for her wasn't Clarence Hightower's unique
ability to clear things up, or that the interest of justice

demanded that he be given an opportunity to do so. Nor was it the fact that both sides had rested, then rested again. It wasn't even that the evidence had to come to an end, or that enough had to be enough already.

No, the clincher was the fact that Jaywalker had already begun delivering his summation.

"It turns out the case law is quite clear," said Levine. "I have the discretion to permit either side to reopen the evidence for good cause and in the interest of justice, even after both sides have rested. Even after rebuttal and surrebuttal and rerebuttal. But once closing statements have begun," she said, glancing up from a law book her law clerk had hastily retrieved and handed her moments earlier, "that discretion comes to an end."

Jaywalker continued to press the point. He happened to know the case the judge was reading from. Knew it by name, in fact. He tried his best to convince Levine that it was distinguishable on its facts. "That case concerned an application to visit a crime scene," he pointed out. "The lawyer hadn't requested it until he heard his adversary say something during his summation. This situation is totally different. Here a previously missing witness suddenly shows up just as summations are beginning. Not only that, but he's ready, willing and able to testify about something absolutely crucial."

"I'm sorry," said the judge. "But unless both sides consent to reopening, I'm not going to permit it. Mr. Pulaski?"

"The People strenuously oppose the application to reopen."

"Then that's my ruling, Counsel. And you have an exception, Mr. Jaywalker."

Meaning that in a year or two, after the conviction and the sentencing, long after Alonzo Barnett had been shipped upstate to spend the rest of his life, Jaywalker could take up the issue with some appellate judge. Only to be told that the trial court had lacked discretion in the matter, and even if that wasn't so, she'd been justified in acting as she had.

"So what's the key to this entire case?" Jaywalker asked the jurors once the trial resumed. "Better yet, *who's* the key?"

It wasn't how he'd started summing up a half an hour earlier. But Kenny Smith's interruption had changed things, prompted him to discard his notes and take a totally different approach. And from the expressions on the jurors' faces, he knew he'd grabbed their attention with those opening questions, knew that the trial was his to win if only he could do it right.

"Despite the fact that the case bears his name, it's not Alonzo Barnett who's the key. Sure, he's the defendant and he's important, and we'll have plenty to say about him, but he's not the key. Nor is Trevor St. James, or Dino Pascarella or Angel Cruz or Lance Bucknell or Olga Kasmirov or Thomas Egan. Nor is Kenny Smith, who so rudely interrupted us this morning. If we count them all, including those who testified a second time on rebuttal, we've heard a total of nine witnesses during the course of this trial. Yet not one of those nine holds the key. Not one of those nine witnesses can unlock the dirty little secret that lies at the very heart of this case.

"But there is someone who can.

"So who is that someone?" Jaywalker asked them. Only to be instantly rewarded by seeing the name form silently on the lips of several jurors.

"That's right. The key to this case is the tenth witness,

the one who never got to testify. The key to this case is Clarence Hightower."

He paused for a moment, letting the notion sink in to those in the jury box who hadn't realized where he was going.

"Let's take a look at what we learn about Mr. Hightower as the trial progresses." His use of the pronoun *we* was a conscious one. He wanted them to make this journey together, the jurors and he, to arrive at the truth simultaneously—even though he himself had arrived at it some time ago.

"We learn that Mr. Hightower is a career criminal, much like Alonzo Barnett. Only where Barnett's record is for drug possession and sales to support his own addiction, Hightower's record is one of predatory crimes. Crimes against property. Crimes against people. And while there came a time when Alonzo Barnett finally overcame his addiction, stopped committing crimes and began the never-ending process of redemption, Clarence Hightower stayed in the life. Still dealing, still scheming, still hustling.

"Next we learn that not too many years earlier, the lives of Alonzo Barnett and Clarence Hightower converged inside the walls of Green Haven prison. And don't let that nice bucolic name fool you. State prisons are terrible places where grown men stab each other, rape each other and kill each other. And there at Green Haven, because of circumstances partly his own fault and partly not, Alonzo Barnett immediately became a target, an inmate with a contract on him.

"A man marked for death.

"And when no one else would save him, Clarence Hightower stepped forward. He offered Barnett a job in the prison barbershop, and by doing that he saved Barnett's life. I'm not speaking figuratively or metaphorically here. Clarence Hightower *saved* this man's life. Literally saved it.

"And from that fact, it's tempting to think of Mr. Hightower as a Good Samaritan, a selfless individual who rode off into the sunset, asking nothing in return for his good deed.

"Not so fast.

"We learn more about Hightower, you and I. We learn that shortly after his release, he comes looking for the man whose life he saved. But not to celebrate, not for old times' sake. No, we learn Hightower has a business opportunity for Alonzo Barnett, a drug deal. But Barnett wants no part of it. We learn next that Hightower's not to be denied. Not only is he persistent, he's creative. He tries to induce and encourage Barnett, first with the promise of money, then with the lure of drugs and next with a tale of personal woe. And remember those words, jurors. *Induce* and *encourage*. They're important.

"Still, Barnett says no. He's clean now. He's got a good job and an apartment of his own. He's reestablished his ties with his young daughters. Six times he's offered an opportunity to make some easy money and score some drugs. Remember that phrase, too, jurors. *Offered an opportunity.*

"Six times Barnett says no to that offer. Six times he turns down that opportunity. Until the seventh time, when Clarence Hightower plays his ace and tells Alonzo Barnett that Barnett owes him this favor in return for Hightower's having saved his life. And on that seventh time, Barnett finally succumbs to the pressure. He gives in.

"But that's not all we learn about Hightower. As the trial progresses, we learn, for example, that he's greedy. Not only does he make money on the deals he convinces

Barnett to get involved in, but he mysteriously ends up with some of the drugs, too. We know where he gets the money from. Barnett gives it to him. The drugs are a different story, something we're left to wonder about. We know he didn't get them from Barnett, because Barnett gave all the drugs he got to Agent St. James. How some of those very same drugs managed to end up in Hightower's pocket later is anyone's guess.

"Or is it?

"Next we learn that Clarence Hightower is one unbelievably lucky man. Because despite the fact that he played a pivotal role in the sales, introducing Agent St. James to Alonzo Barnett, he gets arrested not for felony sales but only for misdemeanor possession. Brought to court, despite his long record, he's allowed to plead down to disorderly conduct, not a crime at all. Disorderly conduct. Fifteen days. Time served. Faced with a parole violation that normally would send him back to prison for years, he instead gets his parole terminated early.

"Were all those things really nothing but dumb luck and happy coincidence? Come on, jurors, we're New Yorkers. We weren't born yesterday. We know what it means when somebody tries to sell us something that sounds too good to be true."

Jaywalker paused for a moment, not only to give himself a moment to rest, but to give the jurors a chance to think about where he was taking them. He'd told them that Clarence Hightower was the key to the case, but he hadn't yet showed them how.

Now it was time.

"So what *really* happened in this case? We've been told a lot of things, you and I. But what *haven't* we been told? What have the cops left out? What is the evidence telling us, even as two of the prosecution's witnesses are trying their hardest to keep us from hearing it?"

He walked to the defense table and retrieved Defendant's Exhibits B and C, the two photos of Clarence Hightower, carried them back to the jury box and placed them on the wooden rail that was all that separated him from the jurors.

"Dino Pascarella would have us believe that this case began with a phone call. He says it was an anonymous call, so we have no way of knowing who supposedly made it. He makes it a blocked call, so we won't be able to know the number where it supposedly originated. And he makes it an unrecorded call, so we won't be able to hear it. Anonymous, untraceable and unpreserved.

"According to Pascarella, Clarence Hightower was a total stranger to the authorities when he showed up on Alonzo Barnett's stoop. According to Pascarella, the first contact he ever had with Hightower was on the afternoon of October 5, 1984, moments after Barnett's arrest, when Hightower walked up to Barnett and managed to get himself arrested, as well.

"Lieutenant Pascarella is lying about that. And these two photographs, Defendant's Exhibits B and C in evidence, tell us that loudly and clearly and beyond any shadow of a doubt."

Jaywalker held the photos up in front of him so the jurors could see them again. Even with them facing away from him, he was able to describe them in detail. Defendant's C. The dated one. Taken at Central Booking later on, on the same day as the arrests. In it, a cleanly shaven Hightower, dressed in a faded blue denim work shirt. And Defendant's B. The undated one. Showing Hightower with a three- or four-day stubble of a beard, this time wearing a gray sweatshirt over a blue T-shirt.

"The undated photo is the one taken by Dino Pascarella. Here are his initials, right on the back of it, admittedly written in his own hand. ASP.

"*A* for Andino.

"*S* for Salvatore.

"*P* for Pascarella.

"Although when first asked, Pascarella denied that that particular combination of letters meant anything at all to him. Think about that for a minute.

"Next, Pascarella inadvertently does us a favor. He admits that after October 5, he never saw Clarence Hightower again. So it follows that he couldn't have taken this undated photo of him after that date. And he admits that.

"What's left?

"He took the photo, but he obviously didn't take it on October 5. And he didn't take it *after* October 5. What does that leave? It leaves only one possibility. And that's that Pascarella took the undated photo of Clarence Hightower *before* October 5. And the reason he did so was because sometime before October 5, Hightower was already working as Pascarella's informer.

"There can be no other explanation.

"Sure, Pascarella denies it. And Captain Egan, taking Pascarella's word for it, backs him up and tells us Hightower's name isn't in the book.

"Well, Captain Egan may have been willing to take Pascarella's word for it, but that doesn't mean we have to. For one thing, you and I have the photo that puts the lie to Pascarella's word. And you and I have seen the lengths Pascarella was willing to go to, and the lie he was willing to orchestrate, in order to keep another informer's name out of this case. Finally, you and I know for a fact that Clarence Hightower ended up with the missing

2.55 grams of heroin that could only have come from Pascarella or someone working under his supervision.

"So what really happened in this case, jurors? It turns out we know that, too. We know because it's the only thing that could possibly have happened. At some point— maybe it was late August, maybe mid-September—Dino Pascarella caught Clarence Hightower doing something. We don't know exactly what, because Pascarella won't tell us. And Hightower? Well, all I can say is that as much as we would have liked to hear what Mr. Hightower might have to say, we never got the chance. But you know what? It doesn't matter. What matters is that on that very same day, whenever and wherever it was, Pascarella *flipped* Hightower, convinced him to become an informer. Had Pascarella sent him on to Central Booking to be put through the system, as Alonzo Barnett was, it would have been all over for Hightower. Jail, prosecution, conviction, parole violation. Back upstate to prison, not for days or weeks or months, but for years. So instead Pascarella offers Hightower a deal on the spot. Exactly as Captain Egan tells us it's sometimes done. 'Make us one good case,' Pascarella tells Hightower, 'and we'll cut you loose.' And because he finds himself stuck between a rock and a hard place, Hightower agrees. So Pascarella never completes the arrest process. He never books Hightower, never sends him to Central Booking, never submits his name to Captain Egan for inclusion in the cross-index. It's all done off the books. All Pascarella does is take a photograph of Hightower for his own records. He uses an old Polaroid camera they keep in the squad room, and he writes his initials, ASP, on the back of it. And then he no doubt forgets all about it. Until at some point last week, when Captain Egan asks Pascarella if he has a photo of Hightower, Pascarella pulls it out without thinking too much about it, and without realizing it could come back and bite him in the asp.

"That's what really happened. Because that's the only thing that could possibly have happened. And now we're going to see why it changes absolutely everything for you."

Jaywalker spent the next thirty minutes giving the jurors a short course in the law of entrapment. He had to be careful to avoid usurping the judge's prerogative to define the law. But that didn't stop him from reading them section 40.05 of the Penal Law in its entirety. He paused at the term *affirmative defense,* explaining how those two words placed the burden of proof upon him and required him to convince them by a preponderance of the evidence.

"But that's a burden we welcome," he told them. "That's a burden we're delighted to shoulder." He readily conceded that Alonzo Barnett had made the first two sales and was in the process of completing the third one when he'd been arrested. "But only because he'd been both *induced* and *encouraged* to do so by *a person acting in cooperation with a public servant.* Specifically, Clarence Hightower, acting in cooperation with Dino Pascarella.

"And make no mistake about it," he told them. "Without Hightower's unrelenting pressure—without his seven different attempts on seven different days, and finally without his insistence that Alonzo Barnett had to help him out in payment for Hightower's having saved his life—those sales simply wouldn't have happened. This wasn't a case of the police merely providing an opportunity for someone already disposed to commit a crime," Jaywalker told the jurors. "This was a case in which the police, acting through their informer, *manufactured* a crime that would never have taken place otherwise, not in a million years.

"That's what makes it entrapment, jurors. And that's why it becomes your duty to find Alonzo Barnett not guilty of each and every charge in the indictment."

His voice was hoarse, and he was just about finished, but not quite. "There's one other thing I want to tell you," he said. "And it's absolutely essential you understand this. When you come back into this courtroom at the conclusion of your deliberations to deliver your verdict, you should harbor no reservation whatsoever. And a week from now, or a month or a year from now, should someone walk up to you and suggest out of ignorance or stupidity that you acquitted a guilty man, you're going to look that person squarely in the eye. And you're going to say in a calm voice, 'No, we didn't. We acquitted a man who had succeeded in redeeming himself. A man who never would have broken the law but for the fact that the police and their informer first targeted him and then entrapped him into doing so.' So you tell that person you've got one word for what you accomplished through your verdict. And that word is *justice.*

"Nothing more, nothing less.

"Justice."

Two hours and two minutes after he'd begun, Jaywalker turned from the jurors, walked back to the defense table and sat down. Gathering his notes while listening to the judge sending the jurors off to lunch, he felt Alonzo Barnett lean toward him. "No matter what happens," whispered Barnett, "I want to thank you. You did everything a man possibly could have done for me, and I'll never forget it as long as I live."

They were nice words to hear, but Jaywalker wasn't so

sure they were accurate. He'd actually had more to tell the jury. He'd been prepared to argue agency as an alternative defense. But the entrapment argument had gone so well, and the jurors' reactions to it had seemed so favorable, that at the last minute Jaywalker had decided to forget about agency altogether.

Now he hoped that decision wouldn't turn out to be a mistake. Which was vintage Jaywalker, of course. Here he'd hit a top-of-the-ninth, bases-clearing triple to give his side a convincing three-run lead, only to blame himself for not having tried to stretch it into an inside-the-park home run.

The other thing he'd left out was the reason the jurors had never heard the testimony of Clarence Hightower. Jaywalker had lost the legal battle to reopen the case, and it would have been improper for him to complain to the jurors about either Pulaski's opposition or the judge's ruling. So he'd had to settle for the rather innocuous comment that he shared the jurors' frustration over never having had an opportunity to hear from Hightower. Hopefully that would help them recall that it had been Pulaski who jumped up and shouted "Objection!" the moment Jaywalker had tried to call Hightower to the stand. Hopefully, too, they'd be able to draw their own conclusions from Pulaski's obstructionism.

Other than those concerns, Jaywalker was pretty pleased at the way things had gone. Although he never, ever allowed himself to feel confident about his chances, he did celebrate after a fashion by treating himself to lunch, something he hadn't done for two weeks straight.

If, that is, you're willing to stretch things and consider a container of iced tea and a bag of Wheat Thins lunch.

* * *

Jaywalker's self-indulgence and good spirits lasted him all of an hour, ending about thirty seconds into Daniel Pulaski's summation on behalf of the prosecution.

Pulaski spoke that afternoon for only half as long as Jaywalker had that morning. And although Jaywalker would have loved to say that Pulaski spoke only half as well, that decidedly wasn't the case. In fact, Pulaski proceeded to deliver a truly impassioned summation, heaping ridicule upon Jaywalker's assumptions about Clarence Hightower's having been an informer. "Inferences upon inferences," he called them. "Pure speculation. Totally unsupported by the evidence. And the proof is in the pudding. Both Lieutenant Pascarella and Captain Egan were absolutely forthright in their testimony. They stepped up and volunteered that Investigator Bucknell had been less than honest when he said he saw the defendant push the button for the twelfth floor. Rather than allow that inaccuracy to stand, they came forward on their own and corrected it. In so doing, they not only risked their ranks and reputations, they revealed the name of an important confidential informer. So why on earth should they hesitate to do as much if another informer had been involved? The answer is as plain and simple as it can be. Clarence Hightower wasn't an informer. He never was, and he never will be. You have the sworn testimony of not one but *two* high-ranking police officials to tell you that. A captain and a lieutenant. You've got the word of an experienced federal agent. You've got your own good common sense. Why in God's name would all three of those men get together and decide to risk everything and lie about that? To convict this defendant? To protect Hightower?

"But if that's not enough for you, there's even more. You've got the official record, the NYPD's cross-index of all informers. Let me say that again. *All informers.* And Clarence Hightower's name isn't in it. How does Mr. Jaywalker explain that inconvenient detail? He doesn't. He doesn't because he *can't.*

"Ladies and gentlemen, when it comes right down to it, this is as simple a case as it could possibly be. This defendant, Alonzo Barnett, a man who's been selling drugs for most of his life, sold drugs once again. But this time he sold them to an undercover officer. Not just drugs, but heroin. Not just in small amounts, but large ones. Wholesale amounts. A-1 felony amounts. And not just once or twice, but three times, if you count the third time, when he was interrupted in the process. His claim that he did all that to repay a debt is supported by nothing but his own words, and is belied by his own admission that he kept—and was about to keep once again—part of the money he skimmed off the top. That's not the act of someone who's repaying a debt. That's the act of someone who's looking to profit from his own criminal acts.

"What a shame the defendant couldn't own up and take responsibility for those criminal acts. Instead he asks you to believe that he was forced into committing them, that the Devil made him do it. Only this particular devil, he tells you, was named Clarence Hightower. How convenient—and how cowardly.

"Well, ladies and gentlemen, just because the defendant refuses to take responsibility for his criminal acts doesn't mean you can't assign responsibility to him. How do you go about doing that? Very simple. Tomorrow, right after the judge has finished instructing you on the law, she's going to tell you that you may retire to the jury room to begin your deliberations. You know what you're going to do? You're going to tell her that won't be necessary. Because there's nothing to deliberate about in this case. The defendant takes the stand and admits selling or trying to sell heroin to Agent St. James on the three dates specified in the indictment, exactly as Agent St. James testified. Agent Angel Cruz tells you that when he arrested the defendant he searched him and found more than four ounces of white powder and five hundred dollars. The serial numbers on those five hundred dollars match the numbers of the bills given the defendant by Agent St. James some twenty minutes earlier. Finally, a United States chemist comes in and verifies that it was indeed heroin each time, and that the weights more than satisfied the requirements of the statutes the defendant is charged with violating. End of case. Forget about this entrapment nonsense. That's nothing but a red herring brought in by a desperate defense lawyer in order to distract you. A smoke screen to keep you from focusing on your job.

"So," Pulaski told them, "you tell the judge that there's no need to retire, and no issues to deliberate. You tell her that the defendant may not think people are responsible for their actions, but you do. You tell her that you find the defendant guilty as charged."

And turning to face the defense table, he added, "Now that, Mr. Jaywalker, is what justice *really* is in this case."

There are lawyers who sleep like babies after summing up. All the pressure is finally over. All that's left are the judge's charge, the jurors' deliberations and the reading of the verdict.

Jaywalker, of course, is different.

Even though it had been more than two weeks since he'd gotten a good night's sleep, that night would be no exception. Daniel Pulaski's surprisingly strong summation had unnerved him, caused him to have second thoughts—make that third thoughts—about not having gone into the alternative defense of agency. He was convinced he'd picked a bad jury, not smart enough to understand the nuances of something as complicated as entrapment. Shirley Levine's upcoming charge worried him. Worst of all, he'd noticed that the same jurors who'd struck him as receptive during his summation had seemed equally attentive to Pulaski's arguments. He should have called other members of the backup team, on the theory that one of them might have slipped up and confirmed that Hightower had been an informer. He shouldn't have spent so much time cross-examining the chemist and numbing the jurors with nonsense about weights and additives and percentages. He should have stayed at the DEA, or gone to medical school instead of law school.

Because by now it was absolutely clear: Alonzo Barnett was going to be convicted. Jaywalker was going to lose.

Again.

The last time he looked at the clock beside the bed it said two forty-four.

20

Jury-watching

Among the many things he is, Jaywalker is a jury watcher. He watches potential jurors as they first enter a courtroom at a point when they have no idea about the type of case they're being screened for. He studies their reactions like a hawk as the judge reads off the charges or reveals something particularly distasteful about the facts. He looks for the jurors' reactions to himself and to his adversary, trying to gauge which one of them is going to be their favorite. He checks to see whom they've chosen to sit next to in the audience, and whether they whisper to the man on their left or the woman on their right once they've been seated in the jury box. What are they wearing? What have they brought with them? Are they excited at the idea of being there, or do they see jury duty as an imposition? If a recess is called, are they willing to walk close by the defense table as they enter or leave the courtroom, or do they instinctively go out of their way to give the defendant a wide berth?

These things count, every one of them and a hundred more like them. And even early in his career, even as early as 1986, Jaywalker had learned to read jurors the same way a sailor learns to read clouds or a firefighter learns to read smoke.

And as he watched and tried to read the jurors' faces that Tuesday morning as they sat and listened to Shirley Levine's charge, he was almost immediately seized by panic.

They weren't listening.

Oh, they were listening, but not *really* listening. Not perched on the edges of their seats as they should have been, leaning forward to make sure they didn't miss a single word. Not listening the way they had during his summation or Pulaski's.

And right then, he knew it was over.

Had the case been a whodunit, or a simple he-said/she-said, he could have lived with their inattentiveness. Other than reasonable doubt and burden of proof, there wouldn't have been too much the judge could have told them that they didn't already know from having heard the evidence.

But the case *wasn't* a whodunit. It *didn't* come down to a straightforward matter of deciding which version of the facts to believe and which to reject. Entrapment was pretty esoteric stuff. Crammed into the single paragraph of section 40.05 were more than half a dozen complex issues—burden of proof, inducement, encouragement, public servant or a person cooperating with one, substantial risk, previous disposition, *active* inducement or cooperation, and mere opportunity to commit an offense. This wasn't the stuff jurors were born knowing about. Each of those phrases had a highly technical, legal meaning. And the outcome of this case depended on how the jurors decided to apply those meanings to the facts they'd heard.

Yet they were barely listening.

They'd already made up their minds.

They'd done exactly what Daniel Pulaski had told them to do. They'd heard Trevor St. James say he'd bought heroin from Alonzo Barnett twice and had been in the process of buying it a third time when Barnett had been arrested. They'd learned that Barnett had not only had an eighth of a kilogram of heroin when he'd been searched, but five hundred dollars of the prerecorded buy money.

That had been all they'd needed to know.

Everything else had gone right over their heads. All the business about the eighth-floor/twelfth-floor, all the nonsense about the weights and additives and percentages, all the suggestions that Clarence Hightower might have been working with the police. They couldn't care less.

And who could blame them? The crack epidemic was taking the city by storm. Drugs were a scourge, and heroin was among the very worst of drugs. There was a war being waged, and men like Trevor St. James and Dino Pascarella were the soldiers in the front line, while scum like Alonzo Barnett and Clarence Hightower were the enemy. In the final analysis, there was no need for nuance, no room for clever defense lawyering. It all came down to a choice between the good guys and the bad guys. And that was no choice at all.

Even Barnett seemed to sense it. At one point he nudged Jaywalker and drew his attention to a juror in the second row, a woman who'd turned away from the judge and was staring out the window. Jaywalker nodded grimly, having already noticed her. Then he shrugged. What was he supposed to do? Point her out to the judge and get the woman admonished? All that would do would be to guarantee her vote for conviction.

Not that it mattered.

Not that any of it mattered anymore.

* * *

Shirley Levine's charge took just under an hour. It helped that Jaywalker had dropped his agency argument from his summation. As a result, the judge barely felt compelled to instruct the jurors on it. But having said she would, she did. And she spent fifteen minutes on entrapment, but they struck Jaywalker as a bland, bloodless fifteen minutes, the highlight of which seemed to be that the defense bore the burden of proof on the issue.

By the time Levine reached the last of her instructions, that the jury's verdict would have to be unanimous and that they were to communicate with her only through written notes from their foreman, Jaywalker found himself looking through his pocket calendar, wondering what might be a good day to come back to court to stand up on Alonzo Barnett's sentencing.

It was that bad.

"Now," the judge was telling them, "you may follow the court officer and retire to the jury room to begin your deliberations."

"That won't be necessary," said the foreman.

21

Up yours, Mac!

It wasn't as if Jaywalker was a complete stranger to convictions. Even if he'd accumulated less than his fair share of them, he'd had enough to know they were a fact of life for every defense lawyer this side of Hollywood. And now he was looking at two in a row. A *losing streak,* in sports parlance. *Back-to-back defeats.*

Worse yet, he'd never had one quite like this.

He'd never had a jury convict without even showing the courtesy to go back to the jury room. He knew that jurors discussed cases long before the evidence was completed and they were told they could begin their deliberations. But to arrive at an actual verdict without retiring to the jury room? If nothing else, they could have sat around and eaten the sandwiches brought in for them at the taxpayers' expense. And even if none of them wanted to wrestle with concepts like entrapment and inducement and encouragement, common decency still dictated that they kill an hour before marching back into the courtroom to convict the defendant. They could have thought of his lawyer, if nothing else.

No, this was a new low.

This was embarrassing.

This was fucking *humiliating,* is what it was.

"*Excuse* me?" The judge was staring at the foreman, a small bald man who'd given his name as Runyon and had described himself as an accountant, although not a CPA.

"I said it won't be necessary for us to retire and deliberate," he repeated in a voice that to Jaywalker sounded somewhere between indifferent and downright cruel. "We've reached our verdict."

"Not another word, sir," cautioned the judge. "Remember that I told you to communicate with the court only through a written note?"

"Here you are," said Runyon—and extended a folded piece of paper that apparently had been in his hand the whole time. Hell, thought Jaywalker, it might have been there for *days,* perhaps a *week.* Why in God's name had he ever let an *accountant* onto the jury? A guy who did nothing but sit around all day crunching numbers, and was either too dumb or too lazy to even get certified?

I deserved this, Jaywalker decided. I really did.

But Alonzo Barnett didn't.

"Objection!" Jaywalker shouted, jumping to his feet. The sudden intensity of his own voice surprised even him. "The jury *has* to deliberate." Even as the judge banged her gavel in an attempt to silence him, he continued to stand, at the same time frantically thumbing through his dog-eared copy of the Criminal Procedure Law. "Here it is!" he shouted triumphantly. "Section three-ten point ten, subdivision one. 'The jury *must* retire to deliberate upon its verdict in a place outside the courtroom. It must be provided with suitable accommoda—'"

"Sit down, Mr. Jaywalker, and please shut up."

The judge's last two words, even with the "please" that prefaced them, accomplished what the banging of her gavel hadn't been able to. Jaywalker sat down, and

he shut up. But even as he did, he held the book aloft for
Levine to see the words. As if she'd be able to make out
the microscopic print from twenty-five feet away.

With Jaywalker's ranting finally cut off, the courtroom
gradually grew quiet, except for a bit of residual snick-
ering coming from the direction of the jury box. *Great,*
he thought, looking down at his shoes, the black one and
the brown one. Not only have they gone and convicted
my client without so much as deliberating, now they're
laughing at me. Well, fuck them. He lifted his gaze and
turned to stare at them. He wanted to see if collectively
they had an ounce of shame left.

Apparently they didn't. They were staring right back at
him, every last one of them. Even the alternates. A couple
of them were even gesturing derisively now. One was
raising and lowering both hands, palms down, as though
trying to calm down an unruly child. Another was rudely
shushing him with a finger pressed to her lips. Yet another,
a guy in the second row, had made a fist and was pointing
his thumb upwards, as if to say, "Up yours, Mac!"

Off to one side, Jaywalker could feel a tugging on his
sleeve. He tried to pull away from it, but it only grew
more insistent. He turned in annoyance. Looking directly
at Alonzo Barnett, he snapped, "Back off, will you? Getting railroaded like this might be okay with you, but it's
not okay with me."

Barnett's only response was to smile gently.

Fucking lunatic, was all Jaywalker could think. Here
he's going off to die in prison, and he's all serene and Zen-
like about it, while I'm the one who's totally bat-shit. "It's
not okay," he told Barnett again. "It's not okay at all."

"I think maybe it actually might be," said Barnett,
pointing toward the jury box. "I think they might be
trying to tell us something."

22

Doyle's pub

The fact that it was barely one o'clock when the courtroom emptied out for the last time didn't stop fourteen of
the sixteen jurors from bodily grabbing Jaywalker in the
hallway and spiriting him off to Doyle's Pub, a local wa-
tering hole and restaurant behind the courthouse. Twice
he tried to break free before giving up. Not only was he
seriously outnumbered, but he soon realized that as kid-
nappings go, this was going to be a pretty benign one.

Standing around a hastily set table of food and
drinks—none of which Jaywalker would be allowed to
contribute a penny toward—the jurors took turns pep-
pering him with questions. Where were Alonzo Barnett's
daughters? Would Lieutenant Pascarella be prosecuted?
What would become of poor Lance Bucknell? Why hadn't
Jaywalker argued agency, when they would have acquitted Barnett just as quickly under that theory? How had
Kenny Smith managed to drag Clarence Hightower down
to court? What had happened to cute little Miki Shaughnessey? Why was Daniel Pulaski such a pompous prick?
And why hadn't Jaywalker realized they were about to
acquit Barnett, rather than convict him?

He did his best to answer the questions he could and

deflect the ones he couldn't. He lost track of how many
Bloody Marys he downed, and he actually ate lunch. Not
Cheez-Its or Wheat Thins, but fresh seeded rye bread
covered with real chicken salad, or maybe it was tuna.
And then, just when he thought the time might be ripe for
him to thank his hosts and make his getaway, there was
a tumultuous roar at the doorway, and the two missing
jurors showed up, flanking a beaming Alonzo Barnett.
They'd stationed themselves outside the Tombs, they explained, and had pounced on him the moment he'd been
released.

To this day, Jaywalker can't tell you how long the cel-
ebration lasted or how much he had to drink before the
jurors finally let him leave. He remembers being surprised
to find it was dark outside when he emerged, and that
he was totally disoriented, having no idea which way to
walk. A friendly cabdriver not only drove him home but
walked him into his building and brought him upstairs to
his apartment, where his wife first sympathized with his
need to drown his sadness, and then, upon learning the
actual outcome of the case, put him to bed and applied
some smothering of her own.

He awoke a day and a half later with a serious headache, a terrible taste in his mouth and an ear-to-ear grin
that wouldn't go away for a week. That said, he did find
enough time to wipe it off and put in a call to Lorraine
Wilson, the clerk who'd assigned him the case more than
two months earlier, just as he'd promised he would. But
he needn't have bothered. She'd already heard. A lot of
people had, it seemed.

The party at Doyle's was by no means the last Jaywalker saw or heard of Alonzo Barnett. Three weeks

after the trial, Barnett called to report on his efforts to reestablish contact with his daughters.

The news wasn't good.

Early on during Barnett's twenty-month confinement, it turned out the girls had been placed with a foster family. The Bureau of Child Welfare had been lucky enough to find a childless couple willing to take them both, no small thing. The placement had gone well enough that the couple now wanted to formally adopt the girls. Under the law, that could happen only if their father's paternal rights were first legally terminated.

A social worker for BCW confided to Barnett that the couple had been reluctant to begin proceedings to do that. Apparently they felt that would be a hurtful thing, not only for Barnett but the girls themselves. There was no mother to worry about, Barnett's wife having died years earlier, the victim of a hit-and-run driver. So BCW itself had submitted a petition, setting forth their reasons to believe that it would be in the best interest of the girls to end their relationship with their father and let the adoptions proceed.

"What do you want to do?" Jaywalker asked Barnett.

"I want to fight to get my daughters back. Will you help me?"

Jaywalker had learned a half a dozen years earlier that a case didn't end when you lost it. Now he was about to learn a corollary to that rule. A case didn't end just because you won it, either. He called a friend, a young woman he'd known at Legal Aid who'd left to practice family law. Over lunch he told her the story of Alonzo Barnett and begged her to help Barnett get his daughters back.

"I'll pay your fee," he said, forgetting that he had nothing to pay it with.

"There won't be a fee," she told him. "But here's the deal. You're going to be my first witness at the hearing."

"What could I possibly contribute?" he asked. "I never even met the girls. I've never once seen Barnett interact with them."

"That may be," she agreed. "But you can contribute something equally important. You can testify to how he's turned his life around."

And so it was that two months later Jaywalker found himself in a cramped makeshift courtroom on the eighth floor of Manhattan Family Court.

The eighth floor.

There was no jury present, and no spectators in sight. The foster parents had already testified on a previous date. Not even the girls themselves were there. In the criminal courts, the Constitution guarantees every defendant the right to a public trial. In family court, privacy reigns supreme.

Jaywalker wasn't three minutes into his testimony when he broke down. He was there to tell the judge what a changed man Alonzo Barnett was, how he'd single-handedly kicked his addiction and turned his life around, and that his arrest two years earlier was no evidence of a relapse. But the story overwhelmed him, and the notion that the state could now step in and take away the man's children left him all but unable to continue. But continue he did, and somehow he got through it. And afterward, outside the courtroom, his friend told him that he'd been terrific, that the judge had been deeply moved, and that it was highly likely that the petition to terminate Alonzo Barnett's paternal rights would be denied.

So it came as a total surprise when Barnett came to see

Jaywalker two weeks later to tell him that he'd decided not to contest the petition after all.

"My girls are becoming teenagers," he said. "They're growing up, getting their periods, having boyfriends, going through issues at school. I don't know anything about that stuff. I grew up in prison. I don't know about periods and boyfriends and school. My lawyer tells me the girls say they're happy where they are, and that they've learned to rely on their foster parents. That's something they could never do with me. Every time they tried to rely on me, I let them down."

"But you're their father," said Jaywalker.

"I know that," said Barnett. "But I have to understand that this isn't about me. This has to be about them."

Jaywalker said nothing. All he could do was think about his own daughter, and what he'd do if anyone ever tried to take her away from him and his wife. But it wasn't the same.

"Do I dream of them?" Barnett asked no one in particular. "Every night. But in my dreams, my girls have become doctors and lawyers, grown women with husbands who go off to work, and children of their own. And they're happy, truly happy. Does it absolutely kill me to let go of them? Sure it does, it tears my guts out. But I've come to understand that it's something I owe them, something I have to do for them."

Right before leaving, Barnett fulfilled a promise made months earlier by handing Jaywalker a sealed manila envelope with what felt like a thin booklet inside it. Opening it twenty minutes later, Jaywalker discovered a collection of handwritten poems, neatly stapled together along the left-hand margin. The poet was identified only by the initials "AB." And though the punctuation was imperfect and the spelling erratic, the sentiments expressed were surprisingly moving. Together they described a man's life-long struggle to reclaim his soul. The title of the slender volume was lifted from the last word in the last line of the last poem.

"Redemption," it was called.

Shirley Levine died two years later. She had no family, and Jaywalker was one of the few who visited her in her hospital room. She was down to seventy pounds by then but still had a sparkle in her eyes. They traded war stories, Levine at last talking about the wartime exploits she'd never before shared with anyone. Jaywalker tried to match her with some stories from his undercover days at the DEA, but they were pale stuff in comparison.

Daniel Pulaski left the Office of the Special Narcotics Prosecutor a year after the trial to run for Congress. He lost, getting twelve per cent of the vote in the Republican primary.

Miki Shaughnessey left, too, disillusioned with the job. She had a brief career doing courtroom commentary, first for Court TV and then for one of the networks, before picking up and moving out to the West Coast.

Clarence Hightower was never heard from again.

None of the detectives, agents or investigators who'd testified at the trial were ever prosecuted or disciplined in any way for being less than honest in their reports and testimony.

A week after the trial, Jaywalker and Kenny Smith got together over cheeseburgers and Coke, and had a good laugh over the stunt they'd managed to pull off.

"How could you be so sure the judge wouldn't let you reopen the evidence and put him on?" Smith wanted to know. "What would you have done then?"

"I'd researched the case law," Jaywalker told him.

"That's why I told you to make certain you waited until I'd begun my summation before you came into the courtroom pretending you had Hightower with you."

"Son of a bitch," said Smith, standing up and coming around to Jaywalker's side of the booth. There they exchanged high fives and hugs, Jaywalker stretching on his tiptoes.

To this day Jaywalker continues to defend men and women charged with crimes. Even the ones who tell him they did exactly what they had been accused of doing. Even the ones he knows are guilty as sin.

Even the Alonzo Barnetts of the world.

And Barnett? In the twenty-five years that he lived following the trial, he stayed completely drug-free and out of trouble. He eventually retired from the restaurant he'd worked at, and toward the end got by on his modest savings and his Social Security check. And up to the very end he volunteered three days a week at a drug rehabilitation facility in the Bronx, and he mentored teenage boys in trouble. He never stopped writing poetry and living in the same apartment in the same building as before. His daughters came to visit him there on a regular basis, having found their way to him with a little help from Jaywalker. Not too long ago the younger one got married, and at her urging and with her adoptive parents' blessing, both her fathers walked her down the aisle, one on either side of her. Jaywalker knows that for a fact, because he was there to witness it. When he mentioned to Barnett how touched he was that Barnett had helped give his daughter away, Barnett replied with a smile that it was something he certainly ought to be good at.

"After all," he explained, "I've had practice."

* * *

So next time you're feeling cynical about the criminal justice system and find yourself tempted to ask some defense lawyer how he can possibly represent somebody he knows is guilty, stop for just a moment and think of Jaywalker.

Better yet, think of Alonzo Barnett.

Think of redemption.

* * * * *

AUTHOR'S NOTE

The story you've just read is drawn from an actual case I myself tried some years ago. Thus there really was an Alonzo Barnett, a Clarence Hightower, a Trevor St. James, a Kenny Smith, and a Shirley Levine. There was even a gathering at Doyle's Pub. That said, I've changed a few things, including the names of the participants from the real-life drama, just as I've substituted Jaywalker's identity for my own.

Best of all, there really was a bunch of jurors who somehow had the collective wisdom to know what to do with a case in which the defendant readily admitted that he'd done exactly what he'd been accused of doing, but nonetheless didn't deserve to be convicted. So if you're looking to find any heroes in the story, look no further than them.

As always, I find myself deeply indebted to my fabulous editor Leslie Wainger, and to my longtime good friend and literary agent Bob Diforio. Between the two of them, they pretty much leave me alone to tell my stories, by far the easiest part of the equation.

I'm equally indebted to you, the reader of these pages, without whom I'd have no one to share my stories with. So I thank each one of you, too, and hope to see you again next time.

I live and write in a truly magical place. My wife,

Sandy, continues to be my first reader, my harshest critic and my biggest fan. My children are never far behind, and these days my grandchildren are getting into the act, too.

What more could I ask of life?